# Pieces of Eight

---

*Richard le Gallienne*

# Contents

# PIECES OF EIGHT

BY

Richard le Gallienne

LIFE BEING OF THE NATURE BOTH OF A TREASURE-HUNT AND A PIRATICAL EXPEDITION, I DEDICATE THIS NARRATIVE TO THE FOLLOWING SAILING COMPANIONS OF MINE ON THIS ENTERTAINING OLD PIRATE CRAFT WE CALL THE EARTH, IN THE HOPE THAT EACH MAY FIND HIS TREASURE, AND, AT LEAST, ESCAPE HANGING AT THE END OF THE TRIP--TO WIT: HARRY DASH JOHNSON, SAM NICHOLSON, BERT WILLSIE AND CHARLEY BETHEL, ALL ENGAGED IN ONE OR ANOTHER OF THE PIRATICAL PROFESSIONS.

# PROLOGUE

(The following MS., the authorship of which I am not at liberty to divulge, came to me in a curious way. Being recently present at a performance of *"Treasure Island"* at The Punch and Judy Theatre in New York City, and, seated at the extreme right-hand end of the front row of the stalls--so near to the ground-floor box that its occupants were within but a yard or two of me, and, therefore, very clearly to be seen--I, in common with my immediate neighbours, could not fail to remark the very striking and beautiful woman who was the companion of a distinguished military-looking man on the youthful side of middle age.

*Still young, a little past thirty, maybe, she was unusually tall and stately of figure, and from her curious golden skin and massive black hair, one judged her to be a Creole, possibly a Jamaican. Her face, which was rather heavily but finely moulded, wore an expression of somewhat poetic melancholy, a little like that of a beautiful animal, but readily lit up with a charming smile now and again at some sally of her companion, with whom she seemed to be on affectionate terms, and with whom, as the play proceeded, she exchanged glances and whispered confidences such as two who have shared an experience together--which the play seems to bring to mind--are seen sometimes to exchange in a theatre.*

*But there was one particular which especially accentuated the singularity of her appearance and was responsible for drawing upon her an interested observation--seemed, indeed, even in her eyes to condone it, for she, as well as her companion, was obviously conscious of it--the two strange-looking gold ornaments which hung from her delicately shaped ears. These continually challenged the eye, and piqued the curiosity. Obviously they were two old coins, of thick gold, stamped with an antique design. They were Spanish doubloons!*

*As, in common with the rest of the audience, I looked at this picturesque pair, my eyes forsook the lady of the doubloons, and fastened themselves with a half-certainty of recognition upon her companion. Why! surely it was ---- ----, an old dare-devil comrade of mine, whose disappearance from New York some ten years before had been the talk of the two or three clubs to which we both belonged. A curious blending of soldier, poet, and mining engineer, he had been popular with all of us, and when he had disappeared without warning we were sure that he was off on some Knight-errant business--to Mexico or the Moon!*

*He was, indeed, wearing that disguise of Time, which we all come involuntarily to wear--an unfamiliar greyness of his hair at the temples, and a moustache that would soon be a distinguished white; yet the disguise was not sufficient to conceal the youthful vigour of his personality from one who had known him so well as I. The more I looked at him, the more certain I grew that it was he, and I determined to go round to his box at the conclusion of the second act.*

*Then, becoming absorbed in the play, I forgot him and his companion of the doubloons for a while, and when I looked for them again, they had vanished. However, a letter in my mail next morning told me that the observation had not been all on my side. My eyes had not deceived me. It was my friend--and, at dinner with him and his lady, next evening, I heard the story of some of those lost years. Moreover, he confided to me that a certain portion of his adventures had* seemed so romantic that he had been tempted to set them down in a narrative, merely, of course, for the amusement of his family and friends. On our parting, he entrusted me with this manuscript, which I found so interesting that I was able to persuade him to consent to its publication to that larger world which it seemed to me unfair to rob of one of those few romances that have been really lived, and not merely conjured up out of the imaginations of professional romancers.

His consent was given with some reluctance, for, apart from a certain risk which the publication of the manuscript would entail, it contains also matters which my friend naturally regards as sacred--though, in this respect, I feel sure that he can rely upon the delicacy of his readers. He made it a condition that every precaution should be taken to keep secret the name and identity of his wife and himself.

Therefore, in presenting to the world the manuscript thus entrusted to me, I have made various changes of detail, with the purpose of the more surely safeguarding the privacy of my two friends; but, in all essentials, the manuscript is printed as it came originally into my hands.

R. Le G.

# BOOK I

Out of the constant East the breeze
Brings morning, like a wafted rose,
Across the glimmering lagoon,
And wakes the still palmetto trees,
And blows adrift the phantom moon,
That paler and still paler glows--
Up with the anchor! let's be going!
O hoist the sail! and let's be going!
Glory and glee

*Of the morning sea--*
*Ah! let's be going!*

Under our keel a glass of dreams
  Still fairer than the morning sky,
  A jewel shot with blue and gold,
The swaying clearness streams and gleams,
  A crystal mountain smoothly rolled
O'er magic gardens flowing by--
Over we go the sea-fans waving,
  Over the rainbow corals paving
   The deep-sea floor;
  No more, no more
  Would I seek the shore
  To make my grave in--
*O sea-fans waving*!

# PIECES OF EIGHT
# CHAPTER I

*Introduces the Secretary to the Treasury of His Britannic Majesty's Govern-*
*ment at Nassau, New Providence, Bahama Islands.*

Some few years ago--to be precise, it was during the summer of 1903--I was
paying what must have seemed like an interminable visit to my old friend John
Saunders, who at that time filled with becoming dignity the high-sounding office
of Secretary to the Treasury of His Majesty's Government, in the quaint little town
of Nassau, in the island of New Providence, one of those Bahama Islands that lie
half lost to the world to the southeast of the Caribbean Sea and form a somewhat
neglected portion of the British West Indies.

Time was when they had a sounding name for themselves in the world; during the American Civil War, for instance, when the blockade-runners made their dare-devil trips with contraband cotton, between Nassau and South Carolina; and before that again, when the now sleepy little harbour gave shelter to rousing freebooters and tarry pirates, tearing in there under full sail with their loot from the Spanish Main. How often those quiet moonlit streets must have roared with brutal revelry, and the fierce clamour of pistol-belted scoundrels round the wine-casks have gone up into the still, tropic night.

But those heroic days are gone, and Nassau is given up to a sleepy trade in sponges and tortoise-shell, and peace is no name for the drowsy tenor of the days under the palm trees and the scarlet poincianas. A little group of Government build-ings surrounding a miniature statue of Queen Victoria, flanked by some old Spanish cannon and murmured over by the foliage of tropic trees, gives an air of old-world distinction to the long Bay street, whose white houses, with their jalousied veran-das, ran the whole length of the water-front, and all the long sunny days the air is lazy with the sound of the shuffling feet of the child-like "darky" population and the chatter of the bean-pods of the poincianas overhead.

Here a handful of Englishmen, clothed in the white linen suits of the tropics, carry on the Government after the traditional manner of British colonies from time immemorial, each of them, like my friend, not without an English smile at the hu-mour of the thing, supporting the dignity of offices with impressive names--Lord Chief Justice, Attorney General, Speaker of the House, Lord High Admiral, Colonial Secretary and so forth--and occasionally a figure in gown and barrister's wig flits across the green from the little courthouse, where the Lord Chief Justice in his scar-let robes, on a dais surmounted by a gilded lion and unicorn, sustains the majesty of British justice, with all the pomp of Westminster or Whitehall.

My friend the Secretary of the Treasury is a man possessing in an uncommon degree that rare and most attractive of human qualities, companionableness. He is a quiet man of middle age, an old white-headed bachelor with a droll twinkling expression, speaking seldom, and then in a curious silent fashion, as though the drowsy heat of the tropics had soaked him through and through. With his white hair, his white clothes, his white moustachios, his white eyelashes, over eyes that seem to hide away among quiet mirthful wrinkles, he carries about him the sort of silence that goes with a miller, surrounded by the white dusty quiet of his mill.

As we sit together in the hush of his snuggery of an evening, surrounded by guns, fishing-lines, and old prints, there are times when we scarcely exchange a dozen words between dinner and bed-time, and yet we have all the time a keen and satisfying sense of companionship. It is John Saunders's gift. Companionship seems quietly to ooze out of him, without the need of words. He and you are there in your comfortable arm-chairs, with a good cigar, a whisky-and-soda, or a glass of that old port on which he prides himself, and that is all that is necessary. Where is the need of words?

And occasionally, we have, as third in those evening conclaves, a big slow-smiling, broad-faced young merchant, of the same kidney. In he drops with a nod and a smile, selects his cigar and his glass, and takes his place in the smoke-cloud of our meditations, radiating, without the effort of speech, that good thing--humanity; though one must not forget the one subject on which now and again the good Charlie Webster achieves eloquence in spite of himself--duck-shooting. That is the only subject worth breaking the pleasant brotherhood of silence for.

John Saunders's subject is shark-fishing. Duck-shooting and shark-fishing. It is enough. Here, for sensible men, is a sufficient basis for life-long friendship, and unwearying, inexhaustible companionship.

It was in this peace of John Saunders's snuggery, one July evening, in 1903, the three of us being duly met, and ensconced in our respective arm-chairs, that we got on to the subject of buried treasure. We had talked more than usual that evening--talked duck and shark till those inexhaustible themes seemed momentarily exhausted. Then it was I who started us off again by asking John what he knew about buried treasure.

At this, John laughed his funny little quiet laugh, his eyes twinkling out of his wrinkles, for all the world like mischievous mice looking out of a cupboard, took a sip of his port, a pull at his cigar, and then:

"Buried treasure!" he said, "well, I have little doubt that the islands are full of it--if one only knew how to get at it."

"Seriously?" I asked.

"Certainly. Why not? When you come to think of it, it stands to reason. Weren't these islands for nearly three centuries the stamping ground of all the pirates of the Spanish Main? Morgan was here. Blackbeard was here. The very governors themselves were little better than pirates. This room we are sitting in was the den of one of the biggest rogues of them all--John Tinker--the governor when Bruce was here building Fort Montague, at the east end yonder; building it against pirates, and little else but pirates at the Government House all the time. A great old time Tinker gave the poor fellow. You can read all about it in his 'Memoirs.' You should read them. Great stuff. There they are," pointing to an old quarto on some well lined shelves, for John is something of a scholar too; "borrow them some time."

"Yes, but I want to hear more about the treasure," interrupted I, bringing him back to the point.

"Well, as I was saying, Nassau was the rendezvous for all the cut-throats of the Caribbean Sea. Here they came in with their loot, their doubloons and pieces of eight"; and John's eyes twinkled with enjoyment of the rich old romantic words, as though they were old port.

"Here they squandered much of it, no doubt, but they couldn't squander it all. Some of them were thrifty knaves too, and these, looking around for some place of safety, would naturally think of the bush. The niggers keep their little hoards there to this day. Fawcett, over at Andros, was saying the other night, that he estimates that they have something like a quarter of a million dollars buried in tin cans among the brush over there now--"

"It is their form of stocking," put in Charlie Webster.

"Precisely. Well, as I was saying, those old fellows would bury their hoards in some cave or other, and then go off--and get hanged. Their ghosts perhaps came back. The darkies have lots of ghost-tales about them. But their money is still here, lots of it, you bet your life."

"Do they ever make any finds?" I asked.

"Nothing big that I know of. A jug full of old coins now and then. I found one a year or two ago in my garden here--buried down among the roots of that old fig tree."

"Then," put in Charlie, "there was that mysterious stranger over at North Cay. He's supposed to have got away with quite a pile."

"Tell me about him," said I.

"Well, there used to be an old eccentric character in the town here--a half-breed by the name of Andrews. John will remember him--"

John nodded.

"He used to go around all the time with a big umbrella, and muttering to himself. We used to think him half crazy. Gone so brooding over this very subject of buried treasure. Better look out, young man!"--smiling at me. "He used to be always grubbing about in the bush, and they said that he carried the umbrella, so that he could hide a machete in it--a sort of heavy cutlass, you know, for cutting down the brush. Well, several years ago, there came a visitor from New York, and he got thick with the old fellow. They used to go about a lot together, and were often off on so-called fishing trips for days on end. Actually, it is believed, they were after something on North Cay. At all events, some months afterward, the New Yorker disappeared as he had come, and has not been heard from since. But since then, they have found a sort of brick vault over there which has evidently been excavated. I have seen it myself. A sort of walled chamber. There, it's supposed, the New Yorker found something or other--"

"An old tomb, most likely," interrupted John, sceptically. "There are some like that over at Spanish Wells."

"Maybe," said Charlie, "but that's the story for what it's worth."

As Charlie finished, John slapped his knee.

"The very thing for you!" he said, "why have I never thought of it before?"

"What do you mean, John?" we both asked.

"Why, down at the office, I've got the very thing. A pity I haven't got it here. You must come in and see it to-morrow."

And he took a tantalising sip of his port.

"What on earth is it? Why do you keep us guessing?"

"Why, it's an old manuscript."

"An old manuscript!" I exclaimed.

"Yes, an old document that came into my hands a short time ago. Charlie, you remember old Wicks--old Billy Wicks--'Wrecker' Wicks, they called him--"

"I should say I do. A wonderful old villain--"

"One of the greatest characters that ever lived. Oh, and shrewd as the devil. Do you remember the story about his--"

"But the document, for heaven's sake," I said. "The document first; the story will keep."

"Well, they were pulling down Wicks's own house just lately, and out of the rafters there fell a roll of paper--now, I'm coming to it--a roll of paper, purporting to be the account of the burying of a certain treasure, telling the place where it is buried, and giving directions for finding it--"

Charlie and I exclaimed together; and John continued, with tantalising deliberation.

"It's in the safe, down at the office; you shall see it to-morrow. It's a statement purporting to be made by some fellow on his deathbed--some fellow dying out in Texas--a quondam pirate, anxious to make his peace at the end, and to give his friends the benefit of his knowledge."

"O John!" said I, "I sha'n't sleep a wink to-night."

"I don't take much stock in it," said John. "I'm inclined to think it's a hoax. Some one trying to fool the old fellow. If there'd been any treasure, I guess one could have trusted old 'Wrecker' Wicks to get after it.... But, boys, it's bed-time, anyhow. Come down to the office in the morning and we'll look it over."

So our meeting broke up for the time being, and taking my candle, I went upstairs, to dream of caves overflowing with gold pieces, and John Tinker, fierce and moustachioed, standing over me, a cutlass between his teeth, and a revolver in each hand.

# CHAPTER II

### *The Narrative of Henry P. Tobias, Ex-Pirate, as Dictated on His Deathbed, in the Year of Our Lord, 1859.*

The good John had scarcely made his leisurely, distinguished appearance at his desk on the morrow, immaculately white, and breathing his customary air of fathomless repose, when I too entered by one door, and Charlie Webster by the other.

"Now for the document," we both exclaimed in a breath.

"Here it is," he said, taking up a rather grimy-looking roll of foolscap from in front of him.

"A little like hurricane weather," said the broadly smiling Charlie Webster, mopping his brow.

The room we were in, crowded with pigeon-holes and dusty documents from ceiling to floor, looked out into an outer office, similarly dreary, and painted a dirty blue and white, furnished with high desks and stools, and railed off with ancient painted ironwork, forlornly decorative, after the manner of an old-fashioned counting-house, or shipping office. It had something quaintly "colonial" about it, suggesting supercargoes, and West India merchants of long ago.

John took a look into the outer office. There was nothing to claim his attention, so he took up the uncouthly written manuscript, which, as he pointed out, was evidently the work of a person of very little education, and began to read as follows:

*"County of Travas "State of Texas "December 1859*

*"I being in very poor health and cannot last long, feeling my end is near, I make the following statement of my own free will and without solicitation. In full exercise of all my faculties, and feel that I am doing my duty by so doing.*

*"My friends have shown me much kindness and taken care of me when sick, and for their kindness I leave this statement in their hands to make the best of it, when I will now proceed to give my statement, which is as follows:--*

"I was born in the city of Liverpool, England (on the 5th day of December 1784). My father was a seaman and when I was young I followed the same occupation. And it happened, that when, on a passage from Spain to the West Indies, our ship was attacked by free-traders, as they called themselves, but they were pirates.

*"We all did our best, but were overpowered, and the whole crew, except three, were killed. I was one of the three they did not kill. They carried us on board their ship and kept us until next day when they asked us to join them. They tried to entice us, by showing us great piles of money and telling us how rich we could become, and many other ways, and they tried to get us to join them willingly, but we would not, when they became enraged and loaded three cannon and lashed each one of us before the mouth of each cannon and told us to take our choice to join them, as they would touch the guns and that dam quick. It is useless to say we accepted everything before death, so we came one of the pirates' crew. Both of my companions were killed in less time than six months, but I was with them for more than two years, in which time we collected a vast quantity of money from*

*different ships we captured and we buried a great amount in two different lots. I helped to bury it with my own hands. The location of which it is my purpose to point out, so that it can be found without trouble in the Bahama Islands. After I had been with them for more than two years, we were attacked by a large warship and our commander told us to fight for our lives, as it would be death if we were taken. But the guns of our ship were too small for the warship, so our ship soon began to sink, when the man-of-war ran alongside of our vessel and tried to bore us, but we were sinking too fast, so she had to haul off again, when our vessel sunk with everything on board, and I escaped by swimming under the stern of the ship, as ours sunk, without being seen, and holding on to the ship until dark, when I swam to a portion of the wrecked vessel floating not far away. And on that I floated. The next morning the ship was not seen. I was picked up by a passing vessel the next day as a shipwrecked seaman.*

*"And let me say here, I know that no one escaped alive from our vessel except myself and those that were taken by the man-of-war. And those were all executed as pirates,--so I know that no other man knows of this treasure except myself and it must be and is where we buried it until to-day and unless you get it through this statement it will remain there always and do no one any good.*

*"Therefore, it is your duty to trace it up and get it for your own benefit, as well as others, so delay not, but act as soon as possible.*

*"I will now describe the places, locations, marks etc., etc., so plainly that it can be found, without any trouble.*

"The first is a sum of one million and a half dollars--($1,500,000)--"

At this point, John paused. We all took a long breath, and Charlie Webster gave a soft whistle, and smacked his lips.

"A million and a half dollars. What ho!"

Then I, happening to cast my eye through the open door, caught sight of a face gazing through the ironwork of the outer office with a fixed and glittering expression, a face anything but prepossessing, the face of a half-breed, deeply pock-marked, with a coarse hook nose, and evil-looking eyes, unnaturally close together. He looked for all the world like a turkey buzzard, eagerly hanging over offal, and it was evident from his expression, that he had not missed a word of the reading.

"There is some one in the outer office," I said, and John rose and went out.

"Good morning, Mr. Saunders," said an unpleasantly soft and cringing voice.

"Good morning," said John, somewhat grumpily, "what is it you want?"

It was some detail of account, which, being despatched, the man shuffled off, with evident reluctance, casting a long inquisitive look at us seated at the desk, and John, taking up the manuscript once more resumed:

*"... a sum of one million and one half dollars--buried at a cay known as Dead Men's Shoes, near Nassau, in the Bahama Islands."*

"'Dead Men's Shoes!' I don't know any such place, do you?" interrupted Charlie.

"No, I don't--but, never mind, let's read it through first and discuss it afterwards," and John went on:

"Buried at a cay known as Dead Men's Shoes, near Nassau, in the Bahama Islands; about fifty feet (50 ft.) south of this Dead Men's Shoes is a rock, on which we cut the form of a compass. And twenty feet (20 ft.) East from the cay is another rock on which we cut a cross (X). Under this rock it is buried four feet (4 ft.) deep.

"The other is a sum of one million dollars ($1,000,000). It is buried on what was known as Short Shrift Island; on the highest point of this Short Shrift Island is a large cabbage wood stump and twenty feet (20 ft.) south of that stump is the treasure, buried five feet (5 ft.) deep and can be found without difficulty. Short Shrift Island is a place where passing vessels stop to get fresh water. No great distance from Nassau, so it can be easily found.

"*The first pod was taken from a Spanish merchant and it is in Spanish silver dollars.*

"*The other on Short Shrift Island is in different kinds of money, taken from different ships of different nations--it is all good money.*

"*Now friends, I have told you all that is necessary for you to know, to recover these treasures and I leave it in your hands and it is my request that when you read this, you will at once take steps to recover it, and when you get it, it is my wish that you use it in a way most good for yourself and others. This is all I ask.*

"*Now thanking you for your kindness and care and with my best wishes for your prosperity and happiness, I will close, as I am so weak I can hardly hold the pen.*

"*I am, truly your friend,*

HENRY P. TOBIAS.

"Henry P. Tobias?" said Charlie Webster. "Never heard of him. Did you, John?"

"Never!"

And then there was a stir in the outer office. Some one was asking for the Secretary of the Treasury. So John rose.

"I must get to work now, boys. We can talk it over to-night." And then, handing me the manuscript: "Take it home with you, if you like, and look it over at your leisure."

As Charlie Webster and I passed out into the street, I noticed the fellow of the sinister pock-marked visage standing near the window of the inner office. The window was open, and any one standing outside, could easily have heard everything that passed inside. As the fellow caught my eye, he smiled unpleasantly, and slunk off down the street.

"Who is that fellow?" I asked Charlie. "He's a queer looking specimen."

"Yes! he's no good. Yet he's more half-witted than bad, perhaps. His face is against him, poor devil."

And we went our ways, till the evening, I to post home to the further study of the narrative. There seated on the pleasant veranda, I went over it carefully, sentence by sentence. While I was reading, some one called me indoors. I put down the manuscript on the little bamboo table at my side, and went in. When I returned, a few moments afterward, the manuscript was gone!

# CHAPTER III

### *In Which I Charter the "Maggie Darling."*

As luck would have it, the loss, or rather the theft, of Henry P. Tobias's narrative, was not so serious as it at first seemed, for it fortunately chanced that John Saunders had had it copied; but the theft remained none the less mysterious. What could be the motive of the thief with whom--quite unreasonably and doubtless unjustly--my fancy persisted in connecting that unprepossessing face so keenly attentive in John Saunders's outer office, and again so plainly eavesdropping at his open window.

However, leaving that mystery for later solution, John Saunders, Charlie Webster, and I spent the next evening in a general and particular criticism of the narrative itself. There were several obvious objections to be made against its authenticity. To start with, Tobias, at the time of his deposition, was an old man--seventy-five years old--and it was more than probable that his experiences as a pirate would date from his early manhood; they were hardly likely to have taken place as late as his fortieth year. The narrative, indeed, suggested their taking place much earlier, and there would thus be a space of at least forty years between the burial of the treasure and his deathbed revelation. It was natural to ask: Why during all those years, did he not return and retrieve the treasure for himself? Various circumstances may have prevented him, the inability from lack of means to make the journey, or what not; but certainly one would need to imagine circumstances of peculiar power that should be strong enough to keep a man with so valuable a secret in his possession so many years from taking advantage of it.

For a long while too the names given to the purported sites of the treasure *caches* puzzled us. Modern maps give no such places as "Dead Men's Shoes" and "Short Shrift Island," but John--who is said to be writing a learned history of the Bahamas--has been for a long time collecting old maps, prints, and documents relating to them; and at last, in a map dating back to 1763, we came upon one of the two names. So far the veracity of Tobias was supported. "Dead Men's Shoes" proved to be the old name for a certain cay some twenty miles long, about a day and a half's sail from Nassau, one of the long string of coral islands now known as the "Exuma Cays." But of "Short Shrift Island" we sought in vain for a trace.

Then the details for identification of the sites left something to be desired in particularity. But that, I reasoned, rather made for Tobias's veracity than otherwise. Were the document merely a hoax, as John continued to suspect, its author would have indulged his imagination in greater elaboration. The very simplicity of the directions argued their authenticity. Charlie Webster was inclined to back me in this view, but neither of my friends showed any optimism in regard to the possible discovery of the treasure.

The character of the brush on the out-islands alone, they said, made the task of search well nigh hopeless. To cut one's way through twenty miles of such stubborn thickets, would cost almost as much in labour as the treasure was worth. And then the peculiar nature of the jagged coral rock, like endless wastes of clinker, almost denuded of earth, would make the task the more arduous. As well look for a particular fish in the sea. A needle in a haystack would be easy in comparison.

"All the same," said I, "the adventure calls me; the adventure and that million and a half dollars--and those 'Dead Men's Shoes'--and I intend to undertake it. I am not going to let your middle-aged scepticism discourage me. Treasure or no treasure, there will be the excitement of the quest, and all the fun of the sea."

"And some duck perhaps," added Charlie.

"And some shark-fishing for certain," said John.

\*     \*     \*     \*     \*

The next thing was to set about chartering a boat, and engaging a crew. In this Charlie Webster's experience was invaluable, as his friendly zeal was untiring.

After looking over much likely and unlikely craft, we finally decided on a two-masted schooner of trim but solid build, the *Maggie Darling,* 42 feet over all and 13 beam; something under twenty tons, with an auxiliary gasolene engine of 24 horse power, and an alleged speed of 10 knots. A staunch, as well as a pretty, little boat, with good lines, and high in the bows; built to face any seas. "Cross the Atlantic in her," said the owner. Owners of boats for sale always say that. But the *Maggie Darling* spoke for herself, and I fell in love with her on the spot.

Next, the crew.

"You will need a captain, a cook, an engineer, and a deck-hand," said Charlie, "and I have the captain, and the cook all ready for you."

That afternoon we rounded them all up, including the engineer and the deck-hand, and we arranged to start, weather permitting, with the morning tide, which set east about six o'clock on July 13, 1903. Charlie was a little doubtful about the weather, though the glass was steady.

"A northeaster's about due," he said, "but unless it comes before you start, you'll be able to put in for shelter at one or two places, and you will be inside the reef most of the way."

Ship's stores were the next detail, and these, including fifty gallons of gasolene, over and above the tanks and three barrels of water, being duly got aboard, on the evening of July 12, all was ready for the start; an evening which was naturally spent in a parting conclave in John Saunders's snuggery.

"Why, one important thing you've forgotten," said Charlie, as we sat over our pipes and glasses. "Think of forgetting that. Machetes--and spades and pickaxes. And I'd take a few sticks of dynamite along with you too. I can let you have the lot, and, if you like, we'll get them aboard to-night."

"It's a pity you have to give it away that it's a treasure hunt," said John,--"but, then you can't keep the crew from knowing. And they're a queer lot on the subject of treasure, have some of the rummest superstitions. I hope you won't have any trouble with them."

"Had any experience in handling niggers?" asked Charlie.

"Not the least."

"That makes me wish I were coming with you. They are rum beggars. Awful cowards, and just like a pack of children. You know about sailing anyhow. That's a good thing. You can captain your own boat, if need be. That's all to the good. Particularly if you strike any dirty weather. Though they're cowards in a storm, they'll take orders better than white men--so long as they see that you know what you are about. But let me give you one word of advice. Be kind, of course, with them--but keep your distance all the same. And be careful about losing your temper. You get more out of them by coaxing--hard as it is, at times. And, by the way, how would you like to take old 'Sailor' with you?"

"Sailor" was a great Labrador retriever, who, at that moment, turned up his big head, with a devoted sigh, from behind his master's chair.

"Rather," I said. So "Sailor" was thereupon enrolled as a further addition to the crew.

"Of course, you needn't expect to start on time," said Charlie, with a laugh;

"you'll be lucky if the crew turns up an hour after time. But that's all in the game. I know them--lazy beggars."

And the morning proved the truth of Charlie's judgment.

"Old Tom," the cook, was first on hand. I took to him at once. A simple, kindly old "darky" of "Uncle Tom's Cabin" type, with faithfulness written all over him, and a certain sad wisdom in his old face.

"You'll find Tom a great cook," said Charlie, patting the old man on the shoulder. "Many a trip we've taken together after duck, haven't we, Tom?" said he kindly.

"That's right, suh. That's right," said the old man, his eyes twinkling with pleasure.

Then came the captain--Captain Jabez Williams--a younger man, with an intelligent, self-respecting manner, somewhat non-committal, business-like, evidently not particularly anxious as to whether he pleased or not, but looking competent, and civil enough, without being sympathetic.

Next came the engineer, a young hulking bronze giant, a splendid physical specimen, but rather heavy and sullen and not over-intelligent to look at. A slow-witted young animal, not suggesting any great love of work, and rather loutish in his manners. But, he knew his engine, said Charlie. And that was the main thing. The deck-hand proved to be a shackly, rather silly effeminate fellow, suggesting idiocy, but doubtless wiry and good enough for the purpose.

While they were busy getting up the anchor of the *Maggie Darling,* I went down into my cabin, to arrange various odds and ends, and presently came the captain, touching his hat.

"There's a party," he said, "outside here, wants to know if you'll take him as passenger to Spanish Wells."

"We're not taking passengers," I answered, "but I'll come and look him over."

A man was standing up in a rowboat, leaning against the ship's side.

"You'd do me a great favour, sir," he began to say in a soft, ingratiating voice.

I looked at him, with a start of recognition. He was my pock-marked friend, who had made such an unpleasant impression on me, at John Saunders's office. He was rather more gentlemanly looking than he had seemed at the first view, and I saw that, though he was a half-breed, the white blood predominated.

"I don't want to intrude," he said, "but I have urgent need of getting to Spanish Wells, and there's no boat going that way for a week. I've just missed the mail."

I looked at him, and, though I liked his looks no more than ever, I was averse from being disobliging, and the favour asked was one often asked and granted in those islands, where communication is difficult and infrequent.

"I didn't think of taking any passengers," I said.

"I know," he said. "I know it's a great favour I ask." He spoke with a certain cultivation of manner. "But I am willing, of course, to pay anything you think well, for my food and my passage."

I waived that suggestion aside, and stood irresolutely looking at him, with no very hospitable expression in my eyes, I dare say. But really my distaste for him was an unreasoning prejudice, and Charlie Webster's phrase came to my mind--"His face is against him, poor devil!"

It certainly was.

Then at last I said, surely not overgraciously: "Very well. Get aboard. You can help work the boat"; and with that I turned away to my cabin.

# CHAPTER IV

### *In Which Tom Catches an Enchanted Fish, and Discourses of the Dangers of Treasure Hunting.*

The morning was a little overcast, but a brisk northeast wind soon set the clouds moving as it went humming in our sails, and the sun, coming out in its glory over the crystalline waters, made a fine flashing world of it, full of exhilaration and the very breath of youth and adventure, very uplifting to the heart. My spirits, that had been momentarily dashed by my unwelcome passenger, rose again, and I felt kindly to all the earth, and glad to be alive.

I called to Tom for breakfast.

"And you, boys, there; haven't you got a song you can put up? How about 'The *John B.* sails?'" And I led them off, the hiss and swirl of the sea, and the wind making a brisk undertone as we sang one of the quaint Nassau ditties:

Come on the sloop *John B.*
My grandfather and me,
 Round Nassau town we did roam;
  Drinking all night, ve got in a fight,
Ve feel so break-up, ve vant to go home.


   *Chorus*    So h'ist up the *John B.* sails,
   See how the mainsail set,
Send for the captain--shore, let us go home,
Let me go home, let me go home,
I feel so break-up, I vant to go home.


The first mate he got drunk,
 Break up the people trunk,
  Constable come aboard, take him away;
 Mr. John--stone, leave us alone,
I feel so break-up, I vant to go home.


   *Chorus*
So h'ist up the *John B.* sails, *etc., etc.*


Nassau looked very pretty in the morning sunlight, with its pink and white houses nestling among palm trees and the masts of its sponging schooners, and soon we were abreast of the picturesque low-lying fort, Fort Montague, that Major Bruce, nearly two hundred years ago, had had such a time building as a protection against pirates entering from the east end of the harbour. It looked like a veritable piece of the past, and set the imagination dreaming of those old days of Spanish galleons and the black flag, and brought my thoughts eagerly back to the object of my trip, those doubloons and pieces of eight that lay in glittering heaps somewhere out in those island wildernesses.

We were passing cays of jagged cinder-coloured rock covered with low bushes and occasional palms, very savage and impenetrable. Miles of such ferocious vegetation separated me from the spot where my treasure was lying. Certainly it was tough-looking stuff to fight one's way through; but those sumptuous words of Henry P. Tobias's narrative kept on making a glorious glitter in my mind: "*The first is a sum of one million and one half dollars.... The other is a sum of one million dollars.... The first pod was taken from a Spanish merchant and it is in Spanish silver dollars. The other on Short Shrift Island is in different kinds of money, taken from different ships of different nations ... it is all good money.*"

In fact I found to my surprise that I had the haunting thing by heart, as though it had been a piece of poetry; and over and over again it kept on going through my head.

Then Tom came up with my breakfast. The old fellow stood by to serve me as I ate, with a pathetic touch of the old slavery days in his deferential, half-fatherly manner, dropping a quaint remark every now and again; as, when drawing my attention to the sun bursting through the clouds, he said, "The poor man's blanket is coming out, sah"--phrases in which there seemed a whole world of pathos to me.

Presently, when breakfast was over, and I stood looking over the side into the incredibly clear water, in which it seems hardly possible that a boat can go on floating, suspended as she seems over gleaming gulfs of liquid space, down through which at every moment it seems she must dizzily fall, Tom drew my attention to the indescribably lovely "sea-gardens" over which we were passing--waving purple fans, fairy coral grottoes, and jewelled fishes, lying like a rainbow dream under our rushing keel. Well might the early mariners people such submarine paradises with sirens and beautiful water-witches, and imagine a fairy realm down there far under the sea.

As Tom and I gazed down lost in those rainbow deeps, I heard a voice at my elbow saying with peculiarly sickening unction:

"The wonderful works of God."

It was my unwelcome passenger, who had silently edged up to where we stood. I looked at him, with the question very clear in my eyes as to what kind of disagreeable animal he was.

"Precisely," I said, and moved away.

I had been trying to feel more kindly toward him, wondering whether I could summon up the decency to offer him a cigar, but "the wonderful works of God" finished me.

"Hello! Captain," I said presently, pointing to some sails coming up rapidly behind us. "What's this? I thought we'd got the fastest boat in the harbour."

"It's the **Susan B.,** sponger," said the Captain.

The Captain was a man of few words.

The **Susan B.** was a rakish-looking craft with a black hull, and she certainly could sail. It made me feel ashamed to watch how quickly she was overhauling us, and, as she finally came abreast and then passed us, it seemed to me that in the usual salutations exchanged between us there was mingled some sarcastic laughter; no doubt it was pure imagination, but I certainly did fancy that I noticed our passenger signal to them in a peculiar way.

I confess that his presence was beginning to get on my nerves, and I was ready to get "edgy" at anything or nothing--an irritated state of mind which I presently took out on George the engineer, who did not belie his hulking appearance, and who was for ever letting the engine stop, and taking for ever to get it going again. One could almost have sworn he did it on purpose.

My language was more forcible than classical--had quite a piratical flavour, in fact; and my friend of "the wonderful works of God" looked up with a deprecating air. Its effect on George was nil, except perhaps to further deepen his sulks.

And this I did notice, after a while, that my remarks to George seemed to have set up a certain sympathetic acquaintance between him and my passenger, the shackly deck-hand being apparently taken in as a humble third. They sat for'ard, talking together, and my passenger read to them, on one occasion, from a piece of printed paper that fluttered in the wind. They listened with fallen lower jaws and occasional attempts to seem intelligent.

The Captain was occupied with his helm, and the thoughts he didn't seem to feel the necessity of sharing; a quiet, poised, probably stupid man, for whom I could not deny the respect we must always give to content, however simple. His hand was on the wheel, his eyes on the sails and the horizon, and, though I was but a yard away from him, you would have said I was not there at all, judging by his face. In fact, you would have said that he was all alone on the ship, with nothing to think of but her and the sea. He was a sailor, and I don't know what better to say of a man.

So for companionship I was thrown back upon Tom. I felt, too, that he was my only friend on board, and a vague feeling had come over me that, within the next few hours, I might need a friend.

Fishing occurred to me as a way of passing the time.

"Are we going too fast for fishing, Tom?" I asked.

"Not too fast for a barracouta," said Tom; so we put out lines and watched the stretched strings, and listened to the sea. After awhile, Tom's line grew taut, and we hauled in a 5-foot barracouta, a bar of silver with a long flat head, all speed and ferocity, and wonderful teeth.

"Look!" said Tom, as he pointed to a little writhing eel-like shape, about nine inches long, attached to the belly of the barracouta.

"A sucking fish!" said Tom. "That's good luck;" and he proceeded to turn over the poor creature, and cut from his back, immediately below his head, a flat inch and a half of skin lined and stamped like a rubber sole--the device by which he held on to the belly of the barracouta much as the circle of wet leather holds the stone in a school-boy's sling.

"Now," he said, when he had it clean and neat in his fingers, "we must hang this up and dry it in the northeast wind; the wind is just right--nor'-nor'east--and there is no mascot like it, specially when--" Old Tom hesitated, with a slyly innocent smile in his eyes.

"What is it, Tom?" I asked.

"Have I your permission to speak, sah?" he said.

"Of course, you have, Tom."

"Well, sar, then I meant to say that this particular part of a sucking fish, properly dried in the northeast wind, is a wonderful mascot--when you're going after treasure." Tom looked frightened again, as though he had gone too far.

"Who said I was going after treasure?" I asked.

"Aren't you, sah?" replied Tom, "asking your pardon?"

I looked for'ard where the three delegates seemed to have lost interest for a while in their conversation and the fluttering paper, and appeared to be noticing Tom and me.

"Let's talk it over later on, when you bring me my dinner, Tom."

Later, as Tom stood, serving my coffee, I took it up with him again.

"What was that you were saying about treasure, Tom?" I asked.

"Well, sar, what I meant was this: that going after treasure is a dangerous business ... it's not only the living you've got to think of--." Here Tom threw a careful eye for'ard.

"The crew, you mean?"

He nodded.

"But it's the dead too."

"The dead, Tom?"

"Yes, sar--the dead!"

"All right, Tom," I said, "go on."

"Well, sar," he continued, "there was never a buried treasure yet that didn't claim its victim. Not one or two, either. Six or eight of them, to my knowledge--and the treasure just where it was for all that. I das'say it sounds all foolishness, but it's true for all that. Something or other'll come, mark my word--just when they think they've got their hands on it: a hurricane, or a tidal wave, or an earthquake. As sure as you live, something'll come; a rock'll fall down, or a thunderbolt, and somebody gets killed--And, well, the ghost laughs, but the treasure stays there all the same."

"The ghost laughs?" I asked.

"Eh! of course; didn't you know every treasure is guarded by a ghost? He's got to keep watch there till the next fellow comes along, to relieve sentry duty, so to speak. He doesn't give it away. My no! He dassn't do that. But the minute some one else is killed, coming looking for it, then he's free--and the new ghost has got to go on sitting there, waiting for ever so long till some one else comes looking for it."

"But, what has this sucking fish got to do with it?" And I pointed to the red membrane already drying up in Tom's hand.

"Well, the man who carries this in his pocket won't be the next ghost," he answered.

"Take good care of it for me then, Tom," I said, "and when it's properly dried, let me have it. For I've a sort of idea I may have need of it, after all."

And just then, old Sailor, the quietest member of the crew, put up his head into my hands, as though to say that he had been unfairly lost sight of.

"Yes, and you too, old chap--that's right. Tom, and you, and I."

And then I turned in for the night.

# CHAPTER V

### *In Which We Begin to Understand our Unwelcome Passenger.*

Charlie Webster had hinted at a nor'easter--even a hurricane. As a rule, Charlie is a safe weather prophet. But, for once, he was mistaken. There hadn't been much of any wind as we made a lee at sunset; but as I yawned and looked out of my cabin soon after dawn, about 4.30 next morning, there was no wind at all.

There was every promise of a glorious day--calm, still, and untroubled. But for men whose voyaging depended on sails, it was, as the lawyers say, a *dies non.* In fact, there was no wind, and no hope of wind.

As I stood out of the cabin hatch, however, there was enough breeze to flutter a piece of paper that had been caught in the mainsail halyard; it fluttered there lonely in the morning. Nothing else was astir but it and I, and I took it up in my hand, idly. As I did so, George reared his head for'ard--

"Morning, George," I said; "I guess we've got to run on gasolene to-day. No wind in sight--so far as I can see."

"That's right, sar," said George, rubbing the sleep out of his eyes. Presently, he came to me in his big hulking way, and said:

"There ain't no gasolene, sir--"

"No gasolene?" I exclaimed.

"It's run out in the night."

"The tanks were filled when we started, weren't they?" I asked.

"Yes, sir."

"We can't have used them up so soon...."

"No sir,--but some one has turned the cocks...."

I stood dazed for a moment, wondering how this could have happened,--then a thought slowly dawned upon me.

"Who has charge of them?" I said.

George looked a little stupid, then defiant.

"I see," I said; and, suddenly, without remembering Charlie Webster's advice not to lose your temper with a negro--I realised that this was no accident, but a deliberate trick, something indeed in the nature of a miniature mutiny. That flutter-ing paper I had picked from the halyard lay near my breakfast table. I had only half read it. Now its import came to me with full force. I had no firearms with me. Hav-ing a quick temper, I have made it a habit all my life never to carry a gun--because they go off so easily. But one most essential part of a gentleman's education had been mine, so I applied it instantly on George, with the result that a well-directed blow under the peak of the jaw sent him sprawling, and for awhile speechless, in the cockpit.

"No gasolene?" I said.

And then my passenger--I must give him credit for the courage--put up his head for'ard, and called out:

"I protest against that; it's a cowardly outrage. You wouldn't dare to do it to a white man."

"O I see," I rejoined. "So *you* are the author of this precious paper here, are you? Come over here and talk it over, if you've the courage."

"I've got the courage," he answered, in a shaking voice.

"All right," I said; "you're safe for the present--and, George, who is so fond of sleep, will take quite a nap for a while, I think."

"You English brute!" he said.

"You English brute!" he had said; and the words had impelled me to invite him aft; for I cannot deny a certain admiration for him that had mysteriously grown up in me. It can only have been the admiration we all have for courage; for, certainly I cannot have suggested that he had any other form of attractiveness.

"Come here!" I said, "for your life is safe for the time being. I would like to discuss this paper with you."

He came and we read it together, fluttering as I had seen it flutter in his fingers as he read it for'ard to the engineer and to the deck-hand. George, meanwhile, was lying oblivious to the rhetoric with which it was plentifully garnished, not to speak of the Latin quotations, taking that cure of bleeding, which was the fashionable cure of a not-unintelligent century. It began:--

"THINK HOW MANY WE ARE!--THINK WHAT WE COULD DO! *It isn't ei-ther that we haven't intelligence--if only we were to use it. We don't lack leaders--we don't lack courage--we don't lack martyrs; All are ready--*"

I stopped reading.

"Why don't you start then?" I asked.

"We have a considerable organisation," he answered.

"You have?" I said. "Why don't you use it then?"

"We're waiting for Jamaica," he answered; "she's almost ready."

"It sounds a pretty good idea to me," I remarked, "from your point of view. 'From your point of view,' remember, I said; but you mustn't think that yours is mine--not for one moment--O dear no! On the contrary, my point of view is that of the Governor of Nassau, or his representative, quite near by, at Harbour Island, isn't it?"

My pock-marked friend grew a trifle green as I said this.

"We have sails still, remember," I resumed. "George and the lost gasolene are not everything. Five hours, with anything of a wind, would bring us to Harbour Island, and--with this paper in my hand it would be--what do you think yourself?--the gallows?"

My friend grew grave at that, and seemed to be thinking hard inside, making resolutions the full force of which I didn't understand till later, but the immediate result of which was a graciousness of manner which did not entirely deceive me.

"O" he said, "I don't think you quite mean that. You're impulsive--as when you hit that poor boy down there--"

"Well," I observed, "I'm willing to treat you better than you deserve. At the same time, you must admit that your manifesto, as I suppose you would call it, is justified neither by conditions nor by your own best sense. You yourself are far more English than you are anything else--you know it; you know how hard it is for white men to live with black men, and--to tell the truth--all they do for them. The mere smell of negroes is no more pleasant to you than it is to many other white men. Englishmen have exiled themselves, for absurdly small salaries, to try to make life finer and cleaner for those dark--and, I'll admit, pathetic--barbarians. You can't deny it. And you've too much sense to deny it. So, I'll say nothing about this, if you like" (pointing to the manuscript), "and if the wind holds, put you ashore to-morrow at Spanish Wells. I like you in spite of myself. Is it a bargain?"

On this we parted, and, as I thought, with a certain friendliness on both sides.

There was no sailing wind, so there was nothing to do but stay where we were all day. The boys fished and lay around; and I spent most of the time in my cabin, reading a novel, and, soon after nine, I fell asleep in a frame of mind unaccountably trustful.

I suppose that I had been asleep about three hours when I was disturbed by a tremendous roar. It was Sailor (who always slept near me) out on the cockpit with a man under his paws--his jaws at the man's throat. I called him off, and saw that it was my pock-marked friend, with his right hand extended in the cockpit and a revolver a few inches away from it. So far as I knew it was the only firearm on the ship. "Let's get hold of that first, Sailor," I said, and I slipped it into my hip pocket.

"It's too bad that we can't be decent to people, Sailor, isn't it? It makes life awfully sad," I said.

Sailor wagged his tail.

The stars were fading on the eastern islands.

"Wake up, Tom," I called, and, "wake up, Captain!" Meanwhile, I took out the revolver from my hip pocket, and held it over the man I seemed to grow more and more sorry for.

"We've not only got a mutiny aboard," I told the captain, "but we've got treason to the British Government. Do you want to stand for that? Or shall I put you ashore with the rest?"

Unruffled as usual, he had nothing to say beyond

"Ay, ay, sir!"

"Take this cord then," I ordered him and Tom, "and bind the hands and feet of this pock-marked gentleman here; also of George, engineer; and also of Theodore, the deck-hand. Bind them well. And throw them into the dingy, with a bottle of water apiece, and a loaf of bread. By noon, we'll have some wind, and can make our way to Harbour Island, and there I'll have a little talk with the Commandant."

And as I ordered, all was done. Tom and I rowed the dingy ashore, with our three captives bound like three silly fowls, and presently threw them ashore with precious little ceremony, I can tell you; for the coral rock is not all it sounds in poetry. Then we got back to the *Maggie Darling,* with imprecations in our ears, and particularly the promises of the pock-marked rebel, who announced the certainty of our meeting again.

Of course we laughed at such threats, but I confess that, as I went down to my cabin and picked up the "manifesto," which had been forgotten in all the turmoil, I could not escape a certain thrill as I read the signature--for it was: "Henry P. Tobias, Jr."

# CHAPTER VI

### *The Incident of the Captain.*

As we hoisted the sails and the sun came up in all his glory, the smell of Tom's coffee seemed to my prosaic mind the best of all in that beautiful world. I said: "Let's give 'em a song, boys,--to cheer 'em up. How about 'Delia gone!'?"

At this suggestion even the imperturbability of the captain broke into a smile. He was a man hard to move, but this suggestion seemed to tickle him.

> *Some gave a nickel, some gave a dime;*
> *I never gave no red cent--*
> *She was no girl of mine.*
> *Delia gone! Delia gone!*

seemed to throw him into convulsions, and I took the helm awhile to give him a chance to recover. The exquisiteness of its appeal to the scoundrels, so securely trussed there on the island we were swiftly leaving behind, seemed to get him to such a degree that I was almost afraid that he might die of laughing, as has been heard of. He laughed as only a negro can laugh, and he kept it going so infectiously that Tom and I got started, just watching him. Even Sailor caught the infection, his big tongue shaking his jaws with the huge joke of it.

I don't know what they thought had happened to us, the three poor devils there on the jagged coral rock. At all events the laughter did us good by relieving the tension of our feelings, and when at last we had recovered and the captain was at the wheel again, once more sober as a judge, you couldn't have believed such an outbreak possible of him.

The *Maggie Darling* was sailing so fast that it hardly seemed necessary to trouble to call at Harbour Island; but, then, the wind might go down, our adventure was far from over, and gasolene might at any moment be a prime necessity. So we kept her going, with her beautiful sails filled out against the bluest sky you can dream of, and the ripple singing at her bow--the loveliest sight and sound in the world for a man who loves boats and the sea.

"Is there anything like it, Tom?" I asked. "Do you read your Bible? You should; it's the greatest book in the world."

Tom hastened to acquiesce.

"You remember in the Book of Job? *Three things are wonderful to me, The way of a ship on the sea, the way of an eagle in the air, and the way of a man with a maid.*"

"Ay, ay, sir," said Tom, "the way of a ship on the sea--but the way of a man with a maid--"

"What's the matter with that, Tom?"

"They're all very pretty--just like the boat; but you'll not find one near so true. We're better without them, if you ask my advice. A man's all right as long as he keeps on his boat; but the minute he lands--the girls and the troubles begin."

"Ah! Tom," I said; "but I think you told me you've a family--"

"Yes, sar, but the only good one amongst them is in the churchyard, this fifteen years."

"Your wife, Tom?"

"Yes, sar, but she was more than a woman. She was a saint. When I talk of women I don't think of her. No; God be kind to her, she is a saint, and I only wait around till she calls me."

"Tom, allow me to shake hands with you," I said, "and call myself your friend for ever."

The tears rolled down the old fellow's cheeks, and I realised how little colour really matters, and how few white men were really as white as Tom.

And so that night we made Harbour Island, and met that welcome that can only be met at the lonely ends of the earth.

The Commandant and the clergyman took me under their wings on the spot, and, though there was a good hotel, the Commandant didn't consider it good enough for me.

Bless them both! I hope to be able some day to offer them the kind of hospitality they brought me so generously in both hands; lonely men, serving God and the British Empire, in that apparently God-forsaken outpost of the world.

I liked the attitude they took toward my adventure. Their comments on "Henry P. Tobias, Jr." and the paper I had with me, were especially enlightening.

"The black men themselves," they both agreed, "are all right, except, of course, here and there. It's fellows like this precious Tobias, real white trash--the negroes' name for them is apt enough--that are the danger for the friendship of both races. And it's the vein of a sort of a literary idealism in a fellow like Tobias that makes him the more dangerous. He's not all to the bad--"

"I couldn't help thinking that too," I interrupted.

"O! no," they said, "but he's a bit mad, too. That's his trouble. He's got a personal, as well as an abstract, grudge against the British Government."

"Treasure?" I laughed.

"How did you know?" they asked.

"Never mind; I somehow got the idea."

"And he thinks that by championing the nigger he can kill two birds, see?"

"I see," I said. "I'm sorry I didn't nab him while I had him."

"Never mind," they rejoined; "if you stick to your present object, you're bound to meet him again and soon. Only take a word of advice. Have a few guns with you, for you're liable to need them. We're not afraid about nabbing the whole bunch; but we don't want to lose good men going after a bad man. And there's such a thing as having too much courage."

"I agree," I remarked. "I'll take the guns all right, but I'm afraid I'll need some more crew. I mean I'll want an engineer, and another deck-hand."

And, just as I said this, there came up some one post-haste from the village; some one, too, that wanted the clergyman, as well as me, for my captain was ill, and at the point of death.

It was an hour or so after dinner time, and we were just enjoying our cigars.

"What on earth can be the trouble?" I said, but, the three of us, including the Commandant went.

We found the captain lying in his berth, writhing with cramps.

"What on earth have you been doing with yourself, Cap.?" I asked.

"I did nothing, sir, but eat my dinner, and drink that claret you were kind enough to give me."

"That half-bottle of claret?"

"Yes, sir, the very same."

"Well, there was nothing to hurt you in that," I said. "Did you take it half and half with water, as I told you?"

"I did indeed, sir."

"And what did you eat for your dinner?"

"Some pigeon-peas, and some rainbow fish."

"Sure, nothing else?"

"God's truth, sir."

"It's very funny," I said. And then as he began to writhe and stiffen, I called out to Tom: "Get some rum, Tom, and make it boiling hot, quick--quick!"

And Tom did.

"We must get him into a sweat."

Very soon we did. Then I said to Tom:

"What do you make out of this smell that's coming from him, Tom?"

"Kerosene, sar," said Tom.

"I thought the very same," I said.

Tom beckoned me to go with him to the galley, and showed me several quart bottles of water standing on a shelf.

"Two of these were kerosene," he said, "and I suppose Cap. made a mistake"; for one looked as clear as the other.

Then I took one of them back to the captain.

"Was it a bottle like this you mixed with the claret?" I asked.

"Sure it was, sir," he answered, writhing hard with the cramps.

"But my God, man!" I said. "Couldn't you tell the difference between that and water?"

"I thought it tasted funny, boss, but I wasn't used to claret."

And then we had to laugh again, and I thought old Tom would die.

"A nigger's stomach and his head," said the Commandant, "are about the same. I really don't know which is the stronger."

And Tom started laughing so that I believe, if the wind had been blowing that way, you could have heard him in Nassau.

The captain didn't die, though he came pretty near to it. In fact, he took so long getting on his feet, that we couldn't wait for him; so we had practically to look out for a new crew, with the exception of Tom, and Sailor. The Commandant proved a good friend to us in this, choosing three somewhat characterless men, with good "characters."

"I cannot guarantee them," he said; "that's impossible, but, so far as I know, and the parson'll bear me out, they're all quiet, good-living men. The engineer's in love, and got it bad; he is engaged to be married, and is all the gladder of the good pay you're offering--more than usually comes their way--and that always keeps a man straight, at least until after he's married."

The Commandant was a splendid fellow, and he had a knowledge of human nature that was almost Shakespearean, particularly when you considered the few and poor specimens he had to study it by.

As we said good-bye, with a spanking southwest breeze blowing, I could see that he was a little anxious about me.

"Take care of yourself," he said, "for you must remember none of us can take care of you. There's no settlement where you're going--no telegraph or wireless; you could be murdered, and none of us hear of it for a month, or for ever. And the fellows you're after are a dangerous lot, take my word for it. Keep a good watch on your guns, and we'll be on the look out for the first news of you, and anything we can do we'll be there, you bet."

And so the *Maggie Darling* once more bared her whiteness to the breeze, and the world seemed once more a great world.

"It's good to be alive, Tom," I said, "on a day like this, though we get killed to-morrow."

Tom agreed to this, so did Sailor; and so, I felt, did the *Maggie Darling,* the loveliest, proud-sailed creature that ever leaned over and laughed in the grasp of the breeze.

# CHAPTER VII

### *In Which the Sucking Fish Has a Chance to Show Its Virtue.*

The breeze was so strong that we didn't use our engine that day. Besides, I wanted to take a little time thinking over my plans. I spent most of the time studying the charts and pondering John P. Tobias's narrative, which threw very little light on the situation. There was little definite to go by but his mark of the compass engraven on a certain rock in a wilderness of rocks; and such rocks as they were at that.

As I thought of that particular kind of rock, I wondered too about my three friends, trussed like fowls, on their coral rock couches. Of course they had long since cut each other free, and were somewhere active and evil-doing; and the thought of their faces seemed positively sweet to me, for of such faces are made "the bright face of danger" that all men are born to love.

Still the thought of that set me thinking too of my defences. I looked well to my guns. The Commandant had made me accept the loan of a particularly expert revolver that was, I could see, as the apple of his eye. He must have cared for me a great deal to have lent it me, and it was bright as the things we love.

Then I called Tom to me: "How about that sucking fish, Tom?" I asked.

"It's just cured, sar," he said. "I was going to offer it to you this lunch time. It's dried out fine; couldn't be better. I'll bring it to you this minute." And he went and was back again in a moment. "You must wear it right over your heart," he said, "and you'll see there's not a bullet can get near it. It's never been known for a bullet to go through a sucking fish. Even if they come near, something in the air seems to send them aside. It's God's truth."

"But, Tom," I said, "how about you?"

"I've worn one here, sar, for twenty years, and you can see for yourself"--and he bared the brown chest beneath which beat the heart that like nothing else in the world has made me believe in God.

And so we went spinning along, and, if only I had the gift of words, I could make such pictures of the islands we sailed by, the colours of the waters, the joy of our going--the white coral sand beaches and the big cocoanut palms leaning over them, and the white surges that curled along and along the surf reef, over and over again, running like children to meet each other and join each other's hands, or like piano keys rippling white under some master's fingers.

That night we made a good lee, and lay in a pool of stars, very tranquil and alive with travelling lights, great globed fishes filled with soft radiance, and dreaming glimmers and pulsating tremors of glory and sudden errands of fire. Sailor and I stayed up quite late watching the wonder in which we so spaciously floated, and of the two of us, I am sure that Sailor knew more than I.

But one thought I had which I am sure was not his, because it was born of shallower conditions than those with which his instincts have to deal. I thought: What treasure sunk into the sea by whatsoever lost ship--galleons piled up and bursting with the gold and silver of Spain, or strange triangular-sailed boats sailing from Tripoli with the many-coloured jewels of the east, "ivory, apes, and peacocks"--what treasure sunk there by man could be compared with the treasure already stored there by Nature, dropped as out of the dawn and the sunset into these unvisited waters by the lavish hand of God? What diver could hope to distinguish among all these glories the peculiar treasures of kings?

We awoke to a dawn that was a rose planted in the sky by the mysterious hand that seems to love to give the fairest thing the loneliest setting.

But there was no wind, so that day we ran on gasolene. We had some fifty miles to go to where the narrative pointed, a smaller cay, the cay which it will be remembered was, according to John Saunders's old map, known in old days as "Dead Men's Shoes"--but since known by another name which, for various reasons, I do not deem it politic to divulge--near the end of the long cay down which we were running.

Tom and I talked it over, and thought that it might be all the better to take it easy that day and arrive there next morning, when, after a good night's sleep, we should be more likely to feel rested, and ready to grapple with whatever we had to face.

So about twilight we dropped anchor in another quiet bay, so much like that of the night before, as all the bays and cays are along that coast, that you need to have sailed them from boyhood to know one from another.

The cove we were looking for, known by the cheery name of Dead Men's Shoes, proved farther off than we expected, so that we didn't come to it till toward the middle of the next afternoon, an afternoon of the most innocent gold that has ever thrown its soft radiance over an earth inhabited for the most part by ruffians and scoundrels.

The soft lapping beauty of its little cove, in such odd contrast to its sinister name--sunshine on coral sand, and farther inland, the mangrove trees, like walking laurel stepping out into the golden ripples--Ah! I should like to try my hand on the beauty of that afternoon; but we were not allowed to admire it long, for we were far from being alone.

"She's changed her paint," said Tom, at my elbow. And, looking round, I saw that our rakish schooner with the black hull was now white as a dove; and, in that soft golden water, hardly a foot and a half deep, five shadowy young sharks floated, with outstretched fins like huge bats. Our engineer, who was already wading fearlessly in the water, beautifully naked, "shooed" them off like chickens. But it was soon to be evident that more dangerous foes waited for us on the shore.

Yet there was seemingly nothing there but a pile of sponges, and a few black men. The **Susan B.** had changed her colour, it was true, but she was a well-known sponger, and I noticed no one among the group ashore that I recognised.

There was one foolish fellow that reminded me of my shackly deck-hand, whom I had always thought out of his mind, standing there on his head on the rocks, and waving his legs to attract attention.

"Why! There's Silly Theodore," called out the captain.

"Look out!" murmured Tom at my elbow.

"I'm going ashore all the same, Tom," I said.

"I'm going with you too," said the Captain. "You needn't be afraid of me. You're the sort I like. But look after your guns. There's going to be something doing--quiet as it looks."

So we rowed ashore, and there was Theodore capering in front of a pile of sponges, but no other face that I knew. But there were seven or eight negroes whose looks I took no great liking to.

"Like some fancy sponges to send home?" said one of these, coming up to me.

"Cost you five times as much in Nassau."

"Certainly I'd like a few sponges," I said.

And then Theodore came up to me, looking as though he had lost his mind over the rather fancy silk tie I happened to be wearing.

"Give me dat!" he said, touching it, like a crazy man.

"I can't afford to give you that, Theodore."

"I'd die for dat," he declared.

"Take this handkerchief instead;" but, meanwhile, my eyes were opening. "Take this instead, Theodore," I suggested.

"I'd die for dat," he repeated, touching it.

His voice and touch made me sick and afraid, just as people in a lunatic asylum make one afraid.

"Look out!" murmured Tom again at my elbow.

And just then I noticed, hiding in some bushes of seven-year apple trees, two faces I had good reason to know.

I had barely time to pull out the Commandant's revolver from my pocket. I knew it was to be either the pock-marked genius or the engineer. But, for the moment, I was not to be sure which one I had hit. For, as my gun went off, something heavy came down on my head, and for the time I was shut off from whatever else was going on.

# CHAPTER VIII

### *In Which I Once Again Sit Up and Behold the Sun.*

"Which did I hit, Tom?" were my first words as I came back to the glory of the world; but I didn't say them for a long time, and, from what Tom told me it was a wonder I ever said them at all.

"There he is, sar," said Tom, pointing to a long dark figure stretched out near by. "I'm afraid he's not the man you were looking for."

"Poor fellow!" I said; it was George, the engineer; "I'm sorry--but I saw the muzzles of their guns sticking out of the bush there. It was they or me."

"That no lie, sar, and, if it hadn't been for that sucking-fish's skin, you wouldn't be here now."

"It didn't save me from a pretty good one on the head, Tom, did it?"

"No, sar, but that was just it--if it hadn't been for that knock on the head, pulling you down just that minute, that thar pock-marked fellow would have got you. As it was, he grazed your cheek, and got one of his own men killed by mistake--the very fellow that hit you. There he is--over there."

"And who's that other, Tom?" I asked, pointing to another dark figure a few yards away.

"That's the captain, sar."

"The captain? O I'm sorry for that. God knows I'm sorry for that."

"Yas, sar, he was one of the finest gentlemen I ever knowed was Captain Tomlinson; a brave man and a good navigator. And he'd taken a powerful fancy to you, for when you got that crack on the head, he picked up your gun, and began blazing away, with words I should never have expected from a religious man. The others, except our special friend--"

"Let's call him Tobias from now on, Tom," I interposed.

"Well him, sar, kept his nerve, but the others ran for the boats as if the devil was after them; but the captain's gun was quicker, and only four of them got to the *Susan B.* The other two fell on their faces, as if something had tripped them up, in a couple of feet of water. But, just then, Tobias hit the captain right in the heart; ah! if only he had one of those skins--but he always laughed off such things as superstitious.

"There was only me and Tobias then, and the dog, for the engineer boy had gone on his knees to the *Susan B.* fellows, at the first crack, and begged them to take him away with them. I wouldn't have thought it of him--for he wasn't afraid o' them sharks, sar, as you saw, but I suppose it was thinking of his gal--anyway he went off a-praying and blubbering with what was left of the crew of the *Susan B.,* who seemed too scared to notice him, and so let him come; and, as I was saying, there was no one left but Tobias and the dog and me, and I was sure my end was not far off, for I was never much of a shot.

"As God is my witness, sar, I was ready to die, and there was a moment when I thought that the time had come and Martha was calling me; but Tobias suddenly walked away to the top of the bluff and called out to the *Susan B.* that was just running up her sails. At his word, they put out a boat for him, and, while he waited, he came down the hill towards me and the dog that stood growling over you; and for sure, I thought it was the end. But he said: 'Tell that fellow there that I'm not going to kill a defenceless man. He might have killed me once but he didn't. It's bound to be one of us some day or other, but despise me all he likes--I'm not such carrion as he thinks me; and if he only likes to keep out of my way, I'm willing to keep out of his. Tell him, when he wakes up, that as long as he gives up going after what belongs to me--for it was my grandfather's--he is safe, but the minute he sets his foot or hand on what is mine, it's either his life or mine.' And then he turned away and was rowed to the *Susan B.,* and they soon sailed away."

"With the black flag at the peak, I suppose, Tom," said I. "Well, that was a fine speech, quite a flight of oratory, and I'm sure I'm obliged to him for the life that's still worth having, in spite of this ungodly aching in my head. But how about the poor captain there! Where does all his eloquence come in there? He can't call it self-defence. They were waiting ready to murder us all right behind that seven-year apple tree, as you saw. I'm afraid the captain and the law between them are all that is necessary to cook the goose of our friend Henry P. Tobias, Jr., without any help from me--though, as the captain died for me, I should prefer they allowed me to make it a personal matter."

And then I got on my feet, and went and looked at the captain's calm face.

"It's the beginning of the price," said Tom.

"The beginning of the price?"

"It's the dead hand," continued Tom; "I told you, you'll remember, that wherever treasure is there's a ghost of a dead man keeping guard, and waiting till another dead man comes along to take up sentry duty so to say."

"That's what you said, Tom," I admitted. "Several men have been killed, it's true, but no one's put his hand on the treasure."

"All the worse for that!" replied Tom, shaking his head. "These are only a beginning. The ghost is getting busy. And it makes me think that we're coming pretty near to the treasure, or we wouldn't have had all this happen."

"Growing warm, you mean, as the children say?"

"The very thing!" said Tom. "Mark me, the treasure's near by--or the ghost wouldn't be so malicious."

And then, looking around where the captain, and the engineer and Silly Theodore lay, I said:

"The first thing we've got to do is to bury these poor fellows; but where," I added, "are the other two that fell in the water?"

"O," said Tom, "a couple of sharks got them just before you woke up."

# CHAPTER IX

### *In Which Tom and I Attend Several Funerals.*

When Tom and I came to look over the ground with a view to finding a burial-place for the dead, I realised with grim emphasis the truth of Charlie Webster's remarks--in those snuggery nights that seemed so remote and far away--on the nature of the soil which would have to be gone over in quest of my treasure. No wonder he had spoken of dynamite.

"Why, Tom," I said, "there isn't a wheel-barrow load of real soil in a square mile. We couldn't dig a grave for a dog in stuff like this," and, as I spoke, the pewter-like rock under my feet clanged and echoed with a metallic sound.

It was indeed a terrible land from the point of view of the husbandman. No wonder the Government couldn't dispose of it as a gift. It was a marvel that anything had the fierce courage to grow on it at all. For the most part it was of a grey clinker-like formation, tossed, as by fiery convulsions, in shelves of irregular strata, with holes every few feet suggesting the circular action of the sea--some of these holes no more than a foot wide, and some as wide as an ordinary-sized well--and in these was the only soil to be found. In them the strange and savage trees--spined, and sown thick with sharp teeth--found their rootage, and writhed about, splitting the rock into endless cracks and fissures with their fierce effort--sea-grape, with leaves like cymbal-shaped plates of green metal; gum-elemi trees, with trunks of glistening bronze; and seven-year apples, with fruit like painted wood.

Here and there was a thatch-palm, stunted, and looking like the head-dress of some savage African warrior. Inland, the creek, all white sand and golden sunny water at its opening, spread out far and near into noisome swamps overgrown with mangroves. Those strangest of all trees, that had something tender and idyllic as they stepped out into the ripple with their fresh child-like laurel-line leaves and dangling rods of emerald, that were really the suckers of their banyan-like roots, had grown into an obscene and bizarre maturity, like nightmares striding out in every direction with skeleton feet planted in festering mud, and stretching out horned, clawing hands that seemed to take root as one looked, and to throw out other roots of horror like a dream.

Twilight was beginning to add to its suggestions of ***diablerie,*** and the whole land to seem more and more the abode of devils.

"Come along, Tom, I can't stand any more of this. We'll have to leave our funerals till to-morrow, and get aboard for the night"--for the ***Maggie Darling*** was still floating there serenely, as though men and their violence had no existence on the planet.

"We'd better cover them up, against the turkey-buzzards," said Tom, two of those unsavory birds rising in the air as we returned to the shore. We did this as well as we were able with rocks and the wreckage of an old boat strewn on the beach, and, before we rowed aboard--Tom, and Sailor, and I--we managed to shoot a couple of them,--***pour encourager les autres.***

I don't think two men were ever so glad of the morning, driving before it the haunted night, as Tom and I; and Sailor seemed as glad as ourselves, for he too seemed to have been troubled by bad dreams, and woke me more than once, growling and moaning in his sleep in a frightened way.

After breakfast, our first thought was naturally to the sad and disagreeable business before us.

"I tell you what I've been thinking, sar," said Tom, as we rowed ashore, and I managed to pull down a turkey-buzzard that rose at our approach--happily our coverings had proved fairly effective--"I've been thinking that the only one of the three that really matters is the captain, and we can find sufficient soil for him in one of those big holes."

"How about the others?"

"Why, to tell the truth, I was thinking that sharks are good enough for them."

"They deserve no better, Tom, and I think we may as well get rid of them first.

The tide's running out strong and we won't have them knocking about for long."

So it was done as we said, and carrying them by the feet and shoulders to the edge of the bluff--George, and Silly Theodore, and the nameless giant who had knocked me down so opportunely--we skilfully flung them in, and they glided off with scarce a splash.

"See that fin yonder!" cried Tom eagerly; and next minute one of the floating figures was drawn under. "Got him already!" (with a certain grim satisfaction). "That's what I call quick work."

Then we turned to the poor captain, and carried him as gently as we could over the rough ground to the biggest of the banana holes, as the natives call them, and there we were able to dig him a fairly respectable grave.

"Do you know the funeral service, Tom?" I asked.

"No, sar, can't say as I do, though I seem to have heard it pretty often."

"Wait a minute. I've got a Bible aboard, I'll go and get it."

"I'd rather go with you, sar, if you don't mind."

"Why, you're surely not frightened of the poor fellow here, are you, Tom?"

"Well, sar, I don't say as I'm exactly that; but somehow he seems kind of lonesome; and, if you don't mind--"

So we went off, and were back in a few moments with the Bible, and I read those passages, from Job and the Psalms, immemorially associated with the passage of the dead:

*"Man, that is born of woman, is of few days, and full of trouble. He cometh forth like a flower, and is cut down: He fleeth also as a shadow, and continueth not--;* and again:

*Behold Thou hast made my days as a hand-breadth: and mine age is as nothing before Thee: Verily every man at his best state is altogether vanity. Surely every man walketh in a vain show: surely they are disquieted in vain: he heapeth up riches, and knoweth not who shall gather them. When Thou with rebukes dost correct man for iniquity, Thou makest his beauty to consume away like a moth: surely every man is vanity. Have mercy, O Lord, and give ear unto my cry: hold not thy peace at my tears, for I am a stranger with Thee, and a sojourner, as all my fathers were--."*

And, by the time we had got to the end, our tears were falling like rain into a brave man's grave.

# CHAPTER X

### *In Which Tom and I Seriously Start in Treasure Hunting.*

Tom and Sailor and I were now, to the best of our belief, alone on the island, and a lonesomer spot it would be hard to imagine, or one touched at certain hours with a fairer beauty--a beauty wraith-like and, like a sea-shell, haunted with the marvel of the sea. But we, alas!--or let me speak for myself--were sinful, misguided men, to whom the gleam and glitter of God's making spoke all too seldom, and whose hearts were given to the baser shining of such treasure as that of which I for one still dreamed--with an obstinacy all the more hardened by the opposition we had encountered, and by the menace of danger the enterprise now held beyond peradventure--a menace, indeed, to which Tobias's words had given the form of a precise challenge. Perhaps but for that, remembering the count of so many dead men--men who had lost their lives in the prosecution of my probably vain desire--I would have given the whole thing up, and sailed the boat back to less-haunted regions, which Tom and I might easily have done, and as Tom, I could plainly see, would himself have preferred.

But Tobias's challenge made such a course impossible for any man worthy of the name, and I never gave the alternative a moment's consideration. But I did give Tom his choice of staying or going--a choice made possible that day by a schooner sailing close in shore and easy to signal. Yet Tom, while making no secret of his real feelings, would not hear of quitting.

"I sha'n't think a cent worse of you, Tom," I assured him. "Indeed, I won't. It's no doubt a mad business anyway, and I'm not sure I've the right to endanger in it any other lives than my own."

"No, sar," said Tom; "I came with you, you have treated me right, and I am going to see you through."

"You're the real thing; God bless you, Tom," I exclaimed. "But I doubt if I've the right to take advantage of your goodness. I'm not sure that I oughtn't to signal those fellows to take you off with them willy-nilly."

"No, sar, you wouldn't do that, I'm sure. I'm a free man, God be praised, though my mother and father were slaves"--and he drew himself up with pathetic pride--"and I can choose my own course, as they couldn't. Besides, there's no one needs me at home; all my girls and boys are well fixed; and if I have to go, perhaps there's some one needs me more in heaven."

"All right, Tom, and thank you; we'll say no more about it." And so we let the schooner go by, and turned to the consideration of our plans.

First we went over our stores, and, thanks to those poor dead mouths that did not need to be reckoned with any more, we had plenty of everything to last us for at least a month, not to speak of fishing, at which Tom was an expert.

When, however, we turned to our plans for the treasure-hunting, we soon came to a dead stop. No plans seemed feasible in face of that rocky wilderness, all knives to the feet, and writhing serpents of fanged and toothed foliage to the eye, with brambles like barbed-wire fences at every yard.

The indications given by Tobias seemed, in the face of such a terrain, naive to a degree. Possibly the land had changed since his day. Some little, of course, it must have done. Tom and I went over Tobias's directions again and again. Of course, there was the compass carved on the rock, and the cross. There was something definite--something which, if it was ever there at all, was there still--for in that climate the weather leaves things unperished almost as in Egypt.

Sitting on the highest bluff we could find, Tom and I looked around.

"That compass is somewhere among these infernal rocks--if it ever was carved there at all--that's one thing certain, Tom; but look at the rocks!"

Over twenty miles of rocks north and south, and from two to six from east to west. A more hopeless job the mind of man could not conceive. Tom shook his head, and scratched his greying wool.

"I go most by the ghost, sar," he said. "All these men had never been killed if the ghost hadn't been somewhere near. It's the ghost I go by. Mark me, if we find the treasure it'll be by the ghost."

"That's all very well," I laughed. "But how are we going to get the ghost to show his hand? He's got such bloodthirsty ways with him."

"They always have, sar," said Tom, no doubt with some ancestral shudder of voodoo worship in his blood. "Yes, sar, they always cry out for blood. It's all they've got to live on. They drink it like you and me drink coffee or rum. It's terrible to hear them in the night."

"Why, you don't mean to say you've heard them drinking it, Tom," I asked. "That's all nonsense."

"They'll drink any kind,--any they can get hold of,--chickens' or pigs' or cows'; you can hear them any night near the slaughterhouse." And Tom lowered his voice. "I heard them from the boat, the other night, when I couldn't sleep--heard them as plain as you can hear a dog lapping water. And it's my opinion there was two of them. But I heard them as plain as I hear you."

As Tom talked, I seemed to hear Ulysses telling of his meeting with Agamemnon in Hades, and those terrible ghosts drinking from the blood-filled trench, and I shuddered in spite of myself; for it is almost impossible entirely to refuse credence to beliefs held with such certitude of terror across so many centuries and by such different people.

"Well, Tom," I remarked, "you may be right, but of one thing I'm certain; if the ghost's going to get any one, it sha'n't be you."

"We've both got one good chance against them--" Tom was beginning.

"Don't tell me again about that old sucking fish."

"Mind you keep it safe, for all that," said Tom gravely. "I wouldn't lose mine for a thousand pounds."

"Well, all right, but let's forget the damned old ghosts for the present," and I broke out into the catch we had sung on so momentous an occasion--

> *Some gave a nickel, some gave a dime;*
> *But I didn't give no red cent--*
> *She was no girl of mine--*
> *Delia's gone! Delia's gone!*

And it did one good to hear Tom's honest laughter resounding in that beautiful haunted wilderness, as the song brought back to both of us the memories of that morning which already seemed so long ago.

"I wonder what's become of our friend of 'the wonderful works of God,'" I queried.

"Wherever he is, he's up to no good, we may be sure of that," answered Tom.

At last we decided to try a plan that was really no plan at all; that is to say, to seek more or less at random, till we consumed all our stores except just enough to take us home. Meanwhile, we would, each of us, every day, cut a sort of radiating swathe, working single-handed, from the cove entrance. Thus we would prospect as much of the country as possible in a sort of fan, both of us keeping our eyes open for a compass carved on a rock. In this way we might hope to cover no inconsiderable stretch of the country in the three weeks, and, moreover, the country most likely to give some results, as being that lying in a semi-circle from the little harbour where the ships would have lain. It wasn't much of a plan perhaps, but it seemed the most possible among impossibles.

So the next morning, bright and early, we started work, I letting Tom take Sailor with him as company and protection against the spirits of the waste; also we took a revolver apiece and cartridge belts, and it seemed to me that the old fellow showed no little courage to go alone at all, with such hair-raising beliefs as he had. We each took food and a flask of rum and water to last us the day, and we promised to halloo now and again to each other for company, as soon as we got out of sight of each other. This, however, did not happen the first day. Of course, we carried a machete and a mattock apiece, though the latter was but little use, and, if either of us should find any spot worth dynamiting, we agreed to let the other know.

Harder work than we had undertaken no men have ever set their hands to. It would have broken the back of the most able-bodied navvy; and when we reached the boat at sunset, we had scarce strength left to eat our supper and roll into our bunks. A machete is a heavy weapon that needs no little skill in handling with economy of force, and Tom, who had been brought up to it, was, in spite of his years, a better practitioner than I.

I have already hinted at the kind of devil's underbrush we had to cut our way through, but no words can do justice to the almost intelligent stubbornness with which those weird growths opposed us. It really seemed as though they were inspired by a diabolic will-force pitting itself against our wills, vegetable incarnations of evil strength and fury and cunning.

Battalions of actual serpents could scarcely have been harder to fight than these writhing, tormented shapes that shrieked and hissed and bled strangely under our strokes, and seemed to swarm with new life at each onset! And the rock was almost more terrible to grapple with than they. Jagged and pointed, it was like needles and razors to walk on; and it was brittle as it was hard. While it could sometimes resist a hammer, it would at others smash under our feet like a tea-cup. It looked like some metallic dross long since vomited up from the furnaces of hell.

Only once in a while was a softer, limestone, formation--like the pit in which we had buried the captain--with hints at honeycombing, and possibilities that invariably came to nothing. Now again we would come upon a rock of this kind that seemed for a second to hint at mysterious markings made by the hand of man, but they proved to be nothing but some decorative sea-fossilisation, making an accidental pattern, like the marking you sometimes come across on some old weathered stone on a moor. Nothing that the fondest fancy could twist into the likeness of a compass or a cross!

Day after day, Tom and I returned home dead-beat, with hardly a tired word to exchange with each other.

We had now been at it for about a fortnight, and I loved the old chap more every day for the grit and courage with which he supported our terrible labours and kept up his spirits. We had long since passed out of sight of each other, and much time was necessarily wasted by our going to and from the place where we left off each day. Many a time I hallooed to the old man to keep his heart up, and received back his cheery halloo far and far away.

Once or twice we had made fancied discoveries which we called off the other to see, and once or twice we had tried some blasting on rocks that seemed to suggest mysterious tunnellings into the earth. But it had all proved a vain thing and a weariness of the flesh. And the ghost of John P. Tobias still kept his secret.

# CHAPTER XI

### *An Unfinished Game of Cards.*

One evening, as I returned to the ship unusually worn-out and disheartened, I asked Tom how the stores were holding out. He answered cheerfully that they would last another week, and leave us enough to get home.

"Well, shall we stick out the other week, or not, Tom? I don't want to kill you, and I confess I'm nearly all in myself."

"May as well stick it out, sar, now we've gone so far. Then we'll have done all we can, and there's a certain satisfaction in doing that, sar."

Good old Tom! and I believe that the wise old man had the thought behind, that, perhaps, when there was evidently nothing more to be done, I might get rid of the bee in my bonnet, and once more settle down to the business of a reasonable being.

So next morning we went at it again; and the next, and the next again, and then on the fourth day, when our week was drawing to its close, something at last happened to change the grim monotony of our days.

It was shortly after the lunch hour. Tom and I, who were now working too far apart to hear each other's halloes, had fired our revolvers once or twice to show that all was right with us. But, for no reason I can give, I suddenly got a feeling that all was not right with the old man, so I fired my revolver, and gave him time for a reply. But there was no answer. Again I fired. Still no answer. I was on the point of firing again, when I heard something coming through the brush behind me. It was Sailor racing toward me over the jagged rocks. Evidently there was something wrong.

"Something wrong with old Tom, Sailor?" I asked, as though he could answer me. And indeed he did answer as plainly as dog could do, wagging his tail and whining, and turning to go back with me in the direction whence he had come.

But I stopped to shoot off my revolver again. Still no answer.

"Off we go then, old chap," and as he ran ahead, I followed him as fast as I could over those damnable rocks.

It took me the best part of an hour to get to where Tom had been working. It was an extent of those more porous limestone rocks of which I have spoken, almost cliff-like in height, and covering a considerable area. Sailor brushed his way ahead, pushing through the scrub with canine importance. Presently, at the top of a slight elevation, I came among the bushes to a softer spot where the soil had given way, and saw that it was the mouth of a shaft like a wide chimney flue, the earth of which had evidently recently fallen in. Here Sailor stopped and whined, pawing the earth, and, at the same time, I heard a moaning underneath.

"Is that you, Tom?" I called. Thank God, the old chap was not dead at all events.

"Thank the Lord, it's you, sar," he cried. "I'm all right, but I've had a bad fall--and I can't seem able to move."

"Hold on and keep up your heart--I'll be with you in a minute," I called down to him.

"Mind yourself, sar," he called cheerily, and, indeed, it was a problem to get down to him without precipitating the loose earth and rock that were ready to make a landslide down the hole, and perhaps bury him for ever.

But, looking about, I found another natural tunnel in the side of the hill. Into this I was able to worm myself, and in the dim light found the old man, and put my flask to his lips.

"Anything broken, do you think?"

Tom didn't think so. He had evidently been stunned by his fall, and another pull at my flask set him on his feet. But, as I helped him up, and, striking a light, we began to look around the hole he had tumbled into, he gave a piercing shriek, and fell on his knees, jabbering with fear.

"The ghosts! the ghosts!" he screamed.

And the sight that met our eyes was certainly one to try the nerves. We had evidently stumbled upon a series of fairly lofty chambers hollowed out long ago first by the sea, and probably further shaped by man--caverns supported here and there by rude columns of the same rock, and dimly lit from above in one or two places by holes like mine shafts, down one of which fell masses of snake-like roots of the fig tree, a species of banyan.

Within the circle of this light two figures sat at a table--one with his hat tilted slightly, and one leaning sideways in his chair in a careless sort of attitude. They seemed to be playing cards, and they were strangely white--for they were skeletons.

I stood hushed, while Tom's teeth rattled at my side. The fantastic awe of the thing was beyond telling. And, then, not without a qualm or two, which I should be a liar to deny, I went and stood nearer to them. Nearly all their clothes had fallen away, hanging but in shreds here and there. That the hat had so jauntily kept its place was one of those grim touches Death, that terrible humorist, loves to add to his jests. The cards, which had apparently just been dealt, had suffered scarcely from decay--only a little dirt had sifted down upon them, as it had into the rum glasses that stood too at each man's side. And, as I looked at the skeleton jauntily facing me, I noticed that a bullet hole had been made as clean as if by a drill in his forehead of bone--while, turning to examine more closely his silent partner, I noticed a rusty sailor's knife hanging from the ribs where the lungs had been. Then I looked on the floor and found the key to the whole story. For there, within a few yards, stood a heavy sailor's chest, strongly bound around with iron. Its lid was thrown back, and a few coins lay scattered at the bottom, while a few lay about on the floor. I picked them up.

They were pieces of eight!

Meanwhile, Tom had stopped jabbering, and had come nearer, looking on in awed silence. I showed him the pieces of eight.

"I guess these are all we'll see of one of John P. Tobias's treasure, Tom," I said. "And it looks as if these poor fellows saw as little of it as ourselves. Can't you imagine them with it there at their feet--perhaps playing to divide it on a gamble; and, meanwhile, the other fellows stealing in through some of these rabbit runs--one with a knife, the other with a gun--and then: off with the loot and up with the sails. Poor devils! It strikes me as a very pretty tragedy--doesn't it you?"

Suddenly--perhaps with the vibration of our voices--the hat toppled off the head of the fellow facing us, in the most weird and comical fashion--and that was too much for Tom, and he screamed and made for the exit hole. But I waited a minute to replace the hat on the rakish one's head. As I was likely often to think of him in the future, I preferred to remember him as at the moment of our first strange acquaintance.

# BOOK II

*The dotted cays,*
*With their little trees,*
*Lie all about on the crystal floor;*
*Nothing but beauty--*

*Far off is duty,*
*Far off the folk of the busy shore.*

*The mangroves stride*
*In the coloured tide,*
*With leafy crests that will soon be isles;*
*And all is lonely--*
*White sea-sand only,*
*Angel-pure for untrodden miles.*

*In sunny bays*
*The young shark plays,*
*Among the ripples and nets of light;*
*And the conch-shell crawls*
*Through the glimmering halls*
*The coral builds for the Infinite.*

*And every gem*
*In His diadem,*
*From flaming topaz to moon-hushed pearl,*
*Glitters and glances*

*In swaying dances*
*Of waters adream like the eyes of a girl.*

*The sea and the stars,*
*And the ghostly bars*
*Of the shoals all bright 'neath the feet of the moon;*
*The night that glistens,*
*And stops and listens*
*To the half-heard beat of an endless tune.*

*Here Solitude*
*To itself doth brood,*
*At the furthest verge of the reef-spilt foam;*
*And the world's lone ends*
*Are met as friends,*
*And the homeless heart is at last at home.*

# BOOK II
# CHAPTER I

*Once More in John Saunders's Snuggery.*

Need I say that it was a great occasion when I was once more back safe in John Saunders's snuggery, telling my story to my two friends, comfortably enfolded in a cloud of tobacco smoke, John with his old port at his elbow, and Charlie Webster and I flanked by our whiskies and soda, all just as if I had never stirred from my easy chair, instead of having spent an exciting month or so among sharks, dead men, blood-lapping ghosts, card-playing skeletons and such like?

My friends listened to my yarn in characteristic fashion, John Saunders's eyes more like mice peeping out of a cupboard than ever, and Charlie Webster's huge bulk poised almost threateningly, as it were, with the keenness of his attention. His deep-set kind brown eyes glowed like a boy's as I went on, but by their dangerous kindling at certain points of the story, those dealing with our pock-marked friend, Henry P. Tobias, Jr., I soon realised where, for him, the chief interest of the story lay.

"The ---- rebel!" he roared out once or twice, using an adjective peculiarly English.

When I come to think of it, perhaps there is no one in His Britannic Majesty's dominions so wholeheartedly English as Charlie Webster. He is an Englishman of a larger mould than we are accustomed to to-day. He seems rather to belong to a former more rugged era--an Englishman say of Elizabeth's or Nelson's day; big, rough, and simple, honest to the core, slow to anger, but terrible when roused--a true heart of oak, a man with massive, slow-moving, but immensely efficient, "governing" brain. A born commander, utterly without fear, yet always cool-headed and never rash. If there are more Englishmen like him, I don't think you will find them in London or anywhere in the British Isles. You must go for them to the British colonies. There, rather than at home, the sacred faith in the British Empire is still kept passionately alive. And, at all events, Charlie Webster may truly be said to have one article of faith--the glory of the British Empire. To him, therefore, the one unforgivable sin is treason against that; as probably to die for England--after having notched a good account of her enemies on his unerring rifle--would be for him not merely a crown of glory, but the purest and completest joy that could happen to him.

Therefore it was--somewhat, I will own, to my disappointment--that for him my story had but one moral--the treason of Henry P. Tobias, Jr. The treasure might as well have had no existence, so far as he was concerned, and the grim climax in the cave drew nothing from him but a preoccupied nod. And John Saunders was little more satisfactory. Both of them allowed me to end in silence. They both seemed to be thinking deeply.

"Well?" I said, somewhat dashed, as one whose story has fallen down on an anti-climax. Still no response.

"I must say you two are a great audience," I said presently, perhaps rather childishly nettled.

"What's happened to your imagination!"

"It's a very serious matter," said John Saunders, and I realised that it was not my crony, but the Secretary to the Treasury of his Britannic Majesty's Government at Nassau that was talking. As he spoke, he looked across at Charlie Webster, almost as if forgetting me. "Something should be done about it, eh, Charlie?" he continued.

"---- traitor!" roared Charlie, once more employing that British adjective. And then he turned to me:

"Look here, old pal, I'll make a bargain with you, if you like. I suppose you're keen for that other treasure, now, eh?"

"I am," said I, rather stiffly.

"Well then, I'll go after it with you--on one condition. You can keep the treasure, if you'll give me Tobias!"

"Give you Tobias?" I laughed.

"Yes! if you go after the treasure, he'll probably keep his word, and go after you. Now it would do my heart good to get him, as you had the chance of doing that afternoon. Whatever were you doing to miss him?"

"I proposed to myself the satisfaction of making good that mistake," I said, "on our next meeting. I feel I owe it to the poor old captain."

"Never mind; hand the captain's rights over to me--and I'll help you all I know with your treasure. Besides, Tobias is a job for an Englishman--eh, John? It's a matter of 'King and Country' with me. With you it would be mere private vengeance. With me it will be an execution; with you it would be a murder. Isn't that so, John?"

"Exactly," John nodded.

"Since you were away," Charlie began again, "I've bought the prettiest yawl you ever set eyes on--the *Flamingo*--forty-five over all, and this time the very fastest boat in the harbour. Yes! she's faster even than the *Susan B.* Now, I've a holiday due me in about a fortnight. Say the word, and the *Flamingo's* yours for a couple of months, and her captain too. I make only that one condition."

"All right, Charlie," I agreed, "he's yours."

Whereat Charlie shot out a huge paw like a shoulder of mutton, and grabbed my hand with as much fervour as though I had saved his life, or done him some other unimaginable kindness. And, as he did so, his old broad sweet smile came back again. He was thinking of Tobias.

# CHAPTER II

### *In Which I Learn Something.*

While Charlie Webster was arranging his affairs so that he might be able to take his holiday with a free mind, I busied myself with provisioning the *Flamingo,* and in casually chatting with one and another along the water front, in the hope of gathering some hint that might guide us on our coming expedition. I thought it possible, too, that chance might thus bring me some information as to the recent movements of Tobias.

In this way, I made the acquaintance of several old salts, both white and black, one or two of whom time and their neighbours had invested with a legendary savour of the old "wrecking days," which, if rumour speaks true, are not entirely vanished from the remoter corners of the islands. But either their romantic haloes were entirely due to imaginative gossip, or they themselves were too shrewd to be drawn, for I got nothing out of them to my purpose. They seemed to be more interested in talking religion than the sea, and as navigators of Biblical deep seas little visited except by professional theologians they were remarkable. Generally speaking, indeed, piety would seem to have taken the place of piracy among the sea-going population of Nassau; a fact in which, no doubt, right-thinking folk will rejoice, but which I, I am ashamed to say, found disappointing.

Those who would master the art of talking to the Nassau negro should first brush up on their Bibles; for a pious salutation might almost be said to be Nassau etiquette for opening a conversation. Of course, this applies mainly to negroes or those "conchs" in whom negro blood predominates. The average white man in Nassau must not be considered as implicated in this statement, for he seems to take his religion much as the average white man takes it in any other part of the world.

One afternoon, in the course of these rather fruitless if interesting investigations among the picturesque shipyards of Bay Street, I had wandered farther along that historic water front than is customary with sight-seeing pedestrians; had left behind the white palm-shaded houses, the bazaars of the sellers of tortoise-shell, the negro grog-shops and cabins, and had come to where the road begins to be left alone with the sea, except for a few country houses here and there among the surrounding scrub--when my eye was caught by a little store that seemed to have strayed away from the others--a small timber erection painted in blue and white with a sort of sea-wildness and loneliness about it, and with large naive lettering across its lintel announcing itself as an "Emporium" (I think that was the word) "of Marine Curiosities."

A bladder-shaped fish, set thick with spines like a hedgehog, swung in the breeze over the doorway, and the windows on each side of the doorway displayed, without any attempt at arrangement, all sorts of motley treasures of the sea: purple sea-fans; coral in every fairy shape, white as sea-foam; conches patterned like some tessellated pavement of old Rome; monster star-fish, sharks' teeth, pink pearls, and shells of every imaginable convolution and iridescence, and many a weird and lovely thing which I had not the knowledge to name; objects, indeed, familiar enough in Nassau, but here amassed and presented with this attractive difference--that they had not been absurdly polished out of recognition, or tortured into horrible "artistic" shapes of brooch, or earring, or paper-knife, or ash-tray, but had been left with all their simple sea-magic upon them--as they might have been heaped up by the sea itself in some moonlit grotto, paved with white sand.

I pushed open the door. There was no one there. The little store was evidently left to take care of itself. Inside, it was like an old curiosity shop of the sea, every available inch of space, rough tables and walls, littered and hung with the queer and lovely bric-a-brac of the sea. Presently a tiny girl came in as it seemed from nowhere, and said she would fetch her father. In a moment or two he came, a tall weathered Englishman of the sailor type, brown and lean, with lonely blue eyes.

"You don't seem afraid of thieves," I remarked.

"It ain't a jewelry store," he said, with the curious soft sing-song intonation of the Nassau "conch."

"That's just what I was thinking it was," I said.

"I know what you mean," he replied, his lonely face lighting up as faces do at unexpected understanding in a stranger. "Of course, there are some that feel that way, but they're few and far between."

"Not enough to make a fortune out of?"

"O! I do pretty well," he said; "I mustn't complain. Money's not everything, you see, in a business like this. There's going after the things, you know. One's got to count that in too."

I looked at him in some surprise. I had met something even rarer than the things he traded in. I had met a merchant of dreams, to whom the mere handling of his merchandise seemed sufficient profit: "There's going after the things, you know. One's got to count that in too."

Naturally we were neck-deep in talk in a moment. I wanted to hear all he cared to tell me about "going after the things"--such "things"!--and he was nothing loth, as he took up one strange or beautiful object after another, his face aglow, and he quite evidently without a thought of doing business, and told me all about them-- how and where he got them, and so forth.

"But," he said presently, encouraged by my unfeigned interest, "I should like to show you a few rarer things I have in the house, and which I wouldn't sell, or even show to every one. If you'd honour me by taking a cup of tea, we might look them over."

So we left the little store, with its door unlocked as I had found it, and a few steps brought us to a little house I had not before noticed, with a neat garden in front of it, all the garden beds symmetrically bordered with conch-shells. Shells were evidently the simple-hearted fellow's mania, his revelation of the beauty of the world. Here in a neat parlour, also much decorated with shells, tea was served to us by the little girl I had first seen and an elder sister, who, I gathered, made all the lonely dreamer's family. Then, shyly pressing on me a cigar, he turned to show me the promised treasures. He also told me more of his manner of finding them, and of the long trips which he had to take in seeking them, to out-of-the-way cays and in dangerous waters.

All this I really believe the reader would find as attractive as I did; still, as I am under an implied contract to tell him a story, I am not going to palm off on him merely descriptive or informative matter, except in so far as such matter is necessary, and I have only introduced him to my dreamer in "marine curiosities" for a very pertinent reason, which will immediately appear.

He was showing me the last and rarest of his specimens. He had kept, he said, the best to the last. To me, as a layman, it was not nearly so attractive as other things he had shown me--little more to my eye than a rather commonplace though pretty shell; but he explained--and he gave me its learned name, which I confess has escaped me, owing, doubtless, to what he was next to say--that it was found, or had so far been found, only in one spot in the islands, a lovely, seldom-visited cay several miles to the north-east of Andros Island.

"What is it called?" I asked, for it was part of our plan for Charlie to do a little duck-shooting on Andros, before we tackled the business of Tobias and the treasure.

"It's called ---- Cay nowadays," he answered, "but it used to be called Short Shrift Island."

"Short Shrift Island!" I cried, in spite of myself, immediately annoyed at my lack of presence of mind.

"Certainly," he rejoined, looking a little surprised, but evidently without suspicion. He was too simple, and too taken up with his shell.

"It is such an odd name," I said, trying to recover myself.

"Yes! those old pirate chaps certainly did think up some of the rummiest names."

"One of the pirate haunts, was it?" I queried with assumed indifference.

"Supposed to be. But one hears that of every other cay in the Bahamas. I take no stock in such yarns. My shells are all the treasure I expect to find."

"What did you call that shell?" I asked.

He told me the name again, but again I forgot it immediately. Of course I had asked it only for the sake of learning more precisely about Short Shrift Island. He told me innocently enough just where it lay.

"Are you going after it?" he laughed.

"After what?" I enquired in alarm.

"The ----"; (again he mentioned the name of the shell.)

"O! well," I replied, "I am going on a duck-shooting trip to Andros before long, and I thought I might drop around to your cay and pick a few of them up for you."

"It would be mighty kind of you, but they're not easy to find. I'll tell you just exactly--" He went off, dear fellow, into the minutest description of the habitats of ----, while all the time I was eager to rush off to Charlie Webster and John Saunders, and shout into their ears--as, later, I did, at the first possible moment, that evening: "I've found our missing cay! What's the matter with your old maps, John? Short Shrift Island is ----; (I mentioned the name of a cay, which, as in the case of "Dead Men's Shoes," I am unable to divulge.)

"Maybe!" said Charlie, "maybe! We can try it. But," he added, "did you find out anything about Tobias?"

# CHAPTER III

### *In Which I am Afforded Glimpses into Futurity--Possibly Useful.*

Two or three evenings before we were due to sail, at one of our snuggery con-claves, I put the question whether any one had ever tried the divining rod in hunting for treasure in the islands. Charlie took his pipe out of his mouth, the more comfortably to beam his big brotherly smile at me.

"What a kid you are!" he said. "You want the whole bag of tricks, eh?"

But I retorted that he was quite behind the times if he considered the divining rod an exploded superstition. Its efficacy in finding water, I reminded him, was now admitted by the most sceptical science, and I was able to inform him that a great American railway company paid a yearly salary to a "dowser" to guide it in the construction of new roads through a country where water was scarce and hard to find.

Old John nodded, blinking his mischievous eyes. He had more sympathy than Charlie with the foolishness of old romance. It was true enough, he said, and added that he knew the man I wanted, a half-crazy old negro back there in Grant's Town--the negro quarter spreading out into the brush behind the ridge on which the town of Nassau proper is built.

"He calls himself a 'king,'" he added, "and the natives do, I believe, regard him as the head of a certain tribe. Another tribe has its 'queen' whom they take much more seriously. You must not forget that it is not so long ago since they all came from Africa, and the oldest negroes still speak their strange African languages, and keep up their old beliefs and practices. 'Obeah,' of course, is still actively practised.

"Why," he resumed presently, "I may even be said to practise it myself; for I protect that part of my grounds here that abuts on Grant's Town by hanging up things in bottles along the fences, which frighten away at least a percentage of would-be trespassers. You should go and see the old man, if only for fun. The lads call him 'Old King Coffee'--a memory I suppose of the Ashantee War. Any one will tell you where he lives. He is something of a witch-doctor as well as 'king,' and manages to make a little out of charms, philtres and such like, I'm told--enough to keep him in rum anyway. He has a name too as a preacher--among the Holy Jumpers!--but he's getting too old to do much preaching nowadays. He may be a little off his head, but I think he's more of a shrewd old fraud. Go and see him for fun anyway."

So, next morning, I went.

I had hardly been prepared for the plunge into "Darkest Africa" which I found myself taking, as, leaving Government House behind, perched on the crest of its white ridge, I walked a few yards inland and entered a region which, for all its green palms, made a similar sudden impression of pervading blackness on the mind which one gets on suddenly entering a coal-mining district, after travelling through fields and meadows.

There were far more blacks than whites down on Bay Street, but here there were nothing but blacks on every side. The wood of the cabins--most of them neat enough and pleasantly situated in their little gardens of bananas and cocoa-nut palms--was black, as with age or coal dust; and the very foliage, in its suggestion of savage scenes in one's old picture-books, suggested "natives." The innumerable smart little pigs that seemed free of the place were black. The innumerable goats, too, were black. And everywhere, mixed in with the pigs and the goats, were the blackest of picaninnies. Everywhere black faces peered from black squares of windows, most of them cheery and round and prosperous looking, but here and there a tragically old crone with witch-like white hair.

The roads ran in every direction, and along them everywhere were figures of black women shuffling with burdens on their heads, or groups of girls, audaciously merry, most of them bonny, here and there almost a beauty. There were churches, and dance-halls, and saloons--all radiating, so to say, a prosperous blackness. It was from these dance-halls that there came at night that droning and braying of barbaric music, as from some mysterious "heart of darkness," as one turned to sleep in one's civilised Nassau beds--a music that kept on and on into the inner blackness of the night.

At first the effect of the whole scene was a little sinister, even a little frighten-
ing. The strangeness of Africa, the African jungle, was here, and one was a white
man in it all alone among grinning savage faces. But for the figures about one being
clothed, the illusion had been complete; but for that and the kind-hearted salutations from comely white-turbaned mammies which soon sprang up about me, and
the groups of elfish children that laughingly blocked one's progress with requests-
-not in any weird African dialect but in excellent national-school English--for "a
copper please."

This request was not above the maidenly dignity of quite big and buxom lasses.
One of these, a really superb young creature, not too liberally clothed to rob one's
eyes of her noble contours, caught my attention by the singularity of something she
carried. It was an enormous axe, the shining blade balanced easily on her head, and
the handle jutting out horizontally like some savage head-dress. She looked like
a beautiful young headswoman. Even she asked for "a copper, please," but with a
saucy coquetry befitting her adolescence.

"A big girl like you too!" I ventured. She gave a fine savage laugh, without in
the least jeopardising the balance of the axe.

"I'll give you one if you'll tell me where the 'King' lives," said I.

"Ole King Coffee?" she asked, and then fell into a very agony of negro laughter. The poor old king was evidently the best of all possible jokes to this irreverent
young beauty. Then, recovering, she put her finger to her lips, suggesting silence,
and said:

"Come along, I'll show you!"

And, walking by my side, lithe as a young animal, evidently without giving a
thought to her gleaming headdress, she had soon brought me to a cabin much like
the rest, though perhaps a little poorer looking. Stopping a little short of it, she once
more put her finger to her lips.

"Shh! There he is!" and she shook all over again with suppressed giggles.

I gave her a sixpence and told her to be a good girl. Then I advanced up a little
strip of garden to where I had caught a glimpse of a venerable white-haired negro
seated at the window, as if for exhibition, with a great open book in his hands.
This he appeared to be reading with great solemnity, through enormous goggles,

though I thought I caught a side-glint of his eye, as though he had taken a swift reconnoitring glance in my direction--a glance which apparently had but deepened his attention and increased the dignity of his demeanour. That dignity indeed was magnificent, and was evidently meant to convey to the passers-by and the world at large that they were in the presence of royalty.

As I approached the doorway, my eye was caught by a massive decoration glittering immediately above it. It was a design of large gilt wooden letters which I couldn't make out at first, as it had been turned upside down. I didn't realise its meaning till afterward, but I may as well tell the reader now.

Shortly before, King Coffee, feeling in need of some insignia to blazon forth his rank, had appealed to a friend of his, a kindly American visitor, who practically kept the old fellow alive with his bounty. This kind friend was a wag too, and couldn't resist the idea that had come to him. The old man wanted something that glittered. So the American had bethought him of those big lettered signs which on the face of saloons brighten the American landscape--signs announcing somebody or other's "extra." This it was that now glittered in front of me as--the royal arms!

That it was upside down merely added to its mysterious impressiveness for the passer-by, and in no way afflicted the old king since, in spite of that imposing book at the window, he was quite unable to read. That book, a huge, much-gilded family Bible, was merely another portion of the insignia--presented by the same kind friend; as also was the magnificent frock coat, three sizes too big for the shrunken old figure, in which I found him--installed, shall I say?--as I presently stood before him in response to a dignified inclination of his head, welcoming me, at the window.

Remembering that he was not merely royal, but pious also, I made my salutation at once courtier-like and sanctimonious.

"Good day to Your Majesty," I said; "God's good, God looks after his servants."

"De Lord is merciful," he answered gravely; "God takes care of his children. Be seated, sar, and please excuse my not rising, my rheumatism is a sore affliction to me. But de Lord is good, de Lord giveth and de Lord He taketh away--and de holy text includes rheumatism too--as I have told my poor wandering flock many a Sabbath evening."

And he smiled in a sly self-satisfied way at his pious pun. "The old fellow is far from being crazy," I said to myself.

I was not long in getting to the subject of my visit. The old man listened to me with great composure, but with a marked accession of mysterious importance in his manner. So mediaeval astrologers drew down their brows with a solemn assumption of supernatural wisdom when consulted by some noble client--noble, but pitiably mortal in the presence of their hidden knowledge. He had put his book down as I talked. I noticed that he had been holding it--like his royal arms--upside down.

"It's true, sar," he said, when I had finished, "I could find it for you. I could find it for you, sure enough; and I'm de only man in all de islands dat could. But I should have to go wid you, and it's de Lord's will to keep me here in dis chair wid rheumatics. O! I don't murmur. It is de Lord's doing and it is marvellous in our eyes. De rods has turned in dese old hands many a time, and I have faith in de Lord dey would turn again--yes. I'd find it for you; sure enough. I'd find it if any man could--and it was de Lord's will. But mebbe I can see it for you widout moving from dis chair. For when de Lord takes away one gift from his servants, he gives dem another. It is His will dat dese 'ere old legs are stiff and can carry me round no more. So wot does de good Lord do? He says: 'Nebber mind dem ole legs; nebber mind dem ole weary eyes; sit jus' whar yuh are,' says de Lord, 'nebber min' no movin' round.' De Lord do wondrous things to his faithful followers; He opens de eyes of de spirit, so, having no eyes, dey shall see. Hallelujah! Glory be to de Lord!--see down into de bowels of de earth, see thousands of miles away just as plain as dis room--"

He had worked himself up to a sort of religious ecstasy, as I had seen the revivalist sect he belonged to, known as the Holy Jumpers, do at their curious services.

"Do you mean, brother, that the Lord has given you second sight?"

"Dat am it! Glory to His name, Hallelujah!" he answered. "I look in a glass ball--so; and if de spirit helps me I can see clear as a picture far under de ground, far, far away over de sea. It's de Lord's truth, sar--Blessed be His Name!"

I asked him whether he would look into his crystal for me. With a burst of profanity, as unexpected as it was vivid, he cursed "dem boys" that had stolen from him a priceless crystal which once had belonged to his old royal mother, who, before him, had had the same gift of the spirit. But, he added--turning to a table by his side, and lifting from it a large cut-glass decanter of considerable capacity, though at present void of contents--that he had found that gazing into the large glass ball of its stopper produced almost equally good results at times.

He said this with perfect solemnity, though, as he placed the decanter on top of his Bible in front of him, I observed, with an inner smile, that he tilted it slightly on one side, as though remarking, strictly to himself, that, save for a drain of dark-coloured liquid in one corner, it was painfully empty.

Then, with a sigh, he applied himself to his business of seer. First, he asked me to be kind enough to shut the door.

We had to be very quiet, he declared; the spirit could work only in deep silence. And he asked me to be kind enough to close my eyes. Then I heard his voice muttering, in a strange tongue, a queer dark gobbling kind of words, which may have been ancient African spell-words, or sheer gibberish such as magicians in all times and places have employed to mystify their consultants.

I looked at him through the corner of my eye--as, doubtless, he had anticipated, for he was glaring with an air of inspired abstraction into the ball of the decanter stopper. So we sat silent for, I suppose, some ten minutes. Then I heard him give another deep sigh. Opening my eyes, I saw him slowly shaking his head.

"De spirits don't seem communicable dis afternoon," he muttered, once more tilting the decanter slightly on one side and observing it drearily as before.

I had been rather slow, indeed, in taking the hint, but I determined to take it, and see what would happen.

"Do you think, Your Majesty," I asked, with as serious a face as I could assume, "the spirits might work better--if the decanter were to be filled?"

The old man looked at me a little cautiously, as though wondering how to take me. I tried to keep grave, but I couldn't quite suppress a twinkle; catching it, he took courage--seemed to feel that he could trust me. Slapping his knee, he let himself go in a rush of that deep, chuckling, gurgling, child-like negro laughter which is one of the most appealing gifts of his pathetic race.

"Mebbe, sar; mebbe. Spirits is curious things; dey need inspiration sometimes, just like ourselves."

"What kind of inspiration, do you think, gets the best results, Your Majesty?"

"Well, sar, I can't say as dey is very particular, but I'se noticed dey do seem powerful 'tached to just plain good old Jamaica rum."

"They shall have it," I said.

I had noticed that there was a saloon a few yards away, so before many more minutes had passed, I had been there and come back again, and the decanter stood ruddily filled, ready for the resumption of our **seance.** But before we began, I of course accepted the seer's invitation to join him and the spirits in a friendly libation.

Then--I having closed my eyes--we began again, and it was astonishing with what rapidity the thick-coming pictures began to crowd upon that inner vision with which the Lord had endowed his faithful follower!

Of course, I was inclined now to take the whole thing as an amusing imposture; but presently, watching his face and the curious "seeing" expression of his eyes, and noting the exactitude of one or two of his pictures, I began to feel that, however much he might be inventing or elaborating, there was some substratum of truth in what he was telling me. I had had sufficient experience of mediums and clairvoyants to know that, except in cases of absolute fraud, there was usually--beneath a certain amount of conscious "imaginativeness"--a mysterious gift at work, independent of their volition; something they did see, for which they themselves could not account, and over which they had no control. And as he proceeded I became more and more convinced that this was the case also with Old King Coffee.

The first pictures that came to him were merely pictures, though astonishingly clear ones, of Webster's boat, the **Flamingo,** of Webster himself, and of the men and the old dog Sailor; but in all this he might have been visualising from actual knowledge. Yet the details were curiously exact. We were all bathed in moonlight, he said--very bright moonlight, moonlight you could read by. Pictures of us out at sea, passing coral islands and so forth followed, all general in character. But presently, his gaze becoming more fixed:

"I see you anchored under a little settlement. You are rowing ashore. Dere are little pathways running up among de coral rock, and a few white houses. And, yes! Dere is a man in overalls, on de roof of a building, seeming like a little schoolhouse. He waves to you; he is getting down from de roof to meet you. But his face is in a mist, I can't see him right. Now he is gone."

He stopped and waited awhile. Then he resumed:

"Seems to be a forest; big, big trees--not like Nassau trees--and thick brush everywhere; all choked up so thick and dark, can't see nut'n. Wait a minute, dough.

Dere seems to be old houses all sunk in and los', like old ruins. Can't see dem right for de brush. And wait--Lord love you, sar, but I'se afraid--I seem to see a big light coming up trough de brush from far under de ground--just like you see old rotten wood shining in de dark--deep, deep down. Didn't I tell you de Lord gave me eyes to see into de bowels of de earth?--it's de bowels of de earth for sure--all lit up and shining. Praise de Lord!--it am de gold, for certain, all hidden away and shining dere under de ground--"

"Can't you see it closer, clearer?" I exclaimed involuntarily; "get some idea of the place it's in?"

The old man gazed with a renewed intensity.

"No," he said presently, and his disappointed tone seemed to me the best evidence yet of his truth, "I only see a little golden mist deep, deep down under de ground; now it is fading away. It's gone; I can only see de woods and de ruins again."

This brought his visions to an end. The spirits obstinately refused to make any more pictures, though the old man continued to gaze on in the decanter stopper for fully five minutes.

"De wind of de spirit bloweth as it listeth," said he at length, with the note of a more genuine piety in his voice than at the beginning; and there was a certain hushed gravity in his manner as we said good-bye, which made me feel that there had been something in his visions that had even surprised and solemnised himself.

# CHAPTER IV

### *In Which We Take Ship Once More.*

The discovery which--through my friend the dealer in "marine curiosities"--I had made, or believed myself to have made, of the situation of Henry P. Tobias's second "pod" of treasure, fitted in exactly with Charlie Webster's wishes for our trip, small stock as he affected to take in it at the moment.

As the reader may recall, "Short Shrift Island" lay a few miles to the northwest of Andros Island. Now Andros is a great haunt of wild duck, not to speak of that more august bird, the flamingo. Attraction number one for the good Charlie. Then, though it is some hundred and fifty miles long and some fifty miles broad at its broadest, it has never yet, it is said, been entirely explored.

Its centre is still a mystery. The natives declare it to be haunted, or at all events inhabited by some strange people no one has yet approached close enough to see. You can see their houses, they say, from a distance, but as you approach them, they disappear. Here, therefore, seemed an excellent place for Tobias to take cover in. Charlie's duck-shooting preserves, endless marl lakes islanded with mangrove copses, lay on the fringe of this mysterious region. So Andros was plainly marked out for our destination.

But, when Charlie was ready for the start, the wind, which is of the essence of any such contract in the Bahamas, was contrary. It had been blowing stormily from the southwest, the direction we were bound for, for several days, and nothing with sails had, for a week, felt like venturing out across the surf-swept bar. It is but forty miles across the Tongue of Ocean which divides the shores of New Providence and Andros, but you need to pick your weather for that, if you don't want to join the numerous craft that have vanished in that brief but fateful strip of water. However, the wind was liable to change any minute now, Charlie said, so he warned me to hold myself in readiness to jump aboard at an hour's notice.

The summons came at last. I had been out for dinner, and returned home about ten to find the message: "Be ready to sail at midnight."

There was a thrilling suddenness about it that appealed to one's imagination. Here I had been expecting a landsman's bed, with a book and a reading-lamp, surrounded by the friendly security of houses; instead, I was to go faring with the night wind into the mystery of the sea.

It was a night of fitful moonlight, and Nassau, with its white houses and white streets, seemed very hushed and spectral as I made my way down to the wharf, vivid in black and silver.

There is always something mysterious about starting a journey at night, even though it be nothing more out-of-the-way than catching a midnight train out of the city; and the simple business of our embarkation breathed an air of romantic secrecy. The moon seemed to have her finger on her lip, and we talked in lowered voices as though we were bound on some midnight raid. The night seemed to be charged with the expectancy of the unknown, and Sailor, who, of course, was to be a fellow-voyager, whined restlessly from the wharf side at the little yawl that awaited us in the whispering, lapping water.

Sailor had watched his master getting his guns ready for some days, and, doubtless, memories stirred in him of Scotch moors they had shot over together. He raised his head to the night wind, and sniffed impatiently, as though he already scented the wild duck on Andros Island. He was impatient, like the rest of us, because, though it was an hour past sailing-time, we had still to collect two of the crew. The same old story! I marvelled at the good humour with which Charlie--who is really a sleeping volcano of berserker rage--took it. But he reminded me of his old advice as I started for my first trip: "No use getting mad with niggers--till you positively have to!"

Well, the two loiterers turned up at last, and, all preliminaries being at length disposed of, we threw off the mooring ropes, and presently there was heard that most exhilarating of sounds, to any one who loves sea-faring, the rippling of the ropes through the blocks as our mainsail began to rise up high against the moon which was beginning to look out over the huge block of the Colonial Hotel, the sea-wall of which ran along as far as our mooring. A few lights in its windows here and there broke the blank darkness of its facade, glimmering through the avenues of royal palms. I am thus explicit because of something that presently happened, and which stayed the mainsail in its rippling ascent.

A tall figure was running along the sea-wall from the direction of the hotel, calling out, a little breathlessly, in a rich young voice as it ran:

"Wait a minute there, you fellows! Wait a minute!"

We were already moving, parallel with the wall, and at least twelve feet away from it, by the time the figure--that of a tall boy, cow-boy hatted, and picturesquely outlined in the half light--stopped just ahead of us. "Like the herald Mercury," I said to myself. He raised something that looked like a bag in his right hand, calling out "catch" as he did so; and, a moment after, before a word could be spoken, he took a flying leap and landed amongst us, plump in the cock-pit, and was clutching first one of us and then the other, to keep his balance.

"Did it, by Jove!" he exclaimed in a beautiful English accent, and then started laughing as only absurd dare-devil youngsters can.

"Forgive me!" he said, as soon as he could get his breath, "but I had to do it. Heaven knows what the old man will say!"

He seemed to take it all for granted in a delightful, nonchalant way, so that the angry protest which had already started from Charlie's lips stopped in the middle. That fearless leap had taken his heart.

"You're something of a long jump!" said Charlie.

"O! I have done my twenty-two and an eighth on a broad running jump, but I had no chance for a run there," answered the lad, carelessly.

"But suppose you'd hit the water instead of the deck?"

"What of it? Can't one swim?"

"I guess you're all right, young man," said Charlie, softened; "but ... well, we're not taking passengers."

The words had a familiar sound. They were the very ones I had used to To-bias, as he stood with his hand on the gunwale of the *Maggie Darling.* I rapidly conveyed the coincidence--and the difference--to Charlie. It struck me as odd, I'll admit, that our second start, in this respect, should be so like the first. Meanwhile, the young man was answering, or rather pleading, in a boyish way.

"Don't call me a passenger; I'll help work the boat. I'm strong, you'll see--not afraid of hard work; and anyway, won't you help a chap to an adventure?... I'll tell the truth. I heard--never mind *how*--about your trip, and I'm just nutty about bur-ied treasure. Come, be a sport; I've been watching for you all day. Pretty late start-ing, aren't you?... We can let the old guv'nor know, somehow ... and it won't kill him to tear his hair for a day or two. He knows I can take care of myself."

"Well!" said Charlie, after thinking awhile in his slow way, "we'll think it over. You can come along till the morning. Then I can get a good look at you. If I don't like your looks, we'll still be able to put you off at West End; and if I do--well--right-ho!"

"My looks!" exclaimed our young stranger, with a peculiar mellow laugh.

"What's the joke?" demanded Charlie.

"O! I only wondered what my looks had to do with it!"

"Well," laughed Charlie, entering into the spirit of the lad, "you might be pock-marked for all I know in this light--and I have a peculiar prejudice against pock-marked gentlemen."

"Unfeeling of you!" retorted the boy. "Anyhow," he added, with the same curiously attractive laugh, "I'm not pock-marked."

"We'll see at sunrise," said Charlie. "Now, boys," he shouted, "go ahead with the sails."

Once more there was that rippling of the ropes through the blocks, as our mainsail rose up high against the moon and filled proudly with the steady northeast breeze we had been waiting for. The water began to talk along our sides, and the immense freshness of the nocturnal sea took us in its huge embrace. The spray began to fly over our bows as we nosed into the glassy rollers, one of which, on the starboard side, admonished us, by half swallowing us, that only the mighty-limbed immortals might dance with safety on the bar that night, and that it were wise for even 45-foot yawls to hug the land till daylight. So, reluctantly, we kept the shadowy coast-line for our companion, as we steered for the southwestern end of the island; to our right, companions more of our mood, parallel ridges of savage whiteness, where the surf boiled and gleamed along the coral shoals.

How good it seemed to all of us to be out thus in the freedom of the night and the sea--not least to the great noble-headed hound sitting up on his haunches, keen and watchful by the steersman's side. What a strange waste of a life so short to be sleeping there on the land, when one might be out and away on such business as ours!

So two or three hours went by, as we plunged on, to the seething sound of the water, and the singing of our sails, and all the various rumour of wind and sea. After all, it was a good music to sleep to, and, for all my scorn of sleeping landsmen, an irresistible drowsiness stretched me out on the roof of the little cabin, wonderfully rocked into forgetfulness.

My nap came to an end suddenly, as though some one had flung me out through a door of blue and gold into a new-born world. There was the sun rising, the moon still on duty, and the morning star divinely naked in the heaven. And, with these glories, there rushed in again upon my ears the lovely zest and turmoil of the sea, heaving huge and tumultuous about us in gleaming hills and foam-flecked valleys.

And there was Charlie, his broad face beaming with boyish happiness, and something like a fatherly gentleness in his eyes, as he watched his companion at the tiller, whom, for a half-asleep moment of waking, I couldn't account for, till our start all came back to me, when I realised that it was our young scapegrace of over-night. Charlie and he evidently were on the best of terms already.

"Nice sailor you are!" Charlie laughed, as I sat up rubbing my eyes. "Falling asleep on watch! Our young friend here is worth ten of you."

I smiled good morning to our young passenger.

"How about the court-martial on his looks you spoke of last night, Charlie?" I asked.

"Well, he's not pock-marked, at all events, is he?--he told the truth so far. But I've still a question or two to ask him before we leave West End. We'll have break-fast first--to give him courage."

The lad made a humorous face to suggest his fear of the ordeal; as he did so, I took a good look at him. Charlie might easily have said a little more about his looks, had it been in his line, for, so far from being only "not pock-marked," he was something more like a young Apollo: some six feet in height, upstanding like the statue of a Greek athlete; a rich olive skin, through which the pink of youth came and went; and splendid blue-green eyes, fearless, and yet shy as a lad's eyes often are--at that moment of development when a good-looking lad, in spite of his height and muscles, has something of the bloom and purity of a girl, without in the least suggesting effeminacy. So, many tall athletic girls, for a brief period, suggest boys--without there being the least danger of mistake as to their real sex.

He was evidently very young--scarcely more than eighteen--and had a great tendency to blush, for all his attempt at nonchalant grown-up airs. He was the very embodiment of youth, in its sun-tipped morning flower. What Charlie could have to "question" this artless young being--as incapable of plotting, it seemed to me, as a young faun--passed my conjecture; but, as Charlie had given me a quiet wink, as he spoke of the after-breakfast examination, I suspected that it was one of those jokes of his which are apt to have something of the simplicity and roughness of seafaring tradition.

Meanwhile, old Tom had been busy with breakfast, and soon the smells of cof-fee and freshly made "johnny-cake" and frying bacon competed not unsuccessfully with the various fragrances of the morning. Is there anything to match for zest a breakfast like that of ours at dawn on the open sea?

Breakfast over, Charlie filled his pipe, assuming, as he did so, a judicial aspect.

I filled mine, and our young friend followed suit by taking a silver cigarette-case from his pocket, and striking a match on the leg of his khaki knickerbockers with a professional air.

"All set?" asked Charlie, and, after a slight pause, he went on:

"Now, young man, you can see we are nearing the end of the island. Another half-mile will bring us to West End. Whether we put you ashore there, or take you along, depends on your answers to my questions."

"Fire away," answered the youth, blowing a cloud of cigarette smoke in a delicate spiral up into the morning sky; "but I've really told you all I have to tell."

"No; you haven't told us how you came to know of our trip, what we were supposed to be after, and when we were starting."

"That's true!" flushed the lad, momentarily losing his composure. Then, partly regaining it: "Is it necessary to answer that question?"

"Absolutely," answered Charlie, beginning to look really serious.

"Because, if you don't mind ... well, I'd just as soon not."

The boy's cheeks were burning with confusion, and he looked more than ever like a girl.

"For that very reason, I want to know. We are out on a more serious business than perhaps you realise, and your answer may mean more to us than you think."

"I'm sure it cannot be of such importance to you. Really it's nothing--a mere accident; and, besides, it's hardly fair for me to tell. I should have to give away a friend, and that, I'm sure you'll agree, is not cricket."

The boy had such a true innocent air, not to speak of his taking ways which had already quite won my heart, that I protested with Charlie on his behalf. But Charlie was adamant. He'd got Tobias so on the brain that there was no reasoning with him, and the very innocent air of the lad seemed to have deepened his suspicions.

"I'm sorry, but I shall have to insist," replied Charlie, looking very grim, and more and more like an Elizabethan sea-rover.

"All right, then," answered the youth, looking him straight in the eyes, "put me ashore."

"No; I won't do that now, either," declared Charlie, sternly setting his jaw. "I'll put you in irons, rather--and keep you on bread and water--till you answer my questions."

"You will, eh?" retorted the youth, flashing fire from his fine eyes. And as he spoke, quick as thought, he leaped up on to the gunwale, and, without hesitation, dived into the great glassy rollers.

But Charlie was quick too. Like a flash, he grabbed one of the boy's ankles, so that the beautiful dive was spoiled; and there was the boy, hanging by an imprisoned leg over the ship's side, a helpless captive--his arms in the water and his leg struggling vainly to get free. But he might as well have struggled against the grip of Hercules. In another moment Charlie had him hauled aboard again, his eyes full of tears of boyish rage and humiliation.

"You young fool!" exclaimed Charlie. "The water round here is thick with sharks; you wouldn't have gone fifty yards without one of them getting you." ...

"Sharks!" gasped out the boy, contemptuously. "I know more about sharks than you do."

"You seem to know a good many things I don't," said Charlie, whose grimness had evidently relaxed a little at the lad's display of mettle. Meanwhile, my temper was beginning to rise on behalf of our young passenger.

"I tell you what, Charlie," I interposed; "if you are going to keep this up, you'd better count me out on this trip and set us both ashore at West End. You're making a fool of yourself. The lad's all right. Any one can see with half an eye there's no harm in him."

The boy shot me a warm glance of gratitude.

"All right," agreed Charlie, beginning to lose his temper too, "I'm damned if I don't." And, his hand on the tiller, he made as if to turn the boat about and tack for the shore.

"No! no!" cried the boy, springing between us, and appealingly laying one hand on Charlie's shoulder, the other on mine. "You mustn't let me spoil your trip. I'll compromise. And, skipper, I'll tell your friend here all there is to tell--everything--I swear--if you will leave it to his judgment."

Charlie gloomed for a moment or two, thinking it over, while I stood aloof with an injured air.

"Right-O," agreed Charlie at last; so our passenger and I thereupon withdrew for our conference.

It was soon over, and I couldn't help laughing aloud at the simplicity of it all.

"Just as I told you, Charlie," I exclaimed; "it's innocence itself." Turning to the lad, I said: "Dear boy, there is really no need to keep such a small secret as that from the skipper here. You'll really have to let me tell him."

The boy nodded acquiescence.

"All the same, I gave my word," he said

When I told Charlie the innocent secret, he laughed as I had done, and his usual good humour instantly returned.

"But to think, you young scapegrace," he exclaimed, "that you might either have been eaten by a shark, or have broken up an old friendship, for such nonsense as that." And, turning to me, and stretching out his huge paw, "My hand, old man; forgive my bad temper."

"Mine too," said I.

So harmony was restored, and the stubbornly held secret had merely amounted to this: Our lad was acquainted with my conchologist, and had paid him a visit the very afternoon I did, had in fact seen me leaving the house. Answering to the boy's romantic talk of buried treasure and so forth, the shell enthusiast had thought no harm to tell him of our projected trip; and that was the whole of the mysterious matter.

Yet the day was not to end without a little incident which, slight though indeed it was, was momentarily to arouse Charlie's suspicions of our charming young companion once more.

By this we had shaken off the unwelcome convoy of the coast-line, and, having had a thrilling minute or two running the gauntlet of the great combers of the southwest bar, we were at last really out to sea, making our dash under a good sailing breeze, with the engine going, too, across the Tongue of Ocean.

This Tongue of Ocean is but a narrow strip of sea--so narrow indeed that you scarcely lose sight of one coast before you sight the other--yet the oldest sailors cross it with fear, for its appalling depth within its narrow boundaries make it subject to sudden "rages" in certain winds. Even Charlie, who must have made the trip half a hundred times, scanned the western horizon with an anxious eye.

Presently, in the far southwest, tiny points like a row of pins began very faintly to range themselves along the sky-line. They were palm trees, though you could not make them out to be such, or anything in particular, till long after. One darker point seemed closer than the rest.

"There's High Cay!" rang out the rich young voice of our passenger, whom we'd half forgotten in our tense scanning of the horizon. Charlie and I both turned to him together in surprise--and his face certainly betrayed the confusion of one who has let something slip involuntarily.

"Ho! ho! young man," cried Charlie, his face darkening again, "what do you know about High Cay? I thought this was your first trip."

"So it is," answered the boy, with a flush of evident annoyance, "on the sea."

"What do you mean by 'on the sea'?"

"I mean that I've done it many a time--on the chart. I know every bluff and reef and shoal and cay around Andros from Morgan's Bluff to Washerwoman's Cut--"

"You do, eh?"

"On the chart. Why, I've studied charts since I was a kid, and gone every kind of voyage you can think of--playing at buccaneering or whaling, or discovering the North Pole. Every kid does that."

"They do, eh?" said Charlie, evidently quite unimpressed. "*I* never did."

"That's because you've about as much imagination as a turnip in that head of yours," I broke in, in defence of my young Apollo.

"Maybe, if you're so smart," continued Charlie, paying no attention to me, "you can navigate us through the North Bight?"

"Maybe!" answered our youngster pertly, with an odd little smile. He had evidently recovered his nerve, and seemed to take pleasure in piquing Charlie's bearish suspicions.

# CHAPTER V

### *In Which We Enter the Wilderness.*

Andros, as no other of the islands, is surrounded by a ring of reefs stretching all around its coasts. The waters inside this ring are seldom more than a fathom or two deep, and, spreading out for miles and miles above a level coral floor, give something of the effect of a vast natural swimming-bath. Frequently there is no more than four or five feet of water, and in calm weather it would be almost possible to walk for miles across this strange sea-bottom.

Darker and solider grew the point on which our eyes were set, till at length we were up with a thick-set, little scrub-covered island which, compared with the low level of the line of coast stretching dimly behind it, rose high and rocky out of the water. Hence its name, "High Cay," and its importance along a coast where such definite landmarks are few.

We were now inside the breakwater of the reefs, and the rolling swell of ocean gave way at once to a millpond calmness. Through this we sped along for some ten miles or so, following a low, barren coast-line till at length, to our right, the water began to spread out inland like a lake. We were at the entrance of North Bight, one of the three bights which, dotted with numerous low-lying cays, breaks up Andros Island in the middle, and allows a passage through a mazelike archipelago direct to the northwest end of Cuba. Here on the northwest shore is a small and very lonely settlement--one of the two or three settlements on the else-deserted island--Behring's Point.

Here we dropped anchor, and Charlie, who had some business ashore, proposed our landing with him; but here again our passenger aroused his suspicions--though Heaven knows why--by preferring to remain aboard. If Charlie has a fault, it is a pig-headed determination to have his own way--but our passenger was politely obstinate.

"Please let me off," he requested, in his most top-lofty English accent. "You can see for yourself that there's nothing of interest--nothing but a beastly lot of nig-ger cabins, and dirty coral rock that will cut your boots to pieces. I'd much rather smoke and wait for you in peace;" and, taking out his case and lighting a cigarette, he waved it gaily to us as we rowed off.

He had certainly been right about Behring's Point--Charlie was absurdly cer-tain that he had known it before, and had some reason for not landing--for a more forlorn and poverty-stricken foot-hold of humanity could hardly be conceived; a poor little cluster of negro cabins, indeed, scrambling up from the beach, and with no streets but craggy pathways in and out among the grey clinker-like coral rock.

But it was touching to find even here that, though the whole worldly goods of the community would scarcely have fetched ten dollars, the souls of men were still held worth caring for--one handsome youth's contempt notwithstanding--for presently we came upon a pretty little church, with a schoolhouse near by, while from the roof of an adjacent building we were hailed by a pleasant-faced white man, busy with some shingling.

It was the good priest of the little place, Father Serapion, disguised in overalls and the honest grime of his labour; like a true Benedictine, praying with his strong and skilful hands. He was down from his roof in a moment, a youngish man with the face of a practical dreamer, strangely happy-looking in what would seem to most an appalling isolation; there alone, month after month, with his black flock. But evidently his was no such thought, for he showed us with pride the new schoolhouse he was building out of the coral limestone with his own hands, as he had built the church, every stone of it, and the picturesque well, and the rampart-like wall round the churchyard. His garden, too, he was very proud of, as he well might be, wrested as it was out of the solid rock.

Father Serapion and Charlie were old friends, and, when we had accepted the Father's invitation to step into his neat little house--also built with his own hands--and dissipate with him to the extent of some grape juice and an excellent cigar, Charlie took occasion to confide in him with regard to Tobias, and, to his huge delight, discovered that a man answering very closely to his description had dropped in there with a large sponger two days before. He had only stopped long enough to buy rum at the little store near the landing, and had been off again through the bight, sailing west. He might have been making for Cuba or for a hiding-place--of which there were plenty on the western shore of the island itself. Father Serapion, who knew Charlie Webster's shooting ground, promised to send a swift messenger, should anything further of interest to us come to his knowledge within the next week or so. As he was, naturally, in close touch with the natives, this was not unlikely.

And then we had to bid the good priest farewell--not without a reverent hush in our hearts as we pondered on the marvel of noble lives thus unselfishly devoted, and as we thought, too, of the loneliness that would once more close around him when we were gone.

It was not until we had left him that I suddenly recalled King Coffee's first vision. Clearly, Father Serapion was the man in overalls shingling the roof! If only his other visions should prove as true!

Then we sailed away from Behring's Point, due west through the North Bight. But we had spent too much time with the good Father, and in various pottering about--making another landing at a lone cabin in search of fresh vegetables and further loading up our much-enduring craft with three flat-bottomed skiffs, for duck-shooting, marvellously lashed to the sides of the cabin deck--to do much more sailing that day. So at sunset we dropped anchor under the lee of Big Wood Cay, and, long before the moon rose, the whole boat's crew was wondrously asleep.

Morning found us sailing through a maze of low-lying desert islands of a bewildering sameness of shape and size, with practically nothing to distinguish one from another. Even with long experience of them, one is liable to go astray; indeed Charlie and the captain had several friendly disputes, and exchanged bets, as to which was which. Then, too, the curious milky colour of the water (in strange contrast to the jewel-like clearness of the outer sea) makes it hard to keep clear of the coral shoals that shelve out capriciously from every island. In the daylight, the deeper water is seen in a bluish track (something like the "bluing" used in laundry work), edged on either side by "the white water." One has to keep a sharp lookout every foot of the way, and many a time our keel gave an ominous grating, and we escaped some nasty ledges by the mere mercy of Heaven.

We had tried bathing at sunrise, but the water was not deep enough to swim in. So we had paddled around picking up "conches"--those great ornamental shells which house with such fanciful magnificence an animal something like our winkle, the hard white flesh of which, cut up fine, makes an excellent salad; that is, as old Tom made it.

There is no fishing to speak of in these inclosed waters; nothing to go after except sponges, which you see dotting the coral floor in black patches. We gathered one or two, but the sponge in its natural state is not an agreeable object. It is like a mass of slimy india-rubber, and has to "die" and rot out its animal life, which it does with a protesting perfume of great power, the sponge of our bath-tubs being the macerated skeleton of the once living sponge.

We had hoped to reach our camp, out on the other side of the island, that evening, but that dodging the shoals and sticking in the mud had considerably delayed us. Besides, though Charlie and the captain both hated to admit it, we had lost our way. We had been looking all afternoon for Little Wood Cay, but as I said before, one cay was so much like another--all alike flat, low-lying, desolate islands covered with a uniform scrub and marked by no large trees--not unbeautiful if one has a taste for melancholy levels, but unpicturesquely depressing and hopeless for eyes craving more featured and coloured "scenery."

So night began to fall, and, as there is no sailing in such waters at night, we once more cast anchor under a gloomy, black shape of land, exceedingly lonesome and forgotten-looking, which we agreed to call "Little Wood Cay"--till morning.

Soon all were asleep except Sailor and me. I lay awake for a long time watching the square yard of stars that shone down through the hatch in our cabin ceiling like a little window looking into eternity, while the waters lapped and lapped outside, and the night talked strangely to itself. It was a wonderful meeting-place of august lonely things--that nameless, dark island, that shadowy water heaving vast and mournful, that cry of the wind, that swaying vault of the stars, and, framed in the cabin doorway, the great black head of the old dog, grave and moveless and wondering.

Next morning Charlie and the captain were forced to own up that the island, discovered to the day, was not Little Wood Cay. No humiliation goes deeper with a sailing man than having to ask his way. Besides, who was there to ask in that solitude? Doubtless a cormorant flying overhead knew it, but no one thought to ask him.

However, we were in luck, for, after sailing about a bit, we came upon two lonely negroes standing up in their boats and thrusting long poles into the water. They were sponging--most melancholy of occupations--and they looked forlorn enough in the still dawn. But they had a smile for our plight. It was evidently a good joke to have mistaken Sapodilla Cay for Little Wood Cay. Of course, we should have gone--"so." And "so" we presently went, not without rewarding them for their information with two generous drinks of old Jamaica rum. I never before saw two men so grateful for a drink. Their faces positively shone with happiness. Certainly it must have seemed as if that rum had fallen out of the sky, the last thing those chilled and lonesome men could have hoped for out there in the inhospitable solitude.

One of our reasons for seeking Little Wood Cay, which it proved had been close by all the time, was that it is one of the few cays where one can get fresh water. "Good water here," says the chart. We wanted to refill some of our jars, and so we landed there, glad to stretch our legs, while old Tom cooked our breakfast on the beach, under a sapodilla tree. The vegetation was a little more varied and genial than we had yet seen, and some small white flowers, growing in long lines, as if they had been planted, wafted a very sweet fragrance across our breakfast table of white coral sand. While we were eating, two or three little lizards with tails curiously twirled round and round, like a St. Catherine wheel, made themselves friendly, and ate pieces of bread from our hands without fear.

Now that we knew where we were, it was clear, but by no means careless sailing to our camp. By noon we had made the trip through the bight and, passing out of a narrow creek known as Loggerhead Creek, were on the southwest side of the island. A hundred and fifty miles or so of straight sailing would have brought us to Cuba, but our way lay north up the coast, as we had come down the other. Here was the same white water as the day before, with the bluish track showing the deeper channel; the same long, monotonous coast; the same dwarf, rusty-green scrub; not a sign of life anywhere. Nothing but the endless blue-streaked white water and the endless desert shore. We were making for what is known as the Wide Opening, a sort of estuary into which a listless stream or two crawl through mangrove bushes from the interior swamps.

But there is one startlingly pleasant river, curiously out of place in its desolate surroundings, which, after running through several miles of marl swamps, enters upon an oasis of fresher foliage and even such stately timber as mahogany, lignum vitae, and horseflesh; and it was in this oasis, at the close of the third day out, we found ourselves. Here, a short distance from the bank, on some slightly ascending rocky ground, under the spreading shade of something like a stretch of woodland, Charlie, several years ago, had built a rough log shanty for his camp--one of two or three camps he had thus scattered for himself up and down the "out islands," where nearly all the land is no man's, and so every man's, land. The particular camp at which we had now arrived he had not visited for a long time.

"Last time I was here," said Charlie, laughing, as, having dropped anchor, we rowed ashore, "I thought of what seemed to me an infallible test of the loneliness of the place. Let's see how it has worked."

The log shanty stood before us, doorless, comfortably tucked in under an umbrella-headed tamarind tree. There was no furniture in it but a rough table. On the table was a bottle, fallen over on its side. This Charlie snatched up, with a cry of satisfaction.

"What do you think of this?" he said. "Not a soul has been here but the turkey-buzzards. The beggars knocked this over, but otherwise it is just as I left it. Do you want better proof than this?"--and he held out the bottle for me to look at.

It was a quart of Scotch whisky, corked and sealed as it had left the distillery. And it had been there for two years! The more the reader ponders this striking fact, the better will he be able to realise the depth of the solitude in which we now found ourselves. While the boys slung the beds, and Tom busied himself with dinner, we sat and smoked, and savoured together our satisfaction in our complete and grandiose isolation.

"It might well be weeks before any one could find us!" said my friend, eager as a boy lapping up horrors from his favourite author. "Yes, weeks!" And then he added: "It was creeks like this the old pirates used to hide in."

And so we talked of pirates and buried treasure, while the sun set like a flight of flamingoes over a scene that was indeed like a picture torn from a Boy's Own Book of Adventure.

Then Tom brought us our dinner, and the dark began to settle down upon us, thrillingly lonely, and full of strange, desolate cries of night creatures from the mangrove swamps that surrounded our little oasis for miles. Not even when Tom and I had been alone on "Dead Men's Shoes" had I felt so utterly out of and beyond the world.

Charlie smacked his big smiling lips at the savage solitude of it.

"It's great to get away from everything--like this--isn't it?" he remarked, looking round with huge satisfaction into the homeless haunted wild, with its brooding blackness as of primeval chaos.

Sailor lay at our feet, dreaming of to-morrow's duck. His master's thoughts were evidently in the same direction.

"How are you with a gun?" he asked, turning to the boy.

"O! I won't brag. I had better wait till to-morrow. But, of course, you will have to lend me a gun."

"I have a beauty for you--just your weight," replied Charlie, his face beaming as it did only at the thought of his guns, which he kept polished like jewels and guarded as jealously as a violinist his violin, or an Arab his harem.

# CHAPTER VI

*Duck.*

Dawn was just breaking as I felt Charlie's great paw on my shoulder next morning. He was very serious. For a moment, as I sat up, still half asleep, I thought he had news of Tobias. But it was only duck. He had heard a great quacking during the night, and was impatient to make a start. So was Sailor.

I was scarcely dressed when Tom arrived with breakfast, and in a few minutes we had shouldered our guns, and were crossing the half mile of peaty waste that divided us from the marl lakes from which the night wind had carried that provocative quacking. Ahead of us, the crew were carrying the skiffs on their shoulders, and very soon we were each seated in regulation fashion on a canvas chair in front of our respective skiffs, with our guns across our knees, and a negro behind us to do the poling.

Charlie went ahead, with Sailor standing in the bow quivering with excitement. The necessity of absolute silence, of course, had been impressed upon us all by the most severe of all sportsmen. But the admonition was scarcely necessary, for, as the sun rose, the scene that spread before us was beautiful enough to have hushed the most garrulous tongue. Far and near stretched misty levels of milkwhite water, in which the mangrove trees made countless islands, sometimes of considerable extent, impenetrable coppices often thirty or forty feet high. From horizon to horizon there was nothing but white water and these coppice-islands of laurel green--one so like another that I marvelled how Charlie expected to find his way back to camp again in the evening. As the sun rose, flooding the wide floors with lonely splendour, it smote upon what at first I took to be gleaming clouds of purest silver unrolling before it. It was an angelic host of white herons soaring and circling, stainless spirits of the dawn high up in the fathomless blue. As we stole silently along in our skiffs, it seemed to me that we were invading some sanctuary of morning, "occult, withdrawn," at the far limits of the world.

I looked around to see how it was all affecting my young friend. He was close behind, almost at my shoulder--his beautiful young face like that of a Greek god in a dream.

"Isn't it wonderful?" he mused, in that voice like a musical instrument. My heart went out to him in gratitude, for, as I caught sight of Charlie's serious figure ahead--with no thought, I was sure, but duck--I realised how lonely I would have been amid all that solemn morning without my young fellow-worshipper.

Presently, the herons alighted on one of the near-by mangrove coppices, and it was as though the green bushes had suddenly been clothed with miraculous white flowers--or been buried under a fall of virgin snow. High up against the sun, several larger birds were uncouthly gambolling in morning joy. It was hard to believe that they were pelicans--such different birds they seemed from their foolish moping fellows at the Zoo. And ah! yonder, riding innocent of danger, filling the morning air with their peaceful quacking, a huge glittering fleet of--teal.

At the sight, Charlie turned with solemn warning hand--at which I heard my young friend behind me smothering his profane laughter--and made various signs by which Tom (who was poling me) and I understood that our job, and also that of my companion, was to steal behind one mangrove copse after another till we had got on the other side of that unsuspecting squadron--which might then be expected to take flight in Charlie's direction and rush by him in a terrified whirlwind. This not very easy feat of stalking we were able to accomplish, thereby winning Charlie's immense approval and putting him a splendid temper for the rest of the day; for, as the wild cloud swept over him, he was able to bring down no less than seven. Like a true sportsman, in telling the story afterward in John Saunders's snuggery, he averred that the number was nine!

I don't know who was happier; he, or Sailor, again and again splashing through the water and returning with a bird in his mouth. As for me, I'm afraid I am but a half-hearted sportsman, for I noticed that, as the bang-bang-bang of the gun shivered the silence like a crystal mirror, those white spirits of the morning, till then massed in dazzling purity on the mangrove coppice, rose once more in a silver cloud and vanished. It was as though beauty were leaving the world.

And once more I was thankful for the presence of dreaming and worshipful youth.

"I shall hate him in a minute," said the boy, but just then came across the water to him Charlie's jovial challenge to show his marksmanship, and he took it forthwith with the same nonchalant skill as he did everything, making, by long odds, as Charlie generously admitted, the most brilliant shot of the day.

Now duck-hunting, while exciting enough in itself, makes unexciting reading, and when I have recorded that Charlie's bag for the day was no less than seven and a half dozen (I am not sure that our figures will agree) and related one curious incident of the day, I shall leave the reader to imagine the rest. The incident was this:

Early in the afternoon, Charlie had made one notable killing (five, I think it was; he will correct me if I am wrong), but one of the birds, not quite dead, had fluttered away into a particularly dense coppice. Sailor had been sent in after it, but, after a lot of fussing about, came out without his bird. Twice Charlie sent him in; with the same result. So, growing impatient, he got out of his skiff, went splashing through the marl water himself, and disappeared in the coppice. Presently we heard his big laugh, and the next second, his gun. A moment or two after, he reappeared, shouldering a huge black snake. No wonder Sailor had been unable to find his bird, for, as Charlie had entered the coppice, the first thing he saw was this snake coiled up in the centre, with a curious protuberance bulging out his neck. Flying from Charlie's gun, the unfortunate duck had landed right into the jaws of the snake! As Charlie ripped open the snake's side--there, sure enough, was the duck. So he was added to the day's bag; and, if he was among those Tom cooked for dinner when we reached camp again that evening, he had the somewhat unusual experience of being eaten twice in one day.

# CHAPTER VII

### *More Particularly Concerns Our Young Companion.*

The days that now followed for a week might be said to be accurate copies of that first day. Had one kept a diary, it would have been necessary to write only:

"ditto," "ditto," "ditto" under the happenings of the first. Wonderful dawn--ditto; white herons and pelicans--ditto; duck--ditto. But they were none the less delightful for that--for there is a sameness that is far indeed from monotony--though I will confess that, for my own tastes, toward the week-end, the carnage of duck began to partake a little of that latter quality. Still, Charlie and Sailor were so happy that I wouldn't have let them suspect that for the world.

Besides, I had my wonderful young friend, to whom I grew daily more attached. He and I, of course, were of the same mind on the subject of duck, and, as often as possible, would give Charlie the slip and explore the ins and outs of the mangrove islands--merely for beauty's sake, or in study of the queer forms of life dimly and uncouthly climbing the ladder of being in those strange solitudes. In these comradely hours together, I found myself feeling drawn to him as I can imagine a young father is drawn to a young son; and sometimes I seemed to see in his eyes the suggestion of a confidence he was on the edge of making me--a whimsical, pondering expression, as though wondering whether he dare to tell me or not.

"What is it, Jack?" I asked him for once when, early in our acquaintance, we had asked him what we were to call him, he had answered with a laugh: "O! call me Jack--Jack Harkaway." We had laughed, reminding him of the schoolboy hero of that name and he had answered: "Never mind. One name is as good as another. That is my name when I go on adventures. Tell me your adventure names. I don't want your prosaic every-day names." "Well," I had replied, entering into the lad's humour, "my friend here is Sir Francis Drake, and I, well--I'm Sir Henry Morgan."

"What is it, Jack?" I repeated.

But he shook his head.

"No!" he replied, "I like you ever so much--and I wish I could; but I mustn't."

"Somebody else's secret again?" I ventured.

"Yes!" And he added: "This time it's mine too. But--some day perhaps; who knows?--" He broke off in boyish confusion.

"All right, dear Jack," I said, patting his shoulder, "take your own time. We're friends anyway."

"That we are," responded the lad, with a fine glow.

We left it so at the moment, and had ourselves poled in the direction of Charlie's voice, which was breaking mirror after mirror of exquisite lagoon-like silence with demands for our return to camp. He evidently had shot all the duck he wanted, for that day, and was beginning to be hungry for dinner.

Yet, I mustn't be too hard on Charlie, for, as we know, even Charlie had another object in his trip besides duck. As a certain poet brutally puts it, he had anticipated also "the hunting of man." In addition, though it is against the law of those Britannic islands, he had promised me a flamingo or two for decorative purposes. However, flamingoes and Tobias alike kept out of gunshot, and, as the week grew toward its end, Charlie began to grow a little restive.

"It looks," he murmured one evening, as we had completed our fourteenth meal of roast duck, and were musing over our after-duck cigars, "it looks as if I am not going to have any use for this."

He had taken a paper from his pocket. It was a warrant with which he had provided himself, empowering him to arrest the said Henry P. Tobias, or the person passing under that name, on two counts: First, that of seditious practices, with intent to spread treason among His Majesty's subjects, and, second, that of wilful murder on the high seas. I should say that, following my recital of the eventful cruise of the *Maggie Darling,* old Tom and I had been required to make sworn depositions of Tobias's share in the happenings of that cruise, the murder of the captain and so forth, and I too had surrendered as evidence that eloquent manifesto which I had seen Tobias reading to the ill-fated George and "Silly" Theodore, and had afterward discussed with him.

The probabilities were that the Government would treat Tobias's case as that of a dangerous madman, rather than as a hanging matter, but, whatever its point of view, it was clearly undesirable for such an individual to remain at large. So the governing powers in Nassau, with whom Charlie Webster was *persona grata,* had been glad to take advantage of his enthusiastic patriotism and invest him with constabulary powers, hoping that he might have an opportunity of using them. Personally, he was rather ashamed of having to employ such tame legal methods. From his point of view, shooting at sight was all that Tobias deserved, and to give him a trial by jury was an absurdity of legal red-tape. In this respect he agreed with the great Mr. Pickwick, that "the law is a hass." It was always England's way, he said, and, if she didn't mind, this leniency to traitors would some day be her undoing!

Charlie put the despised, yet precious, warrant back into his pocket, and gazed disgustedly across the creek, where the loveliest of young moons was rising behind a frieze of the homeless, barbaric brush.

"There was never such a place in the world," he asserted, "to hide in--or get lost in--or to starve in. I have often thought that it would make the most effective prison in the world. Instead of spending good public money in housing and feeding scoundrels behind bars, and paying officials to keep them there, supporting expensive establishments at Dartmoor and so forth, why doesn't the British Government export her convicts over here, land them on one of those mangrove shoals, and-- give them their freedom! Five per cent. might succeed in escaping. The mangrove swamps would look after the rest."

As I have said, Charlie was a terrifying patriot. For most offences he had the humanity of a vast forgiveness. He was, generally speaking, the softest-hearted man I have ever met. But for any breach of the sacred laws of England he was something like a Spanish Inquisitor. England, in fact, was his religion. I have heard of worse.

The young moon rose and rose, while Charlie sat in the dusk of our shanty, like a meditative mountain, saying nothing, the glowing end of his cigar occasionally hinting at the circumference of his broad Elizabethan face.

"I'll get him, all the same," he said presently, coming out of a sort of trance, in which, as I understood later, his mind had been making a geographical survey of our neighbourhood, going up and down every creek and corner on a radius of fifty miles.

"If," he added, "he knows this island better than I do, I'll give him this warrant to eat for his breakfast.... But let's turn in. I'll think it out by the morning. Night brings counsel."

So we sought our respective cots; but I had scarcely begun to undress, when a foolish accident for which I was responsible happened, an accident that might have had serious consequences, and which, as a matter of fact did have--though not at the moment.

As I told the reader at the beginning of this story, I am not accustomed to guns- -being too afraid of my bad temper. Charlie knew this, and was all the time cautioning me about holding my gun right and so on, and especially about shaking out any unused cartridges at the end of the day's shoot.

Well, this special night, I had forgotten his warnings. Neglecting everything a man should do to his gun when he is finished with it for the day, I had left two cartridges in it, left the trigger on the hair-brink of eternity, and other enormities for which Charlie presently, and quite rightly, abashed me with profanity; in short, my big toe tripped over the beast as it stood carelessly against the wall of my cabin, and, as it fell, I received the contents in the fleshy part of my shoulder.

The explosion brought the whole crew out of their shanty, in a state of gesticulating nature, and, as Charlie, growling like a bear, was helping to bring first aid, suddenly our young friend Jack--whose romantic youth preferred sleeping outside in a hammock slung between two palm trees--put him aside.

"I know better how to do this than you, Sir Francis," he said, laughing.

"Same as the sharks, eh?" said Charlie.

"Just the same ... but, let's have a look at your medicine chest, and give me the lint quick."

So Jack took charge, and acted with such confidence and skill,--finally binding up my wound, which was but a slight one--that Charlie stood by dumbfounded and with a curious soft look in his face which I didn't understand till later. The tears came into my eyes at the wonderful tenderness of the lad, as he bent over me.

"Do I hurt you?" he kept saying. "You and I are pals, you know."

"You don't hurt me a bit, dear Jack," I answered; "what a clever lad you are!"

Then Jack looked up for a moment, and caught Charlie's wondering look; and, it seemed to me that he changed colour, and looked frightened.

"Sir Francis is jealous," he said; "but I've finished now. I guess you'll sleep all right after that dose I gave you. Good night...." And he slipped away.

Jack had proved himself a practised surgeon, and, as he predicted, I slept well--so well and so far into next morning that Charlie at last had to waken me.

"What do you think?" were his first words.

"Why, what?" I asked, sitting up, and wincing from my wounded shoulder.

"Our young friend has skipped in the night!"

"'Skipped?'" I exclaimed, with a curious ache at my heart.

"Sure enough! Gone off on that little nigger sloop that dropped in here yesterday afternoon, I guess."

"You don't mean it?"

"No doubt of it--I wonder whether you've had the same thought as I had."

"What do you mean?"

"You know I always said there was a mystery about that boy?"

"Well, what of it?"

"Did you notice the way he bound your shoulder last night?"

"What of it?"

"Did you ever see a man bind a wound like that?"

"What do you mean?"

"I mean simply that the mystery about our Jack Harkaway was just this: Jack Harkaway was no boy at all--but just a girl; a brick of a dare-devil girl!"

# CHAPTER VIII

### Better Than Duck.

Charlie Webster's discovery--if discovery it was--of "Jack Harkaway's" true sex seemed so far plausible in that it accounted not only for much that had seemed mysterious about him and his manner, but also (though this I did not mention to Charlie) it accounted for certain dim feelings of my own, of which, before, I had been scarcely conscious.

But we were not long left to continue our speculations, being presently interrupted by the arrival of exciting news--news which, I need hardly say, promptly drove all thought of "Jack Harkaway" out of Charlie Webster's head, though it was not so soon to be banished from mine.

The news came in the form of a note from Father Serapion. He had sent it by the captain of a sponging schooner, who, in turn, had sent it by two of his men in a rowboat, not being able to venture up the creek himself owing to the northeast wind which was blowing so hard, that, as sometimes happens on that coast, he might have been left high and dry.

Father Serapion's note simply confirmed his conjecture that it was Tobias who had bought rum at Behring's Point, and that he was probably somewhere in the network of creeks and marl lagoons in our neighbourhood. Telling Tom to give the men a good breakfast, Charlie thought the news over.

"I'll tell you what we'll do," he said presently. "I'm going to leave you here-- and I'm going to charter the sponger out there. This river we are on comes out of a sound that spreads directly south--Turner's Sound. Turner's Sound has two outlets: this, and Goose River ten miles down the shore. Now, if Tobias is inside here, he can only get out either down here, or down Goose River. I am going down in the sponger to the mouth of Goose River, to keep watch there; and you must stay where you are, and keep watch here. Between the two of us, a week will starve him out. Or, if not, I'll chase after him up Goose River; and in that case, he'll have to come down here--and it will be up to you, for I don't believe he'll have the nerve to try walking across the marl ponds to the east coast."

So it was settled, and, presently, Charlie went along with two of his best guns and Sailor, in the rowboat, and I saw him no more for a week. Meanwhile, I kept watch and studied the scenery, and old Tom and I talked about the strange people who inhabited the interior--those houses that moved away into the mist as soon as you caught sight of them. Some day old Tom and I are going to explore the interior, for he is not so much afraid of ghosts as he was, since we tried them out together.

At the end of the week, the wind was blowing strong from the west and the tides ran high. About noon we caught sight of triumphant sails making up the river. It was Charlie back again.

"Got him!" was all he said, as he rowed ashore.

Sailor was with him in the rowboat, but I noticed that he was limping, going on three legs.

"Yes!" said Charlie. "It's lucky for Tobias he only got Sailor's foot, or, by the living God, I'd have stood my trial for manslaughter, or whatever they call it. It'll soon be all right, old man," he said, taking Sailor's wounded paw in his hand, "soon be all right." Sailor wagged his tail vigorously, to show that a gunshot through one of his legs was a mere nothing.

"Yes!" said Charlie, as we sat at lunch in the shack, under the tamarind tree; "we've got him safe there under decks all right; chained up like a buoy. If he can get away, I'll believe in the Devil."

"Won't you tell me about it?" I asked.

"Not much to tell; too easy altogether. I waited a couple of days at the mouth of Goose River. Then I got tired, and left the sponger with the captain and two or three men, while I went up the river with a couple of guns and Sailor, and a man to pole the skiff--just for some duck-shooting, you know. We lay low, for two days, on the marshes, and then Sailor got sniffing the wind one morning, as if there was something around he didn't care much for. The day before, we had heard firing a mile or so inland, and had come upon some duck that some one or other had shot and hadn't had time to pick up. So, that morning, I let Sailor lead the way. We had been out about an hour, and were stealing under the lee of a big mangrove island, after some duck we had sighted a little to the eastward, when, suddenly, apparently without anything to alarm them, they rose from the water and came flying in our direction. But evidently something, or somebody, had startled them. They came right by me. It was hard luck not to be able to take a shot at them. I could have got a dozen of them at least."

"Probably more," I suggested.

"I really believe I could," agreed Charlie, in entire innocence. "Well, as I have said, it was hard luck; but Sailor seemed to have something on his mind, beside duck. As we poled along silently in the direction from which the duck had risen, he grew more and more excited, and, at last, as we neared a certain mangrove copse to which all the time he had been pointing, he barked two or three times, and, I let him go. Poor old fellow!"

As he told the story, Sailor, who seemed to understand every word, rubbed his head against his master's hand.

"He went into the mangroves, just as he'd go after duck, but he'd hardly gone in, when there were two shots, and he came out limping, making for me. But, by this, I was close up to the mangroves myself, and in another minute, I was inside; and there, just like that old black snake you remember, was Tobias--his gun at his shoulder. He had a pot at me, but, before he could try another, I knocked him down with my fist--and--Well, we've got him all right. And now you can go after your treasure, as soon as you like. I'll take him over to Nassau, and you can fool around for the next month or so. Of course we'll need you at the trial, but that won't come off for a couple of months. Meanwhile, you can let me know where you are, in case I should need to get hold of you."

"All right, old man," I said, "but I wish you were coming along with me."

"I've got all the treasure I want," laughed Charlie. "But don't you want to come and interview our friend? He might give you some pointers on your treasure hunt."

"How does he take it?" I asked.

"Pretty cool. He talked a little big at first, but now he sits with his head between his hands, and you can't get a word out of him. Something up his sleeve, I dare say."

"I don't think I'll bother to see him, Charlie," I said. "I'm kind of sorry for him." Charlie looked at me.

"Sorry for him?"

"Yes! In fact, I rather like him."

"Like him?" Charlie bellowed; "the pock-marked swine!"

"I grant," I said, smiling, and recalling Charlie's own words of long ago, "that his face is against him."

"Rather like him? You must be crazy! You certainly have the rummiest taste."

"At least you'll admit this much, Charlie," I said; "he has courage--and I respect courage even in a cockroach--particularly, perhaps, in a cockroach ..."

"He's a cockroach, all right," said Charlie.

"Maybe," I assented. "I don't pretend to love him, but--"

"If you don't mind," interrupted Charlie, "we'll let it go at 'but'--". And he rose. "The tide's beginning to run out. Send me word where you are, as soon as you get a chance; and good luck to you, old chap, and your doubloons and pieces of eight!"

Then we walked down to his row-boat, and soon he was aboard the sponger. Her sails ran up, and they were off down stream--poor Tobias, manacled, somewhere between decks.

"See you in Nassau!" I shouted.

"Right-O!" came back the voice of the straightest and simplest Englishman in the world.

# BOOK III

*Across the scarce-awakened sea,*
  *With white sail flowing,*
  *And morning glowing,*
*I come to thee--I come to thee.*

*Past lonely beaches,*
*And gleaming reaches,*
*And long reefs foaming,*
*Homing--homing--*
  *A-done with roaming,*
  *I come to thee.*

*The moon is failing,*
 *A petal sailing*
  *Down in the west*
  *That bends o'er thee;*
*And the stars are hiding,*
*As we go gliding*
  *Back to the nest,*
  *Ah! back to thee.*

# BOOK III
# CHAPTER I

## *In Which We Gather Shells--and Other Matters.*

With Charlie gone, and duck-shooting not being one of my passions, there was nothing to detain me in Andros. So we were soon under way, out of the river, and heading north up the western shore of the big monotonous island. We had some fifty miles to make before we reached its northern extremity--and, all the way, we seldom had more than two fathoms of water, and the coast was the same interminable line of mangroves and thatch palms, with occasional clumps of pine trees, and here and there the mouth of a creek, leading into duck-haunted swamps.

It was evident that the island kept its head above water with difficulty, and that the course we were running over was all the time aspiring to be dry land, right away from the coast to the Florida channel. For miles west and north, it would have been impossible to find more than three fathoms. As I said of the east coast, inside the reef, it was a vast swimming bath, but of greater dimensions, a swimming bath with a floor of alabaster, and water that seemed to be made of dissolved moonstones.

For a while, our going seemed very much as though we were sailing a big toy-boat in an illimitable porcelain bathtub. There were no rocks to look out for, no shoals in what was really one vast shoal, and all was smooth as milk. All the afternoon, till the sun set and the stars came out and we dropped our anchor in a luminous nothingness, a child could have navigated us; but, when the next day brought us up to the northwest corner of Andros, we found ourselves face to face with a variety of difficulties: glimmering sandbars, reaches of moon-white shoals, patches of half-made land with pines struggling knee-deep in the tide; here and there a mile of mangroves, and delusive channels of blue water; beauty everywhere spreading out her sweeping laces of foam--a welter of a world still in its making, with no clear passages for any craft drawing more than a canoe. Loveliness everywhere--again the waving purple fans, and the heraldic fish, and the branching coral mysteriously making the world. Loveliness everywhere!--in fact a labyrinth of beauty with no way out.

And the captain, like nearly every captain I have met in the Bahamas, knew as little about it as I did. Charlie had been right; you must know how to sail your own boat when you hoist your sails in Bahaman waters. I confess that I began to regret Charlie's preoccupation with Tobias--for, in spite of his missing his way that day in the North Bight, Charlie seems to know his way in the dark wherever one happens to be on the sea.

However, there was really nothing to worry us. There was no wind. The weather was calm, and there was lots of time. At last, after studying the chart and talking it over with Tom, who though he had only shipped as cook, was the best sailor on board, we decided to run north, and take a channel described on the chart as "very intricate."

At last we came to a little foam-fringed cay, where it was conceivable that the shyest and rarest of shells would choose to make its home--a tiny aristocrat, driven out of the broad tideways by the coarser ambitions and the ruder strength of great molluscs that feed and grow fat and house themselves in crude convolutions of uncouthly striving horn; a little lonely shore, kissed with the white innocence of the sea, where pearls might secretly make themselves perfect, untroubled by the great doings of wind and tide--merely rocked into beauty by ripple and beam, with a teardrop falling, once in a while, into their dim growing hearts, from some wavering distant star.

It was impossible to imagine a cay better answering to my conchologist's description of Short Shrift Island. Its situation and general character, too, bore out the surmise. On landing, also, we found that it answered in two important particulars to Tobias's narrative. We found, as he had declared, that there was good water there for passing ships. Also, we found, in addition to the usual scrub, that cabbage-wood trees grew there very plentifully, particularly, as he said, on the highest part of the island. Our conjectures were presently confirmed by the captain of a little sponging boat that, an hour after our arrival, put in for water. Yes, he said, it was ---- Cay (giving it the name by which it was generally known, and by which the conchologist had first mentioned it to me). So, having talked it all over with Tom, I decided that here we would stay for a time, and try our luck.

But, first, having heard from the sponging captain, that he was en route for Nassau, I gave him a letter to Charlie Webster, telling him of our whereabouts, in case he should have sudden need of me with regard to Tobias.

It was too late to begin treasure-hunting that day, but Tom and I made an early start, the following morning, prospecting the island--I having set the men to work gathering shells, in the hope of being able to oblige my shell-loving friend. The island was but a small cay compared with that of Dead Men's Shoes,--on which we had so memorably laboured side by side--some five miles long and two broad. It was a pretty little island, rising here and there into low hills, and surprising us now and again with belts of pine trees. But, of course, the cabbage-wood tree was our special tree; and, as I said before, this grew plentifully. All too plentifully, indeed; and cabbage-wood stumps, alas! were scarcely more rare.

The reader may recall that Tobias's narrative, in reference to his second "pod" of one million dollars, had run: "***On the highest point of this Short Shrift Island is a large cabbage-wood stump, and twenty feet south of that stump is the treasure, buried five feet deep and can be found without difficulty.***" But which was the highest point? There were several hillocks that might claim to be that--all about equal in height.

We visited them all in succession. There was a "large cabbage-wood stump" on each and all of them! It had seemed an absurdly inadequate direction, even as we had talked the narrative over in John Saunders's snuggery. But, confronted with so many "large cabbage-wood stumps," one began to suspect Henry P. Tobias of having been a humourist, and to wonder whether John Saunders was not right after all, and the whole manuscript merely a hoax for the benefit of buried-treasure cranks like myself.

However, as the high points of the island were only seven in all, it was no difficult matter to try them all out, one by one, as we had plenty of time and plenty of hands for the work. For, of course, it would have been idle to attempt any concealment of my object from the crew. Therefore, I took them from their shell-gathering, and, having duly measured out twenty feet south from each promising cabbage-wood stump, set them to work. They worked with a will, for I promised them a generous share of whatever we found.

Alas! it was an inexpensive promise, for, when we had duly turned up the ground, not only twenty feet, but thirty, forty, and fifty feet, not only south but north, east and west of the various cabbage-wood stumps on the seven various eminences, we were none of us the richer by a single piece of eight. Then we tried the other cabbage-wood stumps on lower ground, and any other likely looking spots, till, after working for nearly a fortnight, we must have dug up most of the island.

And then Tom came to me with the news that our provisions were beginning to give out. As it was, he said, before we returned to Nassau, we should have to put in at Flying Fish Cove--a small settlement on the larger island some five miles to the nor'ard,--for the purchase of various necessities.

"All right, Tom," I said, "I guess the game is up! Let's start out to-morrow morning."

And then I betook myself, like the great philosopher, to gathering shells on the sea-shore, finding some specimens which, to my unlearned eye, seemed identical with that shell so dear to the learned conchologist's heart.

The following afternoon we put in at Flying Fish Cove, a neat little settlement, with a pretty show of sponging craft at anchor, a few prosperous-looking houses on the hill-side, and a sprinkling of white, or half-white, people in the streets. I instructed Tom and the Captain to stock in whatever we needed. We would lie there that night, and in the morning we would make a start, homeward-bound, for Nassau.

"You may as well have your sucking fish back, Tom," I said, laughing in self-disgust. "I shall have no more need of it. I am through with treasure-hunting."

"I'd keep it a little longer, sar," answered Tom; "you never know."

# CHAPTER II

### *In Which I Catch a Glimpse of a Different Kind of Treasure.*

I had, as I have said, made up my mind to start on the homeward trip early the following morning, but something happened that very evening to change my plans. I had dropped into the little settlement's one store, to buy some tobacco, the only kind that Charlie Webster--who carried his British loyalty into the smallest concerns of life, declared fit to smoke--some English plug of uncommon strength, not to say ferocity, a real manly tobacco such as one might imagine the favourite chew of pirates and smugglers.

I stayed chatting with the storekeeper--a lean, astute-looking Englishman, with the un-English name of Sweeney--who made a pretty good thing of selling his motley merchandise to the poor natives, on the good old business principle of supplying goods of the poorest possible quality at the highest possible prices. He was said to hold a mortgage on the lives of half the population, by letting them have goods on credit against their prospective wages from sponging trips, he himself being the owner of three or four sponging sloops, and so doubly insured against loss. His low-ceilinged, black-beamed store, dimly lit with kerosene lamps, was a wilderness of the most unattractive merchandise the mind of man can conceive, lying in heaps on trestles, hanging from the rafters, and cluttering up every available inch of space, so that narrow lanes only were left among dangling tinware, coils of rope, coarse bedding, barrels in which very unappetising pork lay steeping in brine, other barrels overflowing with grimy looking "grits" and sailors' biscuits, drums of kerosene and turpentine, cans of paint, jostling clusters of bananas, strings of onions, dried fish, canned meats, loaves of coarse bread, tea and coffee, and other simple groceries.

Two rough planks laid on barrels made the counter, up to which from time to time rather worn-looking, spiritless negro women and girls would come to make their purchases, and then shuffle off again in their listless way. Once in a while a sturdy negro would drop in for tobacco, with a more independent, well-fed air. The Englishman served them all with a certain contemptuous indifference in which one somehow felt the presence of the whip-hand.

While he was thus attending a little group of such customers, I had wandered toward the back of the store, curiously examining the thousand and one commodities which supplied the strange needs of humanity here in this lost corner of the world; and, thus occupied, I was diverted by a voice like sudden music, a voice oddly rich and laughing and confident for such grim and sinister surroundings. It was one, too, which I seemed to have heard before, and not so very long ago. When I turned in its direction, I was immediately arrested, as one always is by any splendour of vitality; for a startling contrast indeed--to the spiritless, furtive figures that had been coming and going hitherto--was this superb young creature, tall and lithe with proudly carried head on glorious shoulders. Her skin was a golden olive, and it had been hard to say which was the more intensely black--her hair, or the proud eyes which, turning presently in my direction, seemed to strike upon me as with an actual impact of soft fire. I swear I could feel them touch me, as it were, with a warm ray, the radiating glow of her fragrant vitality enfolding me as in a burning golden cloud.

I wondered whether her glance enfolded everything she looked on in the same way. Perhaps it was but the unconsciously exerted force of her superb young womanhood intensely alive. Yet--there was too a significant wild shyness about her. My presence seemed at once to put her on her guard. The music of her voice was suddenly hushed, as though she had hurriedly, almost in terror, thrown a robe of reticence about an impulsive naturalness not to be displayed before strangers. As for the storekeeper, he was evidently a familiar acquaintance. He had known her--he said, after she was gone--since she was a little girl.

While he spoke, my eyes had accidentally fallen on the coin still in his hand, with which she had just paid him.

"Excuse me," I said, "but that is a curious-looking coin."

I thought that a shade of annoyance passed over his face, as though he had been better pleased if I had not noticed it. However, it was too late, and he handed it to me to examine--a large antique-looking gold coin.

"Why!" I said, "this is a Spanish doubloon!"

"That's what it is," said the Englishman laconically.

"But doesn't it strike you as strange that she should pay her bills with Spanish doubloons?" I asked.

"It did at first," he answered; and then, as if annoyed with himself, he was attempting to retrieve an expression that carried an implication he evidently didn't wish me to retain, he added: "Of course, she doesn't always pay in Spanish doubloons."

"But she does sometimes?"

"O! once in a great while," he answered, evasively. "I suppose they have a few old coins in the family, and use them when they run out of others."

It was as lame an explanation as well could be, and no one could doubt that, whatever his reason for so doing, he was lying.

"But haven't you trouble in disposing of them?" I enquired.

"Gold is always gold," he answered, "and we don't see enough of it here to be particular as to whose head is stamped upon it, or what date. Besides, as I said, it isn't as if I got many of them; and you can always dispose of them as curiosities."

"Will you sell me this one?" I asked.

"I see no harm in your having it," he said, "but I'd just as soon you didn't mention where you got it."

"Certainly," I answered, disguising my wonder at his secretiveness. "What is it worth?"

He named the sum of sixteen dollars and seventy-five cents. Having paid him that amount, I bade him good-night, glad to be alone with my eager, glowing thoughts. These I took with me to a bit of coral beach made doubly white by the moon, rustled over by giant palms, and whispered to by the vast living jewel of the sea. Surely my thoughts had a brightness to match even this glitter of the night. I took out my strange doubloon, and flashed it in the moon.

But, brightly as it shone, it hardly seemed as bright as it would have seemed a short while back; or, perhaps, it were truer to say that in another, newer aspect it shone a hundred times more brightly. The adventure to which it called me was no longer single and simple as before, but a gloriously confused goal of cloudy splendours, the burning core of which--suddenly raying out, and then lost again in brightness--were the eyes of a mysterious girl.

# CHAPTER III

### *Under the Influence of the Moon.*

My days now began to drift rather aimlessly, as without apparent purpose I continued to linger on an island that might well seem to have little attraction to a stranger--how little I could see by the mystification of the good Tom, in whom, for once, of course, I could not confide. Yet I had a vague purpose; or, at least, I had a feeling that, if I waited on, something would develop in the direction of my hopes.

That doubloon still suggested that it was the key to a door of fascinating mystery to which Chance might at any moment direct me.

And--why not admit it?--apart from my buried treasure, to the possible discovery of which the doubloon seemed to point, I was possessed with a growing desire for another glimpse of those haunting eyes. They needed not their association with the mysterious gold, they were magnetic enough to draw any man, with even the rudiments of imagination, along the path of the unknown. All the paths out of the little settlement were paths into the unknown, and, day after day, I followed one or another of them out into the wilderness, taking a gun with me, as an ostensible excuse for any spying eye, and bringing back with me occasional bags of the wild pigeons which were plentiful on the island.

One day I had thus wandered unusually far afield, and at nightfall found myself still several miles from home, on a rocky path overhanging the sea. The coastline had been gradually mounting in a series of precipitous headlands, at the foot of which the sea made a low booming that suggested hidden caves. Looking over the edge in places, one could see that it had hollowed out the porous rock well under the base of the cliffs, and here and there fallen masses of boulder told of a gradual encroachment which, in course of time, would topple down into the abyss the precarious pathway on which I stood. Inland the usual level scrub gave place to a stretch of wild forest, very dense, and composed of trees of many varieties, loftier than was usual on the island.

There was no sign of habitation anywhere. It was a wild and lonely place, and presently over its savage beauty stole the glamour of the moon rising far over the sea. I sat down on a ledge of the cliffs, and watched the moonlight grow in intensity, as the darkness of the woods deepened behind me. It was a night full of witchcraft; a night on which the stars, the moon, and the sea together seemed hinting at some wonderful thing about to happen.

Far down in the clear water I could see the giant sea-fans waving in a moony twilight, touched eerily in those glassy depths with sudden rays of the spectral light; soft bowers of phosphorescence spread a secret radiance about dimly branching coral groves. And, all the while, the path of the moon over the sea was growing stronger--laying, it would seem, an even firmer pathway of silver stretching to the very foot of the cliff-side.

I am not given to quoting poetry, but involuntarily there came to my mind some lines remembered from boyhood:

If on some balmy summer night     You rowed across the moon-path white, And saw the shining sea grow fair     With silver scales and golden hair-- What would you do?

"What would you do?" I repeated dreamily, thinking very likely as I said them, of two eyes of mysteriously enfolding fire; and then, as if the fairy night were matching the words with a challenge, what was this bright wonder suddenly present on one of the boulders far down beneath me?--a tall shape of witchcraft whiteness, standing, full in the moon, like a statue in luminous marble of some goddess of antiquity. Only once before, and but for a moment, had I seen a woman's form so proudly flowerlike in its superb erectness!

My eyes and my heart together told me it was she; and, as she hung poised over the edge of the water, in the attitude of one about to dive, a turn of her head gave me that longed-for glimpse of those living eyes filled with moonlight. She stood another moment, still as the night, in her loveliness; and the next, she had dived directly into the path of the moon. I saw her eyes moon-filled again, as she came to the surface, and began to swim--not, as one might have expected, out from the land, but directly in toward the unseen base of the cliffs. The moon-path *did* lead to a golden door in the rocks, I said to myself, and she was about to enter it. It was a secret door known only to herself; and then, for the first time that night, I thought of that doubloon.

Perhaps if I had not thought of it, I should not have done what then I did. There will, doubtless, be those who will censure me. If so, I am afraid they must. At all events, it was the thought of that doubloon that swayed the balance of my hesitation in taking the moon-path in the track of that bright apparition. The pursuit of my hidden treasure had long been so fixed an idea in my mind that a scruple would have had to be strong indeed to withstand my impulse to follow up so exciting a clue. (When, alas! has the pursuit of gold heeded any scruples?) Or it is quite possible that a radically different inclination held this materialistic excuse as a cloak for itself. A moment of such glamorous excitement may well account for some confused psychology.

I leave it to others who, less fortunate than I, were not exposed to the breathless enchantments of that immortal night, those sorceries of a situation lovely as the wildest dreams of the heart. I looked about for a way down to the edge of the sea. It was not easy to find, but after much perilous scrambling, I at length found myself on the boulder which had so lately been the pedestal of that Radiance; and, in another moment, I had dived into the moon-path and was swimming toward the mysterious golden door.

Before me the rocks opened in a deep narrow crevasse, a long rift, evidently slashing back into the cliff, beneath the road on which I had been treading. I could see the moonlit water vanishing into a sort of gleaming lane between the vast over-hanging walls. In a few moments I was near the entrance, but, as yet, I could not touch bottom with my feet, and so I swam on into the giant portal, into a twilight which was still luminous with reflections, and to which my eyes readily accustomed themselves.

Presently I felt my feet rest lightly on firm sand, and, still shoulder deep in the water, I walked on another yard or two--to be brought to a sudden stop. There she was coming toward me, breast high in that watery tunnel! The moon, continuing its serene ascension, lit her up with a sudden beam. O! shape of bloom and glory!

For a moment we both stood looking at each other, as if transfixed. Then she gave a frightened cry, and put her hands up to her bosom; as she did so, a stream of something bright--like gold pieces--fell from her mouth, and two like streams from her opened hands. Then, as quick as light, she had darted past me, and dived into the moon-path beyond. She must have swam under the water a long way, for when I saw her dark head rise again in the glimmering path, it was at a distance of many yards.

I had no thought of following her, but stood in a dream among the watery gleams and echoes.

So, once in a lifetime, for a few fortunate ones, all the various magics of the earth, all the mysterious hints and promises of her loveliness that make the heart overflow with a prophetic sense of some supernatural happiness on the brink of coming to pass, combine in one supreme shape of beauty, given to us by divine ordering, on the starlit summit of one immortal hour.

For me had come that hour of wonder; for me out of that tropic sea, into whose flawless deeps my eyes had so often gone adream, had risen the creature of miracle.

O! shape of moonlit marble! O! holiness of this night of moon and stars and sea!

# CHAPTER IV

### *In Which I Meet a Very Strange Individual.*

Yes! I was in love. Yet I hope, and think, that the reader will not resent this unexpected incursion into the realms of sentiment when he considers that my sudden attack was not, like most such sudden attacks, an interruption in the robuster course of events, but, instead, curiously in the direct line of my purpose. Because the eyes of an unknown girl had thus suddenly enthralled me, I was not, therefore, to lose sight of that purpose.

On the contrary, they had suddenly shone out on the pathway along which I had been blindly groping. But for the accident of being in the dirty little store at so psychological a moment, hearing that strangely familiar voice and catching sight of that mysterious doubloon as well as those mysterious eyes, I should have set sail that very night, and given up John P. Tobias's second treasure in final disgust. As it was, I was now warmly on the track of some treasure--whether his or not--with two bright eyes further to point the way. Never surely did a man's love and his purpose make so practical a conjunction.

When I reached my lodging at last in the early morning following that night of wonders, my eyes and heart were not so dazed with that vision in the cave that I did not vividly recall one important detail of the strange picture--those streams of gold that had suddenly poured out of the mouth and hands of the lovely apparition.

Need I say that over and over again the picture kept coming before me?--haunting me like that princess from my childhood's fairy-book, from whose mouth, as she spoke, poured all manner of precious stones. We all remember that--and had I not seen the very thing itself with my own grown-up eyes? No wonder it all seemed like a dream, when, late next forenoon, I woke from a deep sleep that had been long in overtaking me. Yet, there immediately in my mind's eye, without any shadow of doubt, was the beautiful picture once more, vivid and exact in every detail. Without doubting the evidence of my senses, I was forced to believe that, by the oddest piece of luck, I had stumbled upon the hiding-place of that hoard of doubloons, on which my fair unknown drew from time to time as she would out of a bank.

But who was she?--and where was her home? There had seemed no sign of habitation near the wild place where I had come upon her, though, of course, a solitary house might easily have escaped my notice hidden among all that foliage, particularly at nightfall.

To be sure, I had but to enquire of the storekeeper to learn all I wanted; but I was averse from betraying my interest to him or to any one in the settlement--for, after all, it was my own affair, and hers. So I determined to pursue my policy of watching and waiting, letting a day or two elapse before I again went out wandering with my gun.

Probably she would be making another trip to the settlement, before long. Doubtless, it was for that purpose that she was visiting her very original safety-deposit vault when I had come so embarrassingly upon her.

However, inaction, in the circumstances, was difficult, and when two days had gone without bringing any sign of her, I determined to follow the trail of my last expedition, and find out whether that strip of rocky coast, with its hidden cavern, actually did stand firm somewhere on the solid earth, or was merely a phantom coast fronting

"The foam of perilous seas in faery-land forlorn."

As a matter of fact, I did find it, after having lost my way in the thick brush several times before doing so. I reckoned, when at last I emerged upon it, that it was a distance of some six or seven miles from the settlement, though, owing to my ignorance of the way, it had taken me a whole morning to cover it. Did *she* have to thread these thorny thickets every time she came to the little town? No; doubtless she was acquainted with some easier and shorter path.

However, here was the cliff-bastioned sea-front, and down there was the boulder on which she had stood like a statue in the moonlight. I craned my neck over the edge of the cliffs to catch sight of the entrance to her cave--but in vain. Nor was there apparent any way of reaching it from above. Evidently it was only approachable from the sea.

Then I looked about for some signs of a house; but, though it was full noon-day, the forest presented an unbroken front of close-growing trees, and a rich confusion of various foliage uncommon on those islands. I counted at least a dozen varieties, among which were horseflesh, wild tamarind, redwood, pigeon-plum, poison wood, gum-elemi, fig, logwood, and mahogany.

Evidently there was an unusually thick layer of soil over the coral rock in this part of the island, which was in the main composed of the usual clinker and scrub--where it was not mangrove swamp. Yet in spite of appearances, it was certain that there must be some sort of dwelling there-about, and not so very far off either--unless, indeed, my mysterious girl was but a mermaid after all.

So I left the craggy bluff facing the sea, and plunged into the woods. I had no idea how dark it was going to be, but, coming out of the sun, I was at once bewildered by the deep and complicated gloom of massed branches overhead, and the denser darkness of shrubs and vines so intricately interwoven, as almost to make a solid wall about one. Then the atmosphere was so close and airless that a fear of suffocation combined at once with the other fear of being swallowed up in all this savage green life, without hope of finding one's way out again into the sun. I had fought my way in but a very few yards when both these fears clutched hold of me with a sudden horror, and the perspiration poured from me; I could no longer distinguish between the way I had come and any other part of the wood! Indeed, there was no way anywhere!

It was now only a question of sturdy fighting and squirming one's way through the meshes of a gigantic basketwork of every variety of fantastic branch and stem and stout strangling thorn-set vine, made the denser with snaky roots--not merely twisting about one's feet, but dropping from the boughs in nooses and festoons for one's neck; air-plants too, like birds' nests, further choking up the meshes, and hanging moss, like rotting carpets, adding still more to the murk and curious squalor of a foul fertility where beauty, like humanity, found it impossible to breathe.

I must have battled through this veritable inferno of vegetation for at least an hour--though it seemed a life-time. Clouds of particularly unpleasant midges filled my eyes, not to speak of mosquitoes, and a peculiar kind of persistent stinging fly was adding to my miseries, when at last, begrimed and dripping with sweat, I stumbled out, with a cry of thankfulness, on to comparatively fresh air, and something like a broad avenue running north and south through the wood. It was indeed densely overgrown, and had evidently not been used for many years. Still, it was comparatively passable, and one could at least see the sky, and take long breaths once more.

The rock here emerged again in places through the scanty soil, but it had evidently been levelled here and there, so as to make it serve as a rough but practicable road, though plainly it was years since any vehicles had passed that way. Still, there was no sign of a house anywhere. Presently, however, as I stumbled along, I noticed something looming darkly through the matted forest on my left, that suggested walls. Looking closer, I saw that it was the ruin of a small stone cottage, roofless, and indescribably swallowed up in the pitiless scrub. And then, near by, I descried another such ruin, and still another--all, as it were, sunk in the terrible gloom of the vegetation, as sometimes, at low tide, one can discern the walls of a ruined village at the bottom of the sea.

As I struggled on, and my eyes grew accustomed to looking for them, I detected still more of these ruins, of various shapes and sizes, impenetrably smothered but a few yards inward on each side of the road.

Evidently I had come upon a long-abandoned settlement, and presently, on some slightly higher ground to the left, I thought I could make out the half-submerged walls of a much more ambitious edifice. Looking closer, I noted, with a thrill of surprise, the beginning of a very narrow path, not more than a foot wide, leading up through the scrub in its direction. Narrow as it was, it had clearly been kept open by the not-infrequent passage of feet. With a certain eerie feeling, I edged my way into it, and, after following it for a hundred yards or so, found myself close to the roofless ruin of a spacious stone house with something of the appearance of an old English manor house. Mullioned windows, finely masoned, opened in the shattered wall, and an elaborate stone staircase, in the interstices of which stout shrubs were growing, gave, or once had given, an entrance through an arched doorway--an entrance now stoutly disputed by the glistening trunk of a gum-elemi tree and endless matted rope-like roots of giant vines and creepers that writhed like serpents over the whole edifice. Forcing my way up this staircase, I found myself in a stone hall some sixty feet long, at one end of which yawned a huge fireplace, its flue mounting up through a finely carved chimney, still standing firmly at the top of the southern gable. Sockets in the walls, on either side, where massive beams had once lodged, showed that the building had been in three stories, though all the floors had fallen in and made a mound of rubble in the centre of the hall where I stood.

At my entrance something moved furtively out of the fireplace, and shot with a rustle into the surrounding woods. It looked like a small alligator, and was indeed an iguana, one of the few reptiles of these islands.

At the base of a tall fig tree--flourishing in one of the corners, its dense, wide branching top making a literal roof for the otherwise roofless hall--an enormous ant's nest was plastered, a black excrescence looking like burnt paper, and which crumbled like soft crisp cinder as I poked it with the barrel of my gun, to the dismay of its myriad little red inhabitants--the only denizens it would seem of this once-magnificent hall.

How had this almost baronial magnificence come to be in this far-away corner of a desert island? At first I concluded that here was a relic of the brief colonial prosperity of the Bahamas, when its cotton lords lived like princes, with a slave population for retainers--days when even the bootblacks in Nassau played pitch-and-toss with gold pieces; but as I considered further, it seemed to me that the style of the architecture and the age of the building suggested an earlier date. Could it be that this had been the home of one of those early eighteenth-century pirates who took pride in flaunting the luxury and pomp of princes, and who had perhaps made this his headquarters and stronghold for the storage of his loot on the return from his forays on the Spanish Main? This, as the more spirited conjecture, I naturally preferred, and, in default of exact information, decided to accept.

Who knows but that in this hall where the iguana lurked and the ants laboured at their commonwealth, the redoubtable "Blackbeard"--known in private life as Edward Teach--had held his famous "Satanic" revels, decked out in the absurd finery of crimson damask waistcoat and breeches, a red feather in his hat, and a diamond cross hanging from a gold chain at his neck? There, perhaps, glass in hand, and "doxy on his knee," he had roared out many a blood-curdling ditty in the choice society of ruffians only less ruffianly than himself. Perhaps, too, this other spacious building adjacent to the great hall, and connected with it by a ruinous covered way, had been the sybarite's "harem"; for "Blackbeard"--like that other famous gentle-man whose beard was blue--collected from his unfortunate captive ships treasure other than doubloons and pieces of eight, and prided himself on his fine taste in ladies.

The more I pondered upon this fancy, and remarked the extent of the ruins--including several subsidiary out-houses--and noted, too, one or two choked stone staircases that seemed to descend into the bowels of the earth, the more plausible it seemed. In one or two places where I suspected underground cellars--dungeons for unhappy captives belike, or strong vaults for the storage of the treasure--I tested the floors by dropping heavy stones, and they seemed unmistakably to reverberate with a hollow rumbling sound; but I could find no present way of getting down into them. As I said, the staircases that promised an entrance into them were choked with debris. But I promised myself to come some other day, with pick and shovel, and make an attempt at exploring them.

Meanwhile, after poking about in as much of the ruins as I could penetrate, I stepped out through a gap in one of the walls and found myself again on the path by which I had entered. I noticed that it still ran on farther north, as having a destination beyond. So leaving the haunted ruins behind, I pushed on, and had gone but a short distance when the path began to descend slightly from the ridge on which the ruins stood; and there, in a broad square hollow before me, was the welcome living green of a flourishing plantation of cocoanut palms! It was evidently of considerable extent--a quarter of a mile or so, I judged--and the palms were very thick and planted close together. To my surprise, too, I observed, as at length the path brought me to them after a sharp descent, that they were fenced in by a high bamboo stockade, for the most part in good condition, but here and there broken down with decay.

Through one of these gaps I presently made my way, and found myself among the soaring columns of the palms, hung aloft with clusters of the great green nuts. Fallen palm fronds made a carpet for my feet--very pleasant after the rough and tangled way I had travelled, and now and again one of the cocoa nuts would fall down with a thud amid the green silence. One of these, which narrowly missed my head, suggested that here I had the opportunity of quenching very agreeably the thirst of which I had become suddenly aware. My claspknife soon made an opening through the tough shell, and, seated on the ground, I set my mouth to it, and, raising the nut above my head, allowed the "milk"--cool as spring water--to gurgle deliciously down my parched throat. When at length I had drained it, and my head once more returned to its natural angle, I was suddenly made aware that my poaching had not gone unobserved.

"Ha! ha!" called a pleasant voice, evidently belonging to a man of an unusually tall and lean figure who was approaching me through the palm trunks; "so you have discovered my hidden paradise--my Alcinoues garden, so to say"; and he quoted two well-known lines of Homer in the original Greek, adding: "or if you prefer it in Pope's translation, which I think,--don't you?--remains the best:

"Close to the gates a spacious garden lies,    From storms defended and inclement skies--

"and so on. Alas! for an old man's memory! It grows shorter and shorter--like his life, eh? Never mind, you are welcome, sir stranger, mysteriously tossed up here like Ulysses, on our island coast."

I gazed with natural wonderment at this strange individual, who thus in the heart of the wilderness had saluted me with a meticulously pure English accent, and welcomed me in a quotation from Homer in the original Greek. Who, in the devil's name, was this odd character who, I saw, as I looked closer at him, was, as he had hinted, quite an old man, though his unusual erectness and sprightliness of manner, lent him an illusive air of youth? Who on earth was he?--and how did he happen in the middle of this haunted wood?

# CHAPTER V

### *Calypso.*

Of course a glance, and the first sound of his voice, had told me that I had to do with a gentleman, one of those vagabond English gentlemen in exile who form a type peculiar, I think, to the English race; men that are a curious combination of aristocrat and gipsy, soldier, scholar, and philosopher; men of good family, who have drifted everywhere, seen and seen through everything, but in all their wanderings have never lost their sense and habit of "form," their boyish zest in living, their humorous stoicism, and, above all, their lordly accent.

"Now that you have found us, Sir Ulysses"--continued my eccentric host, mo-

tioning me, with an indescribably princely wave of the hand to accompany him--
"you must certainly give us the pleasure of your company to luncheon. Visitors are
as rare as black swans on this **Ultima Thule** of ours--though, by the way, the black
swan, *cygnus atratus,* is nothing like so rare as the ancients believed. I have shot
them myself out in Australia. Still they are rare enough for the purpose of imagery,
though really not so rare as a human being one can talk intelligently to on this island."

Talk! My friend, indeed, very evidently was a talker--one of those fantastic
monologists to whom an audience is little more than a symbol. I saw that there was
no need for me to do any of the talking. He was more than glad to do it all. Plainly
his encounter with me was to him like a spring in a thirsty land.

"Solitude," he continued, "is perhaps the final need of the human soul. After
a while, when we have run the gamut of all our ardours and our dreams, solitude
comes to seem the one excellent thing, the **summum bonum.**"

I murmured that he certainly seemed to have come to the right place for it.

"Very true, indeed," he assented, with a courtly inclination of his head, as
though I had said something profound; "very true, indeed, and yet, wasn't it the
great Bacon who said: 'Whoever is delighted with solitude is either a beast or a
god'?--and this particular solitude, I confess, sometimes seems to me a little too
much like that enforced solitude of the Pontic marshes of which Ovid wailed and
whimpered in the deaf ears of Augustus."

I could not help noticing at last as he talked on with this fantastic magnificence,
the odd contrast between his speech and the almost equally fantastic poverty of his
clothing. The suit he wore, though still preserving a certain elegance of cut, was so
worn and patched and stained that a negro would hardly have accepted it as a gift;
and his almost painful emaciation gave him generally the appearance of an animated framework of rags and bones, startlingly embodying the voice and the manners
of a prince. Yet the shabby tie about his neck was bound by a ring, in which was set
a turquoise of great size and beauty. Evidently he was a being of droll contrasts, and
I prepared myself to be surprised at nothing concerning him.

Presently, as we loitered on through the palms, we came upon two negroes
chopping away with their machetes, trimming up the debris of broken and decay-
ing palm fans. They were both sturdy, ferocious-looking fellows, but one of them

was a veritable giant.

"Behold my bodyguard!" said my magnificent friend, with the usual possessive wave of his hand; "my Switzers, my Janissaries, so to say."

The negroes stopped working, touched their great straw hats, and flashed their splendid teeth in a delighted smile. Evidently they were used to their master's way of talking, and were devoted to him.

"This chap here is Erebus," said my host, and the appropriateness of the name was apparent, for he was certainly the blackest negro I had ever seen, as superbly black as some women are superbly white.

"And this is Samson. Let's have a look at your muscles, Samson--there's a good boy!"

And, with grins of pleasure, Samson proudly stripped off his thin calico jacket and exposed a torso of terrifying power, but beautiful in its play of muscles as that of a god.

"But since my name is Hercules, the man    Who owes me hatred hides it if he can,

"eh, Samson?" was his master's characteristic comment.

"Yaas, sar!" said Samson, as pleased as a flattered bulldog, and understanding the compliment precisely in the same instinctive fashion.

Leaving Samson and Erebus to continue their savage play with their machetes, we walked on through the palms, which here gave a particularly jungle-like appearance to the scene, from the fact of their being bowed out from their roots, and sweeping upward in great curves. One involuntarily looked for a man-eating tiger at any moment, standing striped and splendid in one of the openings.

Then suddenly to the right, there came a flash of level green, suggesting lawns, and the outlines of a house, partly covered with brilliant purple flowers--a marvellous splash of colour.

"***Bougainvillea! Bougainvillea spectabilis***--of course, you know it. Was there ever such a purple? Not Solomon in all his glory, ***et cetera.*** And here we are at the house of King Alcinoues--a humble version of it indeed."

It was evidently quite impossible for my friend to speak otherwise than in images, picturesque scraps from the coloured rag-bag of a mind stored with memories of the classics, all manner of romantic literature, and tags of Greek and Latin which he mouthed with the relish of an epicure.

It was a large rambling stucco house, somewhat decayed looking, and evidently built on the ruins of an older building. We came upon it at a broad Italian-looking loggia, supported by stone pillars bowered in with vines--very cool and pleasant--with mossy slabs for its floor, here and there tropical ferns set out in tubs, some wicker chairs standing about, and a table at one side on which two little barelegged negro girls were busy setting out yellow fruit, and other appurtenances of luncheon, on a dazzling white cloth.

"Has your mistress returned yet, my children?" asked the master.

"No, sar," said the older girl, with a giggle, twisting and grimacing with embarrassment.

"My daughter," explained my host, "has gone to the town on an errand. She will be back at any moment. Meanwhile, I shall introduce you to a cooling drink of my own manufacture, with a basis of that cocoanut milk which I need not ask you whether you appreciate, recalling the pleasant circumstance of our first acquaintance."

Motioning me to a seat, and pushing toward me a box of cigarettes, he went indoors, leaving me to take in the stretch of beautiful garden in front of me, the trees of which seemed literally to be hung with gold--for they were mainly of orange and grapefruit ranged round a spacious beautifully-kept lawn with the regularity of sumptuous decoration. In the middle of the lawn, a little rock foundation threw up a jet of silver, falling with a tinkling murmur into a broad circular basin from which emerged the broad leaves and splendid pink blossoms of an Egyptian lotus. Certainly it was no far-fetched allusion of my classical friend to speak of the garden of Alcinoues; particularly connected as it was in my mind with the white beach of a desert isle, and that marble statue in the moonlight.

As I sat dreaming, bathed in the golden-green light of the orange trees, and lulled by the tinkling of the fountain, my host returned with our drinks, his learned disquisition on which I will spare the reader, highly interesting and characteristic though it was.

Suffice it that it was a drink, whatever its ingredients--and there was certainly somewhere a powerful "stick" in it--that seemed to have been drawn from some cool grotto of the virgin earth, so thrillingly cold and invigorating it was.

While we were slowly sipping it, and smoking our cigarettes, in an unwonted pause of my friend's fanciful verbosity, I almost jumped in my chair at the sound of a voice indoors. It was instantly followed by a light and rapid tread, and the sound of a woman's dress. Then a tall beautiful young woman emerged on the loggia.

"Ah! there you are!" cried my host, as we both rose; and then turning to me, "this is my daughter--Calypso. Her real name I assure you--none of my nonsense-- doesn't she look it? Allow me, my dear, to introduce--Mr. Ulysses!"--for we had not yet exchanged each other's names....

I am a wretched actor, and I am bound to say that she proved herself no better. For she gave a decided start as she turned those glowing eyes on me, and the lovely olive of her cheeks glowed as with submerged rose-colour. Our embarrassment did not escape the father.

"Why you know each other already!" he exclaimed, with natural surprise.

"Not exactly,"--I was grateful for the sudden nerve with which I was able to hasten to the relief of her lovely distress--"but possibly Miss--Calypso recalls as naturally as I do, our momentary meeting in Sweeney's store, one evening. I had no expectation, of course, that we should meet again under such pleasant circum-stances as this."

She gave me a grateful look as she took my hand, and with it--or was it only my eager imagination?--a shy little pressure, again as of gratitude.

I had tried to get into my voice my assurance that, of course, I remembered no other more recent meeting--though, naturally, as she had given that little start in the doorway, there had flashed on me again the picture of her standing, moonlit, in another resounding doorway, and of the wild start she had given then, as the golden pieces streamed from her lovely surprised mouth, and her lifted hands. And her eyes--I could have sworn--were the living eyes of Jack Harkaway! Had she a brother, I wondered. Yet my mind was too dazzled and confused with her nearness to pursue the speculation.

As we sat down to luncheon, waited upon by the little barelegged black chil-dren--waited on, too, surprisingly well, despite the contortions of their primitive embarrassment--my host once more resumed his character of the classic king wel-coming the storm-tossed stranger to his board.

"Far wanderer," he said, raising his glass to me, "eat of what our board affords, welcome without question of name and nation. But if, when the food and wine have done their genial office, and the weariness of your journeying has fallen from you, you should feel stirred to tell us somewhat of yourself and your wanderings, what manner of men call you kinsman, in what fair land is your home and the place of your loved ones, be sure that we shall count the tale good hearing, and, for our part, make exchange in like fashion of ourselves and the passage of our days in this lonely isle."

We all laughed as he ended--himself with a whinny of laughter. For, odd as such discourse may sound in the reading, it was uttered so whimsically, and in so spirited and humorous a style that I assure you it was very captivating.

"You should have been an actor, my lord Alcinoues," I said, laughing. I seemed already curiously at home, seated there at that table with this fantastic stranger and that being out of fairyland, toward whom I dared only turn my eyes now and again by stealth. The strange fellow had such a way with him, and his talk made you feel that he had known you all your life.

"Ah! I have had my dreams. I have had my dreams!" he answered, his eyes gazing with a momentary wistfulness across the orange trees.

Then we talked at random, as friendly strangers talk over luncheon, though we were glad enough that he should do all the talking--wonderful, iridescent, madcap talk, such as a man here and there in ten thousand, gifted with perhaps the most attractive of all human gifts, has at his command.

And, every now and again, my eyes, falling on the paradoxical squalor of his clothing, would remind me of the enigma of this courtly vagabond; though--need I say it?--my eyes and my heart had other business than with him, throughout that wonderful meal, enfolded as I felt myself once more in that golden cloud of magnetic vitality, which had at first swept over me, as with a breath of perfumed fire, among the salt pork and the tinware of Sweeney's store.

# CHAPTER VI

*Doubloons.*

Luncheon over, the Lady Calypso, with a stately inclination of her lovely head, left us to our wine and our cigars. For, as I realised, we were very much in England, in spite of all the orange trees and the palms, the England of two or three generations ago, and but seldom nowadays to be found in England itself.

The time had come, after the Homeric formula which my host had whimsically applied to the situation, for the far-travelled guest to declare himself, and I saw in my host's eye a courteous invitation to begin. While his fantastic tongue had gone a-wagging from China to Peru, I had been pondering what account to give of myself, and I had decided, for various reasons--of which the Lady Calypso was, of course, first, but the open-hearted charm of her father a close second--to tell him the whole of my story. Whatever his and her particular secret was, it was evident to me that it was an innocent and honourable one; and, besides, I may have had a notion that before long I was to have a family interest in it. So I began--starting in with a little prelude in the manner of my host, just to enter into the spirit of the game:

"My Lord Alcinoues; your guest, the far wanderer, having partaken of your golden hospitality, is now fain to open his heart to you, and tell you of himself and his race, his home and his loved ones across the wine-dark sea, and such of his adventures as may give pleasure to your ears" ... though, having no talents in that direction, I was glad enough to abandon my lame attempt at his Homeric style for a plain straightforward narrative of the events of the past three months.

I had not, however, proceeded very far, when, with a courteous raising of his hand, King Alcinoues suggested a pause.

"If you would not mind," he said, "I would like my daughter to hear this too, for it is of the very stuff of romantic adventure in which she delights. She is a brave girl, and, as I often tell her, would have made a very spirited dare-devil boy, if she hadn't happened to be born a girl."

This phrase seemed to flash a light upon the questionings that had stirred at the back of my mind since I had first heard that voice in Sweeney's store.

"By the way, dear King," I said, assuming a casual manner, "do you happen to have a son?"

"No!" he answered, "Calypso is my only child."

"Very strange!" I said, "we met a whimsical lad in our travels whom I would have sworn was her brother."

"That's odd!" said the "King" imperturbably, "but no! I have no son"; and he seemed to say it with a certain sadness.

Then Calypso came in to join my audience, having, meanwhile, taken the opportunity of twining a scarlet hibiscus among her luxuriant dark curls. I should certainly have told the story better without her, yet I was glad--how glad!--to have her seated there, an attentive presence in a simple gown, white as the seafoam--from which, there was no further doubt in my mind, she had magically sprung.

I gave them the whole story, much as I had told it in John Saunders's snuggery--John P. Tobias, Jr.; dear old Tom and his sucking fish, his ghosts, sharks, skeletons, and all; and when I had finished, I found that the interest of my story was once more chiefly centred in my pock-marked friend of "The wonderful works of God."

"I should like to meet your pock-marked friend," said King Alcinoues, "and I have a notion that, with you as a bait, I shall not long be denied the pleasure."

"I am inclined to think that I have seen him already," said Calypso, using her honey-golden voice for the base purpose of mentioning him.

"Impossible!" I cried, "he is long since safe in Nassau gaol."

"O! not lately," she answered to our interrogative surprise, and giving a swift embarrassed look at her father, which I at once connected with the secret of the doubloons.

"Seriously, Calypso?" asked her father, with a certain stern affection, as thinking of her safety. "On one of your errands to town?"

And then, turning to me, he said:

"Sir Ulysses, you have spoken well, and your speech has been that free, open-hearted speech that wins its way alike among the Hyperboreans that dwell in frozen twilight near the northern star, and those dwarfed and swarthy intelligences that blacken in the fierce sunlight of that fearful axle we call the equator. Therefore, I will make return to you of speech no less frank and true ..."

He took a puff at his cigar, and then continued:

"I should not risk this confession, but that it is easy to see that you belong to the race of Eternal Children, to which, you may have realised, my daughter and I also belong. This adventure of yours after buried treasure has not seriously been for the doubloons and pieces of eight, the million dollars, and the million and a half dollars themselves, but for the fun of going after them, sailing the unknown seas, coral islands, and all that sort of blessed moonshine. Well, Calypso and I are just like that, and I am going to tell you something exciting--we too have our buried treasure. It is nothing like so magnificent in amount as yours, or your Henry P. Tobias's--and where it is at this particular moment I know as little as yourself. In fact it is Calypso's secret...."

I looked across at Calypso, but her eyes were far beyond capture, in un-plummeted seas.

"I will show you presently where I found it, among the rocks near by--now a haunt of wild bees.

"Can you ever forget that passage in the Georgics? It makes the honey taste sweeter to me every time I taste it. We must have some of it for dinner, by the way, Calypso."

I could not help laughing, and so, for a moment, breaking up the story. The dear fellow! Was there any business of human importance from which he could not be diverted by a quotation from Homer or Virgil or Shakespeare? But he was soon in the saddle again.

"Well," he resumed, "one day, some seven years ago, in a little cave below the orange trees, grubbing about as I am fond of doing, I came upon a beautiful old box of beaten copper, sunk deep among the roots of a fig tree. It was strong, but it seemed too dainty for a pirate--some great lady's jewel box more likely--Calypso shall show it to us presently. On opening it--what do you think? It spilled over with golden doubloons--among which were submerged some fine jewels, such as this tie ring you see me wearing. Actually, it was no great treasure, at a monetary calculation--certainly no fortune--but from our romantic point of view, as belonging to the race of Eternal Children, it was El Dorado, Aladdin's lamp, the mines of Peru, the whole sunken Spanish Main, glimmering fifty fathoms deep in mother-of-pearl and the moon. It was the very Secret Rose of Romance; and, also, mark you, it was some money--O! perhaps, all told, it might be some five thousand guineas, or--what would you say?--twenty-five odd thousand dollars; Calypso knows better than I, and she, as I said, alone knows where it is now hid, and how much of it now remains."

He paused to relight his cigar, while Calypso and I--Well, he began again:

"Now my daughter and I," and he paused to look at her fondly, "though of the race of Eternal Children, are not without some of the innocent wisdom which Holy Writ countenances as the self-protection of the innocent--Calypso, I may say, is particularly endowed with this quality, needing it as she does especially for the guardianship for her foolish talkative old father, who, by the way, is almost at the end of his tale. So, when this old chest flashed its bewildering dazzle upon us, we, being poor folk, were not more dazzled than afraid. For--like the poor man in the fable--such good fortune was all too likely to be our undoing, should it come to the ears of the great, or the indigent criminal. The 'great' in our thought was, I am ashamed to say, the sacred British Treasury, by an ancient law of which, forty per cent. of all 'treasure-trove' belongs to His Majesty the King. The 'indigent criminal' was represented by--well, our coloured (and not so very much coloured) neighbours. Of course, we ought to have sent the whole treasure to your friend, John Saunders, of His Britannic Majesty's Government at Nassau, but--Well, we didn't. Some day, perhaps, you will put in a word for us with him, as you drink his old port, in the snuggery. Meanwhile, we had an idea, Calypso and I--"

He paused--for Calypso had involuntarily made a gesture, as though pleading to be spared the whole revelation--and then with a smile, continued:

"We determined to hide away our little hoard where it would be safe from our neighbours, and dispose of it according to our needs with a certain tradesman in the town whom we thought we could trust--a tradesman, who, by the way, quite naturally levies a little tax upon us for his security. No blame to him! I have lived far too long to be hard on human nature."

"John Sweeney?" I asked, looking over at Calypso, with eyes that dared at last to smile.

"The very same, my Lord Ulysses," answered my friend.

And so I came to understand that Mr. Sweeney's reluctance in selling me that doubloon was not so sinister as it had, at the moment, appeared; that it had in fact come of a loyalty which was already for me the most precious of all loyalties.

"Then," said I, "as a fitting conclusion to the confidence you have reposed in me, my Lord Alcinoues; if Miss Calypso would have the kindness to let us have a sight of that chest of beaten copper of which you spoke, I would like to restore this, that was once a part of its contents, wherever the rest of them" (and I confess that I paused a moment) "may be in hiding."

And I took from my pocket the sacred doubloon that I had bought from John Sweeney--may Heaven have mercy upon his soul!--for sixteen dollars and seventy-five cents, on that immortal evening.

# CHAPTER VII

### *In Which the "King" Dreams a Dream--and Tells Us About It.*

The afternoon, under the spell of its various magic, had been passing all too swiftly, and at length I grew reluctantly aware that it was time for me to be returning once more to the solid, not to say squalid, earth; but, as I made a beginning of my farewell address, King Alcinoues raised his hand with a gesture that could not be denied. It was not to be heard of, he said. I must be their guest till to-morrow, sans argument. To begin with, for all the golden light still in the garden, with that silver wand of the fountain laid upon the stillness like a charm, it was already night among the palms, he said, and blacker than our friend Erebus in the woods--and there was no moon.

"No moon?" I said, and, though the remark was meaningless, one might have thought, from Calypso's face--in which rose colour fought with a suggestion of sub-merged laughter--that it had a meaning.

If I had found it difficult going at high noon, he continued, with an immense sunlight overhead, how was I going to find it with the sun gone head-long into the sea, as was about to happen in a few moments. When the light that is in thee has become darkness, how great is that darkness! ***Si ergo lumen quod in te est tenebrae sunt, ipsae tenebrae quantae erunt!*** And he settled it, as he settled everything, with a whimsical quotation.

He had not yet, he said, shown me that haunt of the wild bees, where the golden honey now took the place of that treasure of golden money; and there were also other curiosities of the place he desired to show me. And that led me--his invitation being accepted without further parley--to mention the idea I had conceived as I came along, of exploring those curious old ruined buildings. Need I say that the mere suggestion was enough to set him aflame? I might have known that here, of all men, was my man for such an enterprise. He had meant to do it himself for how many years--but age, with stealing step, *et cetera.*

However, with youth--so he was pleased to flatter me--to lend him the sap of energy, why who knows? And in a moment he had us both akindle with his imaginations of what might--"might"! what a word to use!--no! what, without question, *must* lie unsunned in those dark underground vaults, barricaded with all that deviltry of vegetation, and guarded by the coils of a three-headed dragon with carbuncles for eyes--eyes that never slept--for the advantage of three heads to treasure-guarding dragons, he explained, was that they divided the twenty-four hours into watches of eight hours each as the ugly beast kept ward over that heap of gold--bars of it, drifts of it, banks of it minted into gleaming coins--doubloons, doubloons, doubloons--so that the darkness was bright as day with the shine of it, or as the bottom of the sea, where a Spanish galleon lies sunk among the corals and the gliding water snakes.

"O King!" I laughed, "but indeed you have the heart of a child!"

"To-morrow," he announced, "to-morrow we shall begin--there is not a moment to lose. We will send Samson with a message to your captain--there is no need for you to go yourself; time is too precious--and in a week, who knows but that Monte Cristo shall seem like a pauper and a penny gaff in comparison with the fantasies of our fearful wealth. Even Calypso's secret hoard will pale before the romance of our subterranean millions--I mean billions--and poor Henry Tobias will need neither hangman's rope nor your friend Webster's cartridges for his quietus. At the mere rumour of our fortune, he will suddenly turn a green so violent that death will be instantaneous."

So, for that evening, all was laughingly decided. In a week's time, it was agreed, we should have difficulty in recognising each other. We should be so disguised in cloth of gold, and so blinding to look upon with rings and ropes of pearls. As our dear "King" got off something like this for our good-night, my eyes involuntarily fell upon his present garments--far from being cloth of gold. Why? I wondered. There was no real financial reason, it was evident, for these penitential rags. But I remembered that I had known two other millionaires--millionaires not merely of the imagination--whom it had been impossible to separate from a certain beloved old coat that had been their familiar for more than twenty years. It was some odd kink somewhere in the make-up of the "King," one more trait of his engaging humanity.

When we met at breakfast next morning, glad to see one another again as few people are at breakfast, it was evident that, so far as the "King" was concerned, our dream had lost nothing in the night watches. On the contrary, its wings had grown to an amazing span and iridescence. It was so impatient for flight, that its feet had to be chained to the ground--the wise Calypso's doing--with a little plain prose, a detail or two of preliminary arrangement, and then....

Calypso, it transpired, had certain household matters--of which the "King" of course, was ever divinely oblivious--that would take her on an errand into the town. Those disposed of, we two eternal children were at liberty to be as foolish as we pleased. The "King" bowed his uncrowned head, as kings, from time immemorial have bowed their diadems before the quiet command of the domesticities; and it was arranged that I should be Calypso's escort on her errand.

So we set forth in the freshness of the morning, and the woods that had been so black and bewildering at my coming opened before us in easy paths, and all that tropical squalor that had been foul with sweat and insects seemed strangely vernal to me, so that I could hardly believe that I had trodden that way before. And for our companion all the way along--or, at least, for my other companion--was the Wonder of the World, the beautiful strangeness of living, and that marvel of a man's days upon the earth which lies in not knowing what a day shall bring forth, if only we have a little patience with Time--Time, with those gold keys at his girdle, ready, at any turn of the way, to unlock the hidden treasure that is to be the meaning of our lives.

How should I try to express what it was to walk by her side, knowing all that we both knew?--knowing, or giddily believing that I knew, how her heart, with every breath she took, vibrated like a living flower, with waves of colour, changing from moment to moment like a happy trembling dawn. To know--yet not to say! Yes! we were both at that divine moment which hangs like a dew-drop in the morning sun--ah! all too ready to fall. O! keep it poised, in that miraculous balance, 'twixt Time and Eternity--for this crystal made of light and dew is the meaning of the life of man and woman upon the earth.

As we came to the borders of the wood, near the edge of the little town, we called a counsel of two. As the outcome of it, we concluded that, having in mind the "King's" ambitious plans for our cloth-of-gold future, and for other obvious reasons, it was better that she went into the town alone--I to await her in the shadow of the mahogany tree.

As she turned to leave me, she drew up from her bosom a little bag that hung by a silver chain, and, opening it, drew out, with a laugh--a golden doubloon!

I sprang toward her; but she was too quick for me, and laughingly vanished through an opening in the trees. I was not to kiss her that day.

# CHAPTER VIII

*News!*

Calypso was so long coming back that I began to grow anxious--was, indeed, on the point of going into the town in search of her; when she suddenly appeared, rather out of breath, and evidently a little excited--as though, in fact, she had been running away from something. She caught me by the arm, with a laugh:

"Do you want to see your friend Tobias?" she said.

"Tobias! Impossible!"

"Come here," and she led me a yard or two back the way she had come, and then cautiously looked through the trees.

"Gone!" she said, "but he was there a minute or two ago--or at least some one that is his photograph--and, of course, he's there yet, hidden in the brush, and probably got his eyes on us all the time. Did you see that seven-year apple tree move?"

"His favourite tree," I laughed.

"Hardly strong enough to hang him on though." And I realised that she was

King Alcinoues's daughter.

We crouched lower for a moment or two, but the seven-year apple tree didn't move again, and we agreed that there was no use in waiting for Tobias to show his hand.

"He is too good a poker-player," I said.

"Like his skeletons, eh?" she said.

"But what made you think it was Tobias?" I asked, "and how did it all happen?"

"I could hardly fail to recognise him from your flattering description," she answered, "and indeed it all happened rather like another experience of mine. I had gone into Sweeney's store--you remember?--and was just paying my bill."

"In the usual coinage?" I ventured. She gave me a long, whimsical smile--once more her father's daughter.

"That, I'm afraid, was the trouble," she answered; "for, as I laid my money down on the counter, I suddenly noticed that there was a person at the back of the store ..."

"A person?" I interrupted.

"Yes! suppose we say 'a pock-marked person'; was it you?"

"What a memory you have for details," I parried, "and then?"

"Well! I took my change and managed to whisper a word to Sweeney--a good friend, remember--and came out. I took a short cut back, but the 'person' that had stood in the back of the store seemed to know the way almost better than I--so well that he had got ahead of me. He was walking quietly this way, and so slowly that I had at last to overtake him. He said nothing, just watched me, as if interested in the way I was going--but, I'm ashamed to say, he rather frightened me! And here I am."

"Do you really think he saw the--doubloon--like that other 'person'?" I asked.

"There's no doubt of it."

"Well, then," I said, "let's hurry home, and talk it over with the 'King.'"

The "King," as I had realised, was a practical "romantic" and at once took the matter seriously, leaving--as might have surprised some of those who had only heard him talk--his conversational fantasies on the theme to come later.

Calypso, however, had the first word.

"I always told you, Dad," she said;--and the word "Dad" on the lips of that big statuesque girl--who always seemed ready to take that inspired framework of rags and bones and talking music into her protecting arms--seemed the quaintest of paradoxes--, "I always told you, Dad, what would happen, with your fairy-tales of the doubloons."

"Quite true, my dear," he answered, "but isn't a fairy-tale worth paying for?--worth a little trouble? And remember, if you will allow me, two things about fairy-tales: there must always be some evil fairy in them, some dragon or such like; and there is always--a happy ending. Now the dragon enters at last--in the form of Tobias; and we should be happy on that very account. It shows that the race of dragons is not, as I feared, extinct. And as for the happy ending, we will arrange it, after lunch--for which, by the way, you are somewhat late."

After lunch, the "King" resumed, but in a brief and entirely practical vein:

"We are about to be besieged," he said. "The woods, probably, are already thick with spies. For the moment, we must suspend operations on our Golconda"--his name for the ruins that we were to excavate--"and, as our present purpose--yours no less than ours, friend Ulysses--is to confuse Tobias, my suggestion is this: That you walk with me a mile or two to the nor'ard. There is an entertaining mangrove swamp I should like to show you, and also, you can give me your opinion of an idea of mine that you will understand all the better when I have taken you over the ground."

So we walked beyond the pines, down onto a long interminable flat land of marl marshes and mangrove trees--so like that in which Charlie Webster had shot the snake and the wild duck--that only Charlie could have seen any difference.

"Now," said the "King," "do you see a sort of river there, overgrown with mangroves and palmettos?"

"Yes," I answered, "almost--though it's so choked up it's almost impossible to say."

"Well," said the "King," "that's the idea; you haven't forgotten those old ruins we are going to explore. You remember how choked up they are. Well, this was the covered water-way, the secret creek, by which the pirates--John Teach, or whoever it was, perhaps John P. Tobias himself--used to land their loot. It's so overgrown nowadays that no one can find the entrance but myself and a friend or two; do you understand?"

We walked a little farther, and then at length came to the bank of the creek the "King" had indicated. This we followed for half a mile or so, till we met the fresh murmur of the sea.

"We needn't go any farther," said the "King." "It's the same all the way along to the mouth--all over-grown as you see, all the way, right out to the 'white water' as they call it--which is four miles of shoal sand that is seldom deeper than two fathoms, and which a nor'easter is liable to blow dry for a week on end. Naturally it's a hard place to find, and a hard place to get off!--and only two or three persons besides Sweeney--all of them our friends--know the way in. Tobias may know of it; but to know it is one thing, to find it is another matter. I could hardly be sure of it myself--if I were standing in from the sea, with nothing but the long palmetto-fringed coast-line to go by.

"Now, you see it? I brought you here, because words--"

"Even yours, dear 'King,'" I laughed.

"--could not explain what I suggest for us to do. You are interested in Tobias. Tobias is interested in you. I am interested in you both. And Calypso and I have a treasure to guard."

"I have still a treasure to seek," I said, half to myself.

"Good enough," said the "King." "Now, to be practical. We can assume that Tobias is on the watch. I don't mean that he's around here just now, for, before we left, I spoke to Samson and Erebus and they will pass the word to four men blacker than themselves; therefore we can assume that this square mile or so is for the moment 'to ourselves.' But beyond our fence you may rely that Tobias and his myrmidons--is that the word?" he asked with a concession to his natural foolishness--"are there."

"So," he went on, "I want you to go down to your boat to-morrow morning to say good-bye to the commandant, the parson, and the postmaster; to haul up your sail and head for Nassau. Call in on Sweeney on the way, buy an extra box of cartridges, and say '*Dieu et mon Droit*'--it is our password; he will understand, but, if he shouldn't, explain, in your own way, that you come from me, and that we rely upon him to look out for our interest. Then head straight for Nassau; but, about eight o'clock, or anywhere around twilight, turn about and head--well, we'll map it out on the chart at home--anywhere up to eight miles along the coast, till you come to a light, low down right on the edge of the water. As soon as you see it, drop anchor; then wait till morning--the very beginning of dawn. As soon as you can see land, look out for Samson--within a hundred yards of you--all the land will look alike to you. Only make the Captain head straight for Samson, and just as you think you are going to run ashore--Well, you will see!"

# CHAPTER IX

### Old Friends.

Next morning I did as the "King" had told me to do. The whole programme was carried out just as he had planned it. I made my good-byes in the settlement, as we had arranged, not forgetting to say "***Dieu et mon Droit***" to Sweeney, and watching with some humorous intent how he would take it. He took it quietly, as a man in a signal box takes a signal, with about as much emotion, and with just the same necessary seriousness. But I suppose he felt that the circumstances justified a slight heightening of his usual indifference to all mortal things.

"Tell the boss," he said--of course he meant the "King"--"that we are looking after him. Nothing'll slip through here, if we can help it. Good luck!"

So I went down to the boat--to old Tom once more, and the rest of our little crew, who had long since exhausted the attractions of their life ashore, and were glad, as I was, to "H'ist up the *John B.* Sail." We sang that classic chanty, as we went out with all our canvas spread to a lively northeast breeze--and I realised once more how good the sea was for all manner of men, whatever their colour, for we all livened up and shook off our land-laziness again, spry and laughing, and as keen as the jib stretching out like a gull's wing into the rush and spray of the sea.

Down in my cabin, I looked over some mail that had been waiting for me at the post-office. Amongst it was a crisp, characteristic word from Charlie Webster--for whom the gun will ever be mightier than the pen:

"***Tobias escaped--just heard he is on your island--watch out. Will follow in a day or two.***"

I came out on deck about sunset. We were running along with all our sails drawing like a dream. I looked back at the captain, proud and quiet and happy there at the helm, and nodded a smile to him, which he returned with a flash of his teeth. He loved his boat; he asked nothing better than to watch her behaving just as she was doing. And the other boys seemed quiet and happy too, lying along the sides of the house, ready for the captain's order, but meanwhile content to look up at the great sails, and down again at the sea.

We were a ship and a ship's crew all at peace with one another, and contented with ourselves--rushing and singing and spraying through the water. We were all friends--sea, and sails, and crew together. I couldn't help thinking that a mutiny would be hard to arrange under such a combination of influences.

Tom was sitting forward, plaiting a rope. For all our experiences together, he never implied that he was anything more than the ship's cook, with the privilege of waiting upon me in the cabin at my meals. But, of course, he knew that I had quite another valuation of him, and, as our eyes met, I beckoned to him to draw closer to me.

"Tom," I said, "I have found my treasure."

"You don't say so, sar."

"Yes! Tom, and I rely upon you to help me to guard it. There are no ghosts, this time, Tom," I added--as he said nothing, but waited for me to go on--"and no need of our sucking fish...."

"Are you sure, sar?" he asked, adding: "You can never be sure about ghosts--they are always around somewhere. And a sucking fish is liable at any moment to be useful."

I opened my shirt in answer.

"There it is still, Tom; I agree with you. We won't take any unnecessary chances."

This comforted the old man more than any one could have imagined.

"It's all right then, sar?" he said. "It will come out all right now, I'm sure--though, as I wanted to say"--and he hesitated--"I had hoped that you had forgotten those treasures that--"

"Go on, Tom."

"That moth and rust do corrupt."

"I know, dear old Tom, but neither moth nor rust can ever corrupt the treasure I meant--the treasure I have already found."

"You have found the treasure, sar?" asked Tom, in natural bewilderment.

"Yes, Tom, and I am going to show it to you--to-morrow."

The old man waited, as a mortal might wait till it pleased his god to speak a little more clearly.

"Quite true, Tom," I continued; "you shall see my treasure to-morrow; meanwhile, read this note." Tom was so much to me that I wanted him to know all about the details of the enterprise we shared together, and in which he risked his life no less than I risked mine.

Tom took out his spectacles from some recess of his trousers, and applied himself to Charlie Webster's note, as though it had been the Bible. He read it as slowly indeed as if it had been Sanscrit, and then folded it and handed it back to me without a word. But there was quite a young smile in his old eyes.

"'The wonderful works of God,'" he said presently. "I guess, sar, we shall soon be able to ask him what he meant by that expression."

Then, as sunlight had almost gone, and the stars were trying to come out overhead, and the boys were stringing out our lanterns, I surprised our captain by telling him that I had changed my mind, and that I didn't want to make Nassau that night, but wanted to head back again, but a point or so to the south'ard. He demurred a little, because, as he said, he was not quite sure of his course. We ought to have had a pilot, and the shoals--so much he knew--were bad that way, all "white water," particularly in a northeast wind. This only confirmed what the "King" had said. So, admitting that I knew all the captain said, I ordered him to do as I told him.

So we ruffled it along, making two or three "legs"--I sitting abaft the jib boom, with my back against the mainmast, watching out for Samson and his light.

Soon the long dark shore loomed ahead of us. I had reckoned it out about right. But the Captain announced that we were in shoal water.

"How many feet?" I asked, and a boy threw out the lead.

"Sixteen and a half," he said.

"Go ahead," I called out.

"Do you want to go aground?" asked the Captain.

For answer, I pushed him aside and took the wheel. I had caught the smallest glimmer, like a night-light, floating on the water.

"Drop the anchor," I called.

The light in shore was clear and near at hand, about one hundred yards away, and there was the big murmur and commotion of the long breakers over the dancing shoals. We rolled a good deal, and the Captain moodily took my suggestion of throwing out three anchors and cradling them; though, as he said, with the way the northeast was blowing, we should soon be on dry land. It was true enough. The tide was running out very fast, and the white sand coming ever nearer to our eyes in the moonlight; and Samson's light, there, was keeping white and steady. With the thought of my treasure and the "King" so near by, it was hard to resist the temptation to plunge in and follow my heart ashore. But I managed to control the boyish impulse, and presently we were all snug, and some of us snoring, below decks, rocked in the long swells of the shoal water that gleamed milkily like an animated moonstone under the stars--old Sailor curled up at my feet, just like old times.

# CHAPTER X

### *The Hidden Creek.*

I woke just as dawn was waking too, very still and windless; for the threatening nor'easter had changed its mind, and the world was as quiet as though there weren't a human being in it. Near by, stretched the long low coast-line, nothing but level brush, with an occasional thatch-palm lifting up a shock-head against the quickening sky. Out to sea, the level plains of lucent water spread like a vast floor, immensely vacant--not a sail or even a wing to mar the perfect void.

As the light grew, I scanned the shore to see whether I could detect the entrance of the hidden creek; but, though I swept it up and down again and again, it continued to justify the "King's" boast. There was no sign of an opening anywhere. Nothing but a straight line of brush, with mangroves here and there stepping down in their fantastic way into the water. And yet we were but a hundred yards from the shore. Certainly "Blackbeard"--if the haunt had really been his--had known his business; for an enemy could have sought him all day along this coast and found no clue to his hiding-place.

But, presently, as my eyes kept on seeking, a figure rose, tall and black near the water's edge, a little to our left, and shot up a long arm by way of signal. It was Samson; and evidently the mouth of the creek was right there in front of us--under our very noses, so to say--and yet it was impossible to make it out. However, at this signal, I stirred up the still-sleeping crew, and presently we had the anchors up, and the engine started at the slowest possible speed.

The tide was beginning to run in, so we needed very little way on us. I pointed out Samson to the captain, and, following the "King's" instructions, told him to steer straight for the negro. He grumbled not a little. Of course, if I wanted to run aground, it was none of his affair--etc., etc. Then I stationed the sturdiest of the two deck-hands on the port bow with a long oar, while I took the starboard with another. Very slowly and cautiously we made in, pointing straight for a thick growth of mangrove bushes. Samson stood there and called:

"All right, sar. Keep straight on. You'll see your way in a minute."

And, sure enough, when we were barely fifty feet away from the shore, and there seemed nothing for it but to run dead aground, low down through the floating mangrove branches we caught sight of a narrow gleam starting inland, and in another moment or two our decks were swept with foliage as the *Flamingo* rustled in, like a bird to cover, through an opening in the bushes barely twice her beam; and there before us, snaking through the brush, was a lane of water which immediately began to broaden between palmetto-fringed banks, and was evidently deep enough for a much larger vessel.

"Plenty of water, sar," hallooed Samson from the bank, grinning a huge welcome. "Keep a-going after me," and he started trotting along the creek-side.

As we pushed into the glassy channel, I standing at the bow, my eyes were arrested by a tremendous flashing commotion in the water to the right and left of us--like the fierce zigzagging of steel blades, or the ferocious play of submerged lightning. It was a select company of houndfish and sharks that we had disturbed, lying hellishly in wait there for the prey of the incoming tide. It was a curiously sinister sight, as though one had come upon a nest of water-devils in council, and the fancy jumped into my mind that here were the spirits of Teach and his crew once more evilly embodied and condemned to haunt for ever this gloomy scene of their crimes.

Samson went trotting along the twisting banks, we cautiously feeling our way after him, for something like a quarter of a mile; and then, coming round a sudden bend, the creek opened out into a sort of basin. On the left bank stood two large palmetto shanties. Samson indicated that there was our anchorage; and then, as we were almost alongside of them, the cheery halloos of a well-known voice hailed us. It was the "King"; and, as I answered his welcome, the morning suddenly sang for me--for there too was Calypso, at his side.

The water ran so deep at the creek's side that we were able to moor the *Flamingo* right up against the bank, and, when I had jumped ashore and greeted my friends, and the "King" had executed a brief characteristic fantasia on the manifest advantages of having a hidden pirate's creek in the family, he unfolded his plans, or rather that portion of them that was necessary at the moment.

The crew of the *Flamingo,* he said, had better stay where they were for the present. If they were tired of sleeping aboard, there were his two palmetto palaces, with couches of down on which to stretch their limbs--and, for amusement--poor devils!--he swept his eyes whimsically around that dreariest of landscapes--they might exercise their imaginations by pretending, after the manner of John Teach, that they were on an excursion to Hades--this was the famous River Acheron--and so on. But, seriously, he ended, we would find some way of keeping them from committing hari-kari and, meanwhile, we would leave them in peace, and stroll along toward breakfast.

At that moment, Sailor rubbed his head against my knee.

"Ah!" said the "King," "the heroic canine! He, of course, must not be left behind. We may very well need you in our counsels, eh, old fellow?" and he made friends with Sailor in a moment, as only a man who loves dogs can.

I believe I was second in Sailor's affection from that moment of his meeting the "King." But then, who wouldn't have been?

So then, after a reassuring word or two with Tom and the Captain, we went our ways toward breakfast--the "King's" tongue and Sailor's wagging happily in concert every inch of the way.

# CHAPTER XI

### *An Old Enemy.*

Charlie Webster's laconic note was naturally our chief topic over breakfast. "***Tobias escaped--just heard he is on your island. Watch out. Will follow in a day or two.***" The "King" read it out, when I handed him the note across the table.

"Your friend writes like a true man of action," he added, "like Caesar--and also the electric telegraph. We must send word to Sweeney to be on the look-out for him. I will send Samson the Redoubtable with a message to him this morning. Meanwhile, we will smoke and think."

Then for the next hour the "King" thought--aloud; while Calypso and I sat and listened, occasionally throwing in a parenthesis of comment or suggestion. It was evident, we all agreed, that Calypso had been right. It had been Tobias and none other whose evil eye had sent her so breathless back to me, waiting in the shadow of the woods; and it was the same evil eye that had fallen vulture-like on her golden doubloon exposed on Sweeney's counter.

Now what were we to think of Tobias?--what really were his notions about this supposititious treasure?--and what was likely to be his plan of action? Had he really any private knowledge of the whereabouts of his alleged ancestral treasure?-- or was his first authentic hint of its whereabouts derived from the manuscript--first overheard while eavesdropping at John Saunders's office, and afterward purloined from John Saunders's verandah?

There seemed little doubt that this second surmise was correct; for, if he had had any previous knowledge, he would have had no need of the manuscript and long ago he would have gone after the treasure for himself, and found it or not, as the case might be. Probably there was a tradition in his family of the existence somewhere of his grandfather's treasure; but that tradition was very likely the sum of his inheritance; and doubtless it was the mere accident of his dropping into Saunders's office that morning which had set him on the track.

It was also likely, indeed practically certain, that he had been able to make no more out of the manuscript than I had; that he had concluded that I had somehow or other unearthed more about it than he; and that, therefore, his most promising clue to its discovery would be my actions. To keep me in sight was the first step. So far so good.

But thus far, it would appear to him, I had had no very positive success. Otherwise, I would not still be on the quest. He had probably been aware of my movements, and may have been lying hidden on the island longer than we suspected. From some of his spies he had heard of my presence in the settlement, and, chance having directed him to Sweeney's store at the moment of Calypso's ringing down that Spanish gold on the counter, he had somehow connected Calypso's doubloon with me.

At all events, it was clear that there were such coins on the island in somebody's possession. Then, when he had watched Calypso on her way home--and, without any doubt, been the spectator of our meeting at the edge of the wood though we had been unable to catch sight of him--there would, of course, be a suspicion in his mind that my quest might at last be approaching success, and that his ancestral millions might be almost in my hands. That there might be some other treasure on the island with which neither he nor his grandfather had any concern would not occur to him, nor would it be likely to trouble him if it did. My presence was enough to prove that the treasure was his--for was it not his treasure that I was after? Logic irrefutable! How was he to know that all the treasure so far discovered was that modest hoard--unearthed, as I had heard, in the garden--the present whereabouts of which was known only to Calypso. The "King" had interrupted himself at this point of argument.

"By the way, Calypso, where is it?" he asked unexpectedly, to the sudden confusion of both of us. "Isn't it time you revealed your mysterious Aladdin's cave?"

At the word "cave" the submerged rose in Calypso's cheeks almost came to the surface of their beautiful olive.

"Cave!" she countered manfully, "who said it was a cave?"

"It was merely a figure of speech, which--if I may say so, my dear--might apply with equal fitness, say--to a silk stocking."

And Calypso laughed through another tide of rose-colour.

"No, Dad, not that either. Never mind where it is. It is perfectly safe, I assure you."

"But *are* you sure, my dear? Wouldn't it be safer, after all, here in the house? How can you be certain that no one but yourself will accidentally discover it?"

"I am absolutely certain that *no one will,*" she answered, with an emphasis on the last three words which sent a thrill through me, for I knew that it was meant for me. Indeed, as she spoke, she furtively gave me one of those glances of soft fire which had burnt straight through to my heart in Sweeney's store--a sort of blended challenge and appeal.

"Of course, Dad," she added, "if you insist--you shall have it. But seriously I think it is safer where it is, and if I were to fetch it, how can I be sure that no one"--she paused, with a meaning which I, of course, understood--"Tobias, for instance, would see me going--and follow me."

"To be sure--to be sure," said the "King." "What do you think, friend Ulysses?"

"I think it more than likely that she might be followed," I answered, "and I quite agree with Miss Calypso. I certainly wouldn't advise her to visit her treasure just now--with the woods probably full of eyes. In fact," I added, smiling frankly at her, "I could scarcely answer for myself even--for I confess that she has filled me with an overpowering curiosity."

And in my heart I stood once more amid the watery gleams and echoes of that moonlit cavern, struck dumb before that shining princess from whose mouth and hands had fallen those strange streams of gold.

"So be it then," said the "King"; "and now to consider what our friend here graphically speaks of as those eyes in the woods. 'The woods were full of eyes.' Ah! friend Ulysses, you evidently share my taste for the romantic phrase. Who cares how often it has been used? It is all the better for that. Like old wine, it has gained with age. One's whole boyhood seems to be in a phrase like that--Dumas, Scott, Fenimore Cooper. How often, I wonder, has that divine phrase been written--'the woods were full of eyes.' And now to think that we are actually living it--an old boy like myself even. 'The woods were full of eyes.' Bravo! Ulysses, for it is still a brave and gallant world!"

The "King" then made a determined descent into the practical. The woods, most probably, *were* full of eyes. In plain prose, we were almost certainly being watched. Unless--unless, indeed, my bogus departure for Nassau had fooled Tobias as we had hoped. But, even so, with that lure of Calypso's doubloon ever before him, it was too probable that he would not leave the neighbourhood without some further investigation--"an investigation," the "King" explained, "which might well take the form of a midnight raid; murdered in our beds, and so forth."

That being so, being in fact almost a certainty--the "King" spoke as though he would be a much disappointed man otherwise--we must look to our garrison. After all, besides ourselves, we had but Samson and Erebus, and their dark brethren of doubtful courage, while Tobias probably had command of a round dozen of doughty desperadoes. On the whole, perhaps, he said, it might be best to avail ourselves of the crew of the *Flamingo*--"under cover of the dark," he repeated with a smile.

Yes! that must be the first step. We must get them up there that night, under cover of the dark; keep them well hidden, and--well! await developments. Charlie Webster might be expected any moment with his reinforcements, and then!--"Lay on, Macduff!"

While we had been talking, Samson had long since been on his way with the word to Sweeney to look out for Webster, and, as he had been admonished to hurry back, it was scarcely noon when he returned, bringing in exchange a verbal message from Sweeney.

"The pock-marked party," ran the message as delivered by Samson, "had left the harbour in his sloop that morning. Yes, sar!"

"Ha! ha!" laughed the "King," turning to me. "So two can play at that game, says Henry P. Tobias, Jr. But if we haven't fooled him, let's make sure that he hasn't fooled us. We'll bring up your crew all the same--what do you think?"

"Under cover of the dark," I assented.

# CHAPTER XII

### *In Which the "King" Imprisons Me with Some Old Books and Pictures.*

Nothing further transpired that day, and, at nightfall, we brought the crew of the *Flamingo* up to the house--all but two of them, whom we left on guard. Two out of six was rather more than we had bargained for, but we found that none of them had the courage to face the night there in that dismal swamp alone--and we couldn't blame them, for a more devil-haunted desolation could not be imagined even in the daylight, and the mere thought of what might go on there after dark was enough to uncurl the wool on the head of the bravest negro. And we agreed, too, that the watch should be changed nightly, a fresh pair going on duty each evening.

Then there was nothing to do but sit down and await events--amongst them, the coming of Charlie Webster.

In regard to this, we had decided that it would be as well that, instead of disembarking at the settlement, he should come and join the *Flamingo* in the hidden creek; so Samson was once more despatched down to Sweeney with a letter for him to hand to Charlie on his arrival, giving him direction how to find us. Meanwhile, our two men on the *Flamingo* could keep watch for him by day, and have a light burning for him at the entrance of the creek by night.

The "King's" instructions to me were that I was not to show my nose outside the house. Possibly I might expose the tip of it once in a while, for a little exercise in the garden--where all this time the little silver fountain went on playing amid the golden hush of the orange trees, filling the lotus flowers with big pearls of spray. But, most of the day, I must regard myself as a prisoner, with the entire freedom of his study--a large airy room on the second floor, well furnished with all manner of books, old prints, strange fishes in glass cases, rods, guns, pipe-racks, curiosities of every kind from various parts of the world--India, the South Seas, Australia, not forgetting London and Paris--and all the flotsam and jetsam of a far-wandered man, who--as the "King" remarked, introducing their autobiographic display with a comprehensive wave of his hand--had, like that other wanderer unbeloved of all schoolboys, the pious AEneas, been so much tossed about on land and sea--*vi superum, saevae memorem Junonis ob iram*--that he might found his city and bring safe his household gods from Latium. Touching his hand lightly on a row of old quartos, in the stout calfskin and tarnished gold dear to bookmen, he said:

"These I recommend to you in your enforced leisure."

They were a collection of old French voyages--Dampier and others--embellished with copper-plate maps and quaint engravings of the fauna and flora of the world, still in all the romantic virginity of its first discovery.

"This," he said, pointing to a stout old jar of Devonshire ware, "is some excellent English tobacco--my one extravagance; and here," pointing to a pipe-rack, "are some well-tried friends from that same 'dear, dear land,' 'sceptred isle of kings,' and so forth. And now I am going to leave you, while I go with Samson and Erebus on a little reconnoitring tour around our domains."

So he left me, and I settled down to a pipe and a volume of Dampier; but, interesting as I found the sturdy old pages, my thoughts, and perhaps particularly my heart, were too much in the present for my attention long to be held by even so adventurous a past; so, laying the book down, I rose from my chair, and made a tour of inspection of the various eloquent objects about the room--objects which made a sort of chronicle in bric-a-brac of my fantastic friend's earthly pilgrimage, and here and there seemed to hint at the story of his strange soul.

Among the books, for example, was a fine copy of Homer, with the arms of a well-known English college stamped on the binding, and near by was the faded photograph of a beautiful old Elizabethan house, with mouldering garden walls, and a moat brimming with water-lilies surrounding it. Hanging close by it, was another faded photograph, of a tall stately old lady, who, at a glance, I surmised must be the "King's" mother. As I looked at it, my eyes involuntarily sought the garden with its palms and its orange trees. Far indeed had the son of her heart wandered, like so many sons of stately English mothers, from that lilied moat and those old gables, and the proud old eyes that would look on her son no more forever.

And then in my privileged inspection of these sacred symbols, carried across so many storm-tossed seas from that far-away Latium, I came upon another photograph, hanging over the writing-desk--a tall, Spanish-looking young woman of remarkable beauty. It needed but one glance to realise that here was Calypso's mother; and, as was natural, I stood a long time scanning the countenance that was so like the face which, from my first sight of it, had seemed the loveliest in the world. This was a flower that had been the mother of a flower. It was a face more primitive in its beauty, a little less touched with race, than the one I loved, but the same fearless natural nobility was in it, and the figure had the same wild grace of pose, the same lithe strength of carriage.

As I stood looking at it, lost in thought, I heard the "King's" voice behind me.

His step was so light that I had not heard him enter the room.

"You are looking at Calypso's mother!" he said. "She was a beautiful creature. I will tell you of her some day, Ulysses."

And indeed, that very night, as we sat over our pipes, he told me; and without a word of his, I knew that the loneliness of his heart had singled me out for his friend, since, for all his love of speech, he was not the man to speak easily of the deep things of his heart.

"Beauty is a very mysterious thing, friend Ulysses," he began, his eyes musing on the face above his desk, "as our old friends of the Siege of Troy knew all too well. The eternal Helen! And in nothing is the divinity of youth so clearly shown as in its worship of beauty, its faith that there is nothing the world holds--the power and the glory, the riches and the honours--nothing so well worth fighting for as a beautiful face. When the world was young, the whole world thought that too. Now we make ignoble war for markets, but the Greeks made nobler warfare--for a beautiful face--

"The face that launched a thousand ships,     And burnt the topless towers of Ilium.

"So is it still with every young man. 'Fair Helen! make me immortal with a kiss' is still his cry. Titles and broad lands, and all such earthly gear--what are these to a youth, with his eyes on the face of the eternal Helen?--that face we meet once and once only, and either win--to lose all the rest, or lose--and win what? What is there to win if that be lost? So, at all events, it was with me, who, after winging away from those old gables yonder on all the adventurous winds of the seven seas, and having in truth looked into many a fair face in every corner of the globe, suddenly, in a certain little island of the French West Indies, came upon the face I had been unconsciously seeking.

"So, long years before my coming, had it befallen also with a certain young French nobleman, out there on military service, who had set eyes on Calypso's grandmother in the streets of that quaint little town, where the French soul seems almost more at home than in France itself. All had seemed nothing to him--his ancestral ties, his brilliant future--compared with that glory of a woman. He married her and settled down for good, the world well lost, in that dream island. And the dream he had been faithful to remained faithful to him. He seems to have been a singularly happy man. I never saw him, for he was dead when I set foot on his island--destined, though I knew it not, to live his life again in the love of his daughter.

"She and her mother were living quietly on the small fortune he had left them, in an old palm-shaded house backed by purple mountains, and sung to by the sea. The soul of old France seemed to haunt that old house like a perfume, taking on a richer colour and drawing a more ardent life from the passionate tropic soul that enfolded it. Both had mysteriously met and become visibly embodied in the lovely girl, in whose veins the best blood of France blended with the molten gold of tropic suns. So, as had happened with her mother, again it happened with her--she took the wandering man to her heart"--he paused--"held him there for some happy years"--he paused again--"and the rest is--Calypso."

We did not speak for a long time after he had ended, but his confidence had touched me so nearly that I felt I owed him my heart in exchange, and it was hard not to cry out: "And now I love Calypso. Once more the far-wandered man has found the great light on a lonely shore."

But I felt that to speak yet--believer in the miracle of love though he had declared himself to be--would seem as though I set too slight a value on the miracle itself.

There should be a long hush before we speak, when a star has fallen out of heaven into our hearts.

# CHAPTER XIII

### *We Begin to Dig.*

Two or three days went by, but as yet there was no news of either Charlie Webster or Tobias. Nothing further had been heard of the latter in the settlement, and a careful patrolling of the neighbourhood revealed no signs of him. Either his sailing away was a bona-fide performance, or he was lying low in some other part of the island--which, of course, would not be a difficult thing for him to do, as most of it was wilderness--and as, also, there were one or two coves on the deserted northern side where he could easily bide his time. Between that coast and us, however, lay some ten miles of scrub and mangrove swamps, and it was manifestly out of the question to patrol them too. There was nothing to do but watch and wait.

"*Vigile et ora,*" said the "King."

But in spite of that counsel, watching and praying was not much in the "King's" temperament. Besides, as I could see, he was anxious to begin operations on John Teach's ruined mansion, and was impatient of the delay.

"With Golconda and Potosi beneath our very feet," he exclaimed at last, "to be held up by this scurvy pock-marked ruffian, I swear 'I like it not.' No news from your duck-shooting friend either. It is a slow-moving world, and the Bird of Time has either lost his wings, or been captured as a specimen on behalf of the Smithsonian Institute."

At last there came a message from Charlie Webster, another of his Caesarian notes: "Sorry delayed a few days longer. Any news?"

That seemed to decide the "King."

"What do you say, Ulysses," he said, "if we begin digging to-morrow? There are ten of us--with as many guns, four revolvers and plenty of machetes--not counting Calypso, who is an excellent shot herself."

I agreed that nothing would please me better--so, an early hour of the following morning found us with the whole garrison--excepting Samson, whom it had been thought wise to leave at home as a bodyguard for Calypso--lined up at the old ruined mansion, with picks and shovels and machetes, ready to commence operations.

The first thing was to get rid of the immense web, which, as I have already described, the forest had woven with diabolic ingenuity all around, and in and out the skeleton of the sturdy old masonry. Till that was done, it was impossible to get any notion of the ground plan of the several connected buildings. So the first day was taken up with the chopping and slashing of vegetable serpents, the tearing out of roots that writhed as if with conscious life, the shearing away of all manner of haunted leafage, all those dense fierce growths with which Nature loves to proclaim her luxuriant victory over the work of man's hands--as soon, so to say, as his back is turned for a moment--like a stealthy savage foe ever on the watch in the surrounding darkness and only waiting for the hushing of human voices, for the cessation of human footsteps, to rush in and overwhelm.

"'I passed by the walls of Balclutha and they were desolate'" quoted the "King," touched, as a less reflective mind must have been, by this sinister triumph of those tireless natural forces that neither slumber nor sleep.

"Here," said he, "is the future of London and Paris--in miniature. The flora and fauna will be different. There will be none of these nasty centipedes" (he had just crushed one with his foot), "and oaks, beeches, and other such friendly trees will take the place of these outlandish monstrosities. That pretty creature, the wild rose, will fill the desolation with her sweet breath, but the incredible desolation will be there; and as we here to-day watch this gum-elemi tree, flourishing where the good Teach 'gloried and drank deep,' so the men of future days will hear the bittern booming in the Rue de la Paix and their children will go a-blackberrying in Trafalgar Square. Selah!"

Two days we were at it with axe and machete wearisome work which gave Tom and me occasion to exchange memories of the month we had put in together on the Dead Men's Shoes. We smiled at each other, as the other fellows groaned and sweated. It seemed child's play to us, after what we had gone through.

"They should have been with us, Tom, shouldn't they? They'd have known what work is;" and I added, for the fun of watching his face: "I wonder whether we'll find any gentlemen playing poker downstairs, Tom."

"God forbid, sar! God forbid!" he exclaimed, with a look of terror.

The next step was the clearing away of the mounds of fallen masonry and various rubbish, which still lay between us and our fortune--tedious preliminaries which chafed the boyish heart of the "King." To tell the truth, I believe we had both expected to uncover a glittering hoard with the first stroke of the pick.

"'And metals cry to me to be delivered!'" quoted the "King," whimsically, fuming as he took his long strides, hither and thither amid the rubbish-heaps, so slow to disappear and reveal those underground passages and hidden vaults, by which the fancies of both of us were obsessed.

We had worked for a week before we made a clearance of the ground floor. Then at last we came upon a solidly built stone staircase, winding downward. After clearing away the debris with which it was choked to a depth of some twenty or thirty steps, we came to a stout wooden door studded with nails.

"The dungeon at last," said the "King."

"The kitchens, I bet," said I.

After some battering, the door gave way with a crash, a mouldering breath as of the grave met our nostrils, and a cloud of bats flew in our faces, and set the negroes screaming. A huge cavernous blackness was before us. The "King" called for lanterns.

As we raised these above our heads, and peered into the darkness, we both gave a laugh.

"'*Yo--ho--ho--and a bottle of rum,*'" sang the "King."

For all along the walls stood, or lay prone on trestles, a silent company of hogsheads, festooned with cobwebs, like huge black wings. It was the pirate's wine cellar!

*　　*　　*　　*　　*

Such was our discovery for that day, but there is another matter which I must mention--the fact that, somehow, the news of our excavation seemed to have got down to the settlement. It is a curious fact, as the "King" observed, that if a man should start to dig for gold in the centre of Sahara, with no possible means of communicating with his fellows, on the third day, there would not fail to be some one to drop in and remark on the fineness of the weather. So it was with us. As a general thing, not once in a month did a human being wander into that wilderness where the "King" had made his home. There was nothing to bring them there, and, as I have made clear, the way was not easy. Yet we had hardly begun work when one and another idle nigger strolled in from the settlement, and stood grinning his curiosity at our labours.

"I believe it's them black parrots has told them," said old Tom, pointing to a bird common in the islands--something like a small crow with a parrot's beak. "They're very knowing birds."

I saw that Tom was serious. So I tried to draw him out.

"What language do they speak, Tom?" I asked.

"Them, sar? They speak Egyptian," he answered, with perfect solemnity.

"Egyptian!"

"Yes, sar," said Tom.

"Egyptian?--but who's going to understand them?"

"There's always some old wise man or woman in every village, sar, who understands them. You remember old King Coffee in Grant's Town?"

"Does he know Egyptian?"

"O yaas, sar! He knows 'gyptian right enough. And he could tell you every word them birds says--if he's a mind to."

"I wonder if Tobias knows Egyptian, Tom?"

"I wouldn't be at all surprised, sar," he answered; "he looks like that kind of man," and he added something about the Prince of the Powers of the Air, and suggested that Tobias had probably sold his soul to the devil, and had, therefore, the advantage of us in superior sources of information.

"He's not unlike one of those black parrots himself, is he, Tom?" I added, for Tom's words had conjured up a picture for me of Tobias, with his great beak, and his close-set evil eyes, and a familiar in the form of a black parrot perched on his shoulders, whispering into one of his ugly ears.

However, we continued with our digging, and Tobias continued to make no sign.

But, at the close of the third day from our discovery of John Teach's wine cellar, something happened which set at rest the question of Tobias's knowledge of Egyptian, and proved that he was all too well served by his aerial messengers. The three days had been uneventful. We had made no more discoveries, beyond the opening up of various prosaic offices and cellars that may once have harboured loot but were now empty of everything but bats and centipedes. But, toward evening of the third day, we came upon a passage leading out of one of these cellars; it had such a promising appearance that we kept at work later than usual, and the sun had set and night was rapidly falling as we turned homeward.

As we came in sight of the house, we were struck by the peculiar hush about it, and there were no lights in the windows.

"No lights!" the "King" and I exclaimed together, involuntarily hurrying our steps, with a foreboding of we knew not what in our hearts. As we crossed the lawn, the house loomed up dark and still, and the door opening on to the loggia was a square of blackness, in a gloom of shadows hardly less profound. Not a sound, not a sign of life!

"Calypso!" we both cried out, as we rushed across the loggia. "Calypso! where are you?--but there was no answer; and then, I, being ahead of the "King," stumbled over something dark lying across the doorway.

"Good God! what is this?" I cried, and, bending down, I saw that it was Samson.

The "King" struck a match. Yes! it was Samson, poor fellow, with a dagger firmly planted in his heart.

Near by, something white caught my eye attached to the lintel of the doorway. It was a piece of paper held there with a sailor's knife. I tore it off in a frenzy, and--the "King" striking another match--we read it together. It bore but a few words, written all in capital letters with a coarse pencil:

"WILL RETURN THE LADY IN EXCHANGE FOR THE TREASURE," and it was signed "H.P.T."

# CHAPTER XIV

### *In Which I Lose My Way.*

I stood a full minute with the astonishing paper in my hand, too stunned to speak or move. It seemed too incredible an outrage to realise. Then a torrent of feelings swept over me--wild fear for her I loved, and impotent fury against the miscreant who had dared even to conceive so foul a sacrilege. To think of her beauty subject to such coarse ruffianism! I pictured her bound and gagged and carried along through the brush in the bestial grasp of filthy negroes, and it seemed as though my brain would burst at the thought.

"The audacity of the fellow!" exclaimed the "King," who was the first to recover.

"But Calypso!" I cried.

The "King" laid his hand on my shoulder, reassuringly.

"Don't be afraid for her," he said. "I know my daughter."

"But I love her!" I cried, thus blurting out in my anguish what I had designed to reveal in some tranquil chosen hour.

"I have loved her for twenty years," said the "King," exasperatingly calm. "'Jack Harkaway' can take care of himself."

I was not even astonished at the time.

"But something must be done," I cried. "I will go to the commandant at once and rouse the settlement. Give me a lantern," I called to one of the negroes, who by this had come up to us, and were standing around in a terrified group. I waited only for it to be lit, and then, without a word, dashed wildly into the forest.

"Hadn't you better take some one with you?" I heard the "King" call after me, but I was too distraught to reply, plunging headforemost through the tangled darkness--my brain boiling like a cauldron with anger and a thousand fears, and my heart stung too with wild unreasoning remorse. After all, it was my doing.

"To think! to think! to think!" I cried aloud--leaving the rest unspoken.

I meant that it had all come of my insensate pursuit of that filthy treasure, when all the time the only treasure I coveted was Calypso herself. Poor old ignorant Tom had been right, after all. Nothing good came of such enterprises. There was a curse upon them from the beginning. And then, as I thought of Tobias, my body shook so that I could hardly keep on walking, and, next minute, my hatred of him so nerved me up again that I ran on through the brush, like a madman, my clothes clutched at by the devilish vines and torn at every yard.

I fled past the scene of our excavations, looking more haunted than ever in the flashing gleam of the lantern. With an oath, I left them behind, as the accursed cause of all this evil; but I cannot have gone by them many yards when suddenly I felt the ground giving way beneath me with a violent jerk. My arms went up in a wild effort to save myself, and then, in a panic of fright, I felt myself shooting downward, as one might fall down the shaft of a mine. Vainly I clutched at rocky walls as I sped down in the earth-smelling darkness. I seemed to be falling forever, and for a moment my head cleared and I had time to think of the crash that was coming, at the end of my fall--a crash which, I said to myself, must mean death. It came with sudden crunching pain, a swift tightening round my heart, as though black ropes were being lashed tightly about it, squeezing out my breath; then entire blackness engulfed me, and I knew no more.

*    *    *    *    *

How long I lay there in the darkness I cannot tell. All I remember is my suddenly opening my eyes on intense blackness, and vaguely wondering where I was. My head felt strangely clear and alive, but for a moment I could remember nothing. I was conscious only of a strong earthy smell, and my eyes felt so keen that, as the phrase goes, they seemed to make darkness visible. They seemed, too, to see themselves, as rings of light in the blackness. My head, too, seemed entirely detached from my body, of which, so far, I was unconscious. But, presently, the realisation of it returned, and involuntarily I tried to move--to find, with a sort of indifferent mild surprise, that it was impossible.

So there I lay, oddly content, in the dark--the pungent smell of the earth my only sensation, and my head uselessly clear.

Then, bit by bit, it all came back to me, like returning circulation in a numbed limb; but as yet dreamily, as something long ago and far away. Then I found myself partly risen, leaning on my elbow, and looking about--into nothingness. Then feeling seemed slowly to be coming back to the rest of me. My head was no longer isolated. It was part of a heavy something that lay inert on the ground, and was beginning to feel numbly--to ache dully. Then I found that I could move one of my legs, then the other, and eventually, with a mighty effort, I could almost raise myself. But, for the moment, I had to fall back.

The remembrance of what had happened began to grow in force and keenness and, of a sudden, the thought of Calypso smote me like a sword! Spurred to desperate effort, I stood up on the instant and leaned against a rocky wall. Miracle of miracles! I could stand. I was not dead, after all. I was not, indeed, so far as I could tell, seriously hurt. Badly bruised, of course--but no bones broken. It seemed incredible, but it was so. The realisation made me feel weak again, and I sat down with my back propped up against the rock, and waited for more strength.

Slowly my thoughts fumbled around the situation. Then, as by force of habit, my hand went to my pocket. God be praised! I had matches, and I cried with thankfulness, out of very weakness. But I still sat on in the dark for a while. I felt very tired. After thinking about it for a long time, I took out my precious match-box, which unconsciously I had been hugging with my hand, and struck a light, looking about me in a dazed fashion. The match burnt down to my fingers, and I threw it away, as the flame stung me. I had seen something of my surroundings, enough to last my tired brain for a minute or two. I was at the bottom of a sort of crevasse, a narrow cleft in the rocks which continued on in a slanting downward chasm into the darkness. It was a natural corridor, with a floor of white sand. The sand had accounted for my coming off without any broken bones.

After another minute or two, I struck another match, and lo! another miracle. There was my lantern lying beside me. The glass of it was broken, but that was no matter. As I lit the wick, my hopes leapt up with the flame. At the worst, I had light.

"*Lux in tenebris!*" I seemed to hear the voice of the "King"--inextinguishably gay; and, at the thought of him, my inertia passed. What could he be thinking? His daughter spirited away, and now I too mysteriously vanished. What was happening up there, all this time? Up there! How far was it to "up there"? How far had I fallen? All about me was so terribly still and shut away. I could believe myself at the very centre of the earth, and it seemed ages ago, aeons of time, since I had last seen the "King." What time was it? I felt for my watch. I found but the wreck of it. It was the only thing that had suffered. It was smashed to smithereens.

Then I moved myself again, and, taking up the lantern, raised it aloft, but the chasm down which I had fallen went up and up in a slanting direction, and lost itself in darkness. Bringing the lantern down to the level again, I examined the rock corridor. Behind me, as before me, it continued--a long, deep fissure, splitting its way through the earth. I limped my way along some yards of the section that lay before me, but it seemed to me that it was growing narrower as it went on, as though it were coming to an end; and indeed, after a while, I came to a place too narrow for me to pass.

I swung my lantern aloft, seeking the possibilities of a climb, but everywhere it was sheer, without a ledge or protuberance of any kind to take advantage of, and it was utterly devoid of vegetation--not a sign of a friendly shrub or root to hold by.

So I turned back to try my luck in the other direction. But first I shouted and shouted with all my might. I could not be far away from the ruins, and there was a chance of some one hearing me. However, I had little faith in my effort, and was too tired to keep it up; so I turned with my lantern toward the other end of the corridor. And here it was easy going, along a gently-graded descent, covered, as I have said, with white sand, in which shells were here and there embedded. My heart beat wildly. Perhaps I had only to walk on a little farther to come out on the sea--for here certainly the sea had been once, whether or not it came up there any more. Vain hope!--for when I had followed the corridor some fifty yards or so, it suddenly widened out for a few yards into something of a cavern, and then as suddenly narrowed into a mere slit, and so came to an end.

The deadening of my spark of hope weakened me. I slid down, with my back against the rock, and gave way to despair. As I looked up at the smooth implacable walls that imprisoned me, I felt like some poor insect clinging to the side of a bowl partly filled with water. How frantically the poor creature claws and claws the polished sides, at each effort slipping nearer and nearer to the fatal flood.

I had sense enough to know that I was too tired to think profitably, and drowsiness coming over me told me that an hour or two's sleep would give me the strength I needed to renew with a will, and more chance of success, my efforts to escape.

Light was too precious to waste, so I blew out my lantern, and, curling up on the sand, almost instantly fell asleep. But, before I lapsed into unconsciousness, I had clutched hold of one sustaining thought in the darkness--the assurance of Calypso's safety, so confidently announced by her father: "Don't be afraid for her. I know my daughter." Whatever happened to me, she would come out all right. As her brave shape flashed before my mind's eye, down there under the earth, I could have no doubt of that.

# CHAPTER XV

### *In Which I Pursue My Studies as a Troglodyte.*

My instinct had been right in giving way to my drowsiness, for I woke up from my sleep a new man. How long I had been there, of course, I had no means of knowing; but I fancy I must have slept a good while, for I felt so refreshed and full of determination to tackle my escape in good earnest.

It is remarkable how rest sharpens one's perceptions. When we are weary, we only half see what we look at, and the very thing we are desperately seeking may be right under our nose and we quite unaware.

So I had hardly relit my lantern, when its rays revealed something which it seemed impossible for any one with eyes, however weary, to have overlooked.

In the right-hand corner of the little cavern, five or six feet above my head, was a dark hole, like the entrance to a tunnel, or, more properly speaking, a good-sized burrow--for it was scarcely more than a yard in diameter. It seemed to be something more than a mere cavity in the rock, for, when I flashed my lantern up to it, I could see no end. To climb up to it, at first, seemed difficult; but providentially, I had a stout claspknife in my pocket, and with this I cut a step or two in the porous rock, and so managed it. Lying flat on my stomach, I looked in.

It was, as I had thought, a narrow natural tunnel, snaking through the rocks--as often happens in those curious fantastic coral formations--for all the world, indeed, as if it had been made ages ago by some monstrous primeval serpent, a giant worm-hole no less, leading--Heaven alone knew where.

There was just room to crawl along it on all fours, so I started cautiously, making sure I had my precious matches, and my jackknife all safe.

After all, I said to myself, I was no worse off than thousands of poor devils in mines. I had myself snaked through just such passages in coal-mines. Still, I confess that the choking sense of being shut in this earth-smelling tube, like a fox in a drain, and the sudden realisation of the appalling tonnage of superincumbent earth above me--liable at any moment to loosen, and, as with a giant thumb, press out my poor little insect existence--made the sweat pour from me and my heart stand still. I had to shut my eyes for a moment and command myself back to calmness and courage, before I could go on. Above all things I had to blindfold my imagination, the last companion for such a situation.

After this first flurry of fear, I went on crawling in a methodical way, allowing no thought to enter my mind that did not concern the yard or two of earth immediately ahead of me. So I progressed, I should say, for some twenty or thirty yards when, to my inexpressible relief, I came out, still on all fours, onto a spreading floor; then, standing up, I perceived that I was in a cave of considerable loftiness, and some forty feet or so across. It was good to breathe again such comparatively free air; yet, as I looked about and made the circuit of the walls, I saw that I had but exchanged one prison for another. There was this difference, however: whereas there had only been one passageway from the cave I had just left, there were several similar outlets from that in which I now stood. Two or three of them proved to be nothing but alcoves that ran a few yards and then stopped.

But there were two close by each other which seemed to continue on. There was not much choice between them, but, as both made in the same direction, as far as I could judge the direction in which I had so far progressed, I decided to take the larger one. It proved to be a passage much like the tunnel I had already traversed, only a little roomier, and therefore it was easier going, and it, too, brought me out, as had the other, on another cavern--but one considerably larger in extent.

Here, however, I speedily perceived that it was not a case of one cavern, but several--opening out, by natural archways one into another. I walked eagerly through them, scanning their ceilings for sign of some outlet into the upper air; but in vain. Still, after the strangling embrace of those tunnels, it was good to have so much space to breathe and walk about in. In fact, I had stumbled on something like a Monte Cristo suite of underground apartments. And here for a moment I released my imagination from her blinders, and allowed her to play around these strange halls. And in one of her suggestions there was some comfort. It was hardly likely that caverns of such extent had waited for me to discover them. They must surely have been known to Teach, or whatever buccaneer it was who had occupied the ruined mansion not so very far above-ground. What better place could be conceived for his business? It was even likely--more than likely, almost certain--that there was some secret passageway connecting this series of caves with the old house--if one could only find it. And so the dear creature prattled on to me, till I thought it was time to blindfold her again--and return to business.

Still, there was something in what she had said, and I set about the more carefully to examine every nook and corner. And, if I didn't find anything so splendid as she had dreamed, I did presently find evidence that, as she had said, I was not the first human being to stand where now I stood. Two iron staples imbedded in one of the walls, with rusting chains and manacles attached, were melancholy proof of one of the uses to which the place had once been put. Melancholy for certain unhappy souls long since free of all mortal chains, but for me--need I say it?--exceedingly joyous. For if there had been a way to bring prisoners here, it was none the less evident that there had been a way to take them out. But how and where? Again I searched every nook and cranny. There was no sign of entrance anywhere.

Then a thought occurred to me. What if the entrance were after the manner of a mediaeval oubliette--through the ceiling! There was a thought indeed to send one's hopes soaring. I ran in my eagerness through one cavern after another, holding my lantern aloft. That must be the solution. There could be no other way. I sought and sought, but alas! it was a false hope, and I threw myself down in a corner in despair, deciding that the prisoners must have been forced to crawl in as I had--though it was hardly like jailers to put themselves to such inconvenience.

I leaned back against the wall and gazed listlessly upward. Next moment I had bounded to my feet again. Surely I had seen some short regular lines running up the face of the rock, like a ladder. I raised my lantern. Sure enough, they were iron rounds set in the face of the rock, and they mounted up till I lost them in the obscurity, for the cave here must have been forty feet high. Blessed heaven! I was saved!

But alas! they did not begin till some six feet above my head, and the wall was sheer. How was I to reach the lowest rung? The rock was too sheer for me to cut steps in, as I had done farther back. I looked about me. Again the luck was with me. In one of the caves I had noticed some broken pieces of fallen rock. They were terribly heavy, but despair lent me strength, and after an hour or two's work, I had managed to roll several of them to the foot of the ladder, and--with an effort of which I would not have believed myself capable--had been able to build them one on top of another against the wall. So, I found myself able to grasp the lowest rung with my hands. Then, fastening the lantern round my neck with my necktie, I prepared to mount.

The climb was not difficult, once I had managed to get my feet on the first rung of the ladder, but there was always the chance that one of the rungs might have rusted loose with time, in which case, of course, it would have given way in my grasp, and I should have been precipitated backward to certain death below.

However, the man who had mortised them had done an honest piece of work, and they proved as firm as on the day they were placed there. Up and up I went, till I must have been forty feet above the floor, and, then, as I neared the roof, instead of coming to a trap door, as I had conjectured, I found that the ladder came to an end at the edge of a narrow ledge, running along the ceiling much as a clerestory runs near the roof of some old churches. On to this I managed to climb. It was barely a yard wide, and the impending roof did not permit of one's standing erect. It was a dizzy situation, and it seemed safest to crawl along on all fours, holding the lantern in front of me. Presently it brought me up sharp in a narrow recess. It had come to an end.

Yes! but imagine my joy! it had come to an end at a low archway rudely cut in the rock. Deep set in the archway was a stout wooden door. My first thought was that I was trapped again, but, to my infinite surprise and gratitude, it proved to be slightly ajar, and a vigorous push sent it grinding back on its hinges. What next! I wondered. At all events, I was no longer lost in the bowels of the earth; step by step, I was coming nearer to the frontiers of humanity.

But I was certainly not prepared for what next met my eyes, as I pushed through the low doorway with my lantern, and looked around. Yes! indeed, man had certainly been here, man, too, very purposeful and businesslike. I was in a sort of low narrow gallery, some forty feet long, to which the arching rock made a crypt-like ceiling. At my first glance, I saw that there was another door at the far end similar to the one I had entered by; and on the left side of the gallery, built of rough stones from the low ceiling to the floor, was a series of compartments, each with locked wooden door. They were strong and grim looking, and might have been taken for prison cells, or family vaults, or possibly wine-bins. The massive locks were red with rust, and there was plainly no possibility of my opening them.

On the other side of the gallery there was a litter of old chains, and some boards, probably left over from the doors. Yes! and there were two old flintlock guns, and several cutlasses, all eaten away with rust, also a rough seaman's chest open and falling to pieces. At the sight of that, a wild thought flashed through my brain. What if--Good God!--What if this was John Teach's treasury!--behind those grim doors. I threw myself with all my force against one and then the other. For the moment I forgot that my paramount business was to escape. But I might as well have hurled myself against the solid rock. And, at that moment, I noticed that the place was darker than it had been. My lantern was going out. In a moment or two, I should be in the pitch dark, and I had discovered that the door at the end of the gallery was as solid as the others.

I was to be trapped, after all; and I pictured myself slowly dying there of hunger--the pangs of which I was already beginning to feel--and some one, years hence, finding me there, a mouldering skeleton--some one who would break open those doors, uncover those gleaming hoards, and moralise on the irony of my end; condemned to die there of starvation, with the treasure I had so long sought on the other side of those unyielding doors. Old Tom's words suddenly flashed over me, and I could feel my hair literally beginning to rise. "There never was a buried treasure yet that didn't claim its victim." Great God!--and I was to be the ghost, and keep guard in this terrible tomb till the next dead man came along to relieve me of my sentry duty!

Frantically I turned up the wick of my lantern at the thought--but it was no use; it was plainly going out. I examined my match-box; I had still a dozen or so matches left. And then my eye fell on that shattered chest. There were those boards, too. At all events I could build a fire and make torches of slivers of wood, so long as the wood lasted.

And then I had an idea. Why not make the fire against the door at the end of the gallery, and so burn my way through. Bravo! My spirits rose at the thought, and I set to at once--splitting some small kindling with my knife. In a few minutes I had quite a sprightly little fire going at the bottom of the door; but I saw that I should have to be extravagant with my wood if the fire was to be effective. However, it was neck or nothing; so I piled on beams and boards till my fire roared like a furnace, and presently I had the joy of seeing it begin to take hold of the door--which, after a short time, began to crackle and splutter in a very cheering fashion.

Whatever lay beyond, it was evident that I should soon be able to break my way through the obstacle, and, indeed, so it proved; for, presently, I used one of the boards as a battering ram, and, to my inexpressible joy, it went crashing through, with a shower of sparks, and it was but the work of a few more minutes before the whole door fell flaming down, and I was able to leap through the doorway into the darkness on the other side.

As I stood there, peering ahead, and holding aloft a burning stick--which proved, however, a poor substitute for my lantern--a wonderful sound smote my ears. I could not believe it, and my knees shook beneath me. It was the sound of the sea.

Yes! it was no illusion. It was the sound that the sea makes singing and echoing through hollow caves--the sound I heard that night as I stood at the moonlit door of Calypso's cavern, and saw that vision which my heart nearly broke to remember. Calypso! O Calypso! where was she at this moment? Pray God that she was indeed safe, as her father had said. But I had to will her from my mind, to keep from going mad.

And my poor torch had gone out, having, however, given me light enough to see that the door which I had just burnt through let out on to a narrow platform on the side of a rock that went slanting down into a chasm of blackness, through which, as in a great shell, boomed that murmuring of the sea. It had a perilous ugly look, and it was plain that it would be foolhardy to attempt it at the moment without a light; and my fire was dying down. Besides, I was beginning to feel light-headed and worn out, partly from lack of food, no doubt.

As there was no food to be had, I recalled the old French proverb, "He eats who sleeps"--or something to that effect--and I determined to husband my strength once more with a brief rest. However, as I turned to throw some more wood on my fire--preparing to indulge myself with a little camp-fire cheerfulness as I dozed off--my eyes fell once more on that grim line of locked doors; and my curiosity, and an idea, made me wakeful again. I had burned down one door--why not another? Why not, indeed?

So I raked over my fire to the family vault nearest to me, and presently had it roaring and licking against the stout door. It was, apparently, not so solid as the gallery door had been. At all events, it kindled more easily, and it was not long before I had the satisfaction of battering that down too.

As I did so, I caught sight of something in the interior that made me laugh aloud and behave generally like a madman. Of course, I didn't believe my eyes--but they persisted in declaring, nevertheless, that there in front of me was a great iron-bound oaken chest, to begin with. It might not, of course, contain anything but bones--but it might--! The thing was too absurd. I must have fallen asleep--must be already dreaming! But no! I was labouring with all my strength to open it with one of those rusty cutlasses. It was a tough job, but my strength was as the strength of ten, for the old treasure-hunting lust was upon me, and I had forgotten everything else in the world.

At last, with a great wooden groan, as though its heart were breaking at having to give up its secret at last, it crashed open. I fell on my knees as though I had been

struck by lightning, for it was literally brimming over with silver and gold pieces-
-doubloons and pieces of eight; English and French coins, too--guineas and louis
d'or: "all"--as Tobias's manuscript had said--"all good money."

For a while I knelt over it, dazed and blinded, lost; then I slowly plunged my
hands into it, and let the pieces pour and pour through them, literally bathing them
in gold and silver, as I had read of misers doing.

Meanwhile, I talked insanely to myself, made all sorts of inarticulate noises,
sang shreds of old songs. Rising at length, I capered up and down the gallery, talking aloud to the "King" as though he had been there, and anon breaking out again
into absurd song, roaring it out at the top of my voice, laughing and war-whooping
between:

"There was chest on chest of Spanish gold,   With a ton of plate in the middle
hold,    And the cabin's riot of loot untold."

Then suddenly I broke out into an Irish jig--never having had any notion of
doing such a thing before.

In fact I behaved as I have read of men doing, whom a sudden fortune has
bereft of reason. For the time, at all events, I was a gibbering madman. Certainly,
there was to be no sleep for me that night! But, in the full tide of my frenzy, I suddenly noticed something that brought me up sharp. Out beyond the doorway it was
growing light. It was only a dim tremulous suffusion of it, indeed, but it was real
daylight--oozing in from somewhere or other--the blessed, blessed, daylight! God
be praised!

# CHAPTER XVI

### *In Which I Understand the Feelings of a Ghost!*

So, I surmised, I had been underground a whole day and two nights, and this
was the morning of the second day after Calypso's disappearance. What had been
happening to her all this time! My flesh crept at the thought, and, with that daylight
stealing in like a living presence, and the sound and breath of the sea, my anguish
returned a hundredfold. It was like coming to, after an anaesthetic, for I realised

that, actively as I had been occupied in trying to escape, I had been, all the time, under a curious numbing spell. Just as my ears had seemed muffled with a silence that was more than the stillest silence above ground; silence that was itself a captive, airless and gasping, so to say, with the awful pressure of all that oblivious earth above and around; a silence that made me realise with a dreadful reality what had been a mere phrase before, "the silence of the grave"; silence literally buried alive, with eyes fixed in a trance of horror; just in the same way, all my feelings of mind and heart, memory and emotion, had likewise been deadened, as with some heavy narcotic of indifference, so that I felt and yet did not feel--remembered and yet did not remember.

The events of a few hours before, and the dearly loved friends taking part in them, seemed infinitely remote, for all their clearness, as when we see a figure waving to us from a distance, and know that it is calling to us, but yet we cannot hear a word. Even so one lies back in the grip of a deadly sickness, and all that formerly had been so important and moving seems like a picture, definite yet remote, in which one has no part any more.

I think one would die soon and easily underground, as creatures in a vacuum, for the will to live has so little to nourish itself on. One's whole nature falls into a catalepsy; all one's faculties seem asleep, save the animal impulse to escape--an impulse that would soon grow weary too. So, it seemed to me, as I saw a little light and drew the breath of the living world once more, that even my love for Calypso had, so to say, been in a state of suspended animation during an entombment which was heavy with the poppy of the grave, and made me understand why the dead forget us so soon.

But now, as I stood on the little rocky platform outside the door through which I had burned my way, and looked down into the glimmering chasm beneath, and heard the fresh voice of the sea huskily rumbling and reverberating about hidden grottoes and channels, all that Calypso was to me came back with the keenness of a sword through my heart. Ah! there was my treasure--as I had known when my eyes first beheld her--compared with which that gold and silver in there, whose gleam had made me momentarily distraught, was but so much dust and ashes. Ardently as I had sought it, what was it compared to one glance of her eyes? What if, in the same hour, I had lost my true treasure, and found the false? At the thought, that glittering heap became abhorrent to me, and, without looking back, I sought for some way by which I could descend.

As my eyes grew accustomed to the dim light, I saw that there were some shallow steps cut diagonally in the rock, and down these I had soon made my way, to find myself in a roomy corridor, so much like that in which I had seen Calypso standing in the moonlight, that, for a moment, I dreamed it was the same, and started to run down it, thinking, indeed, that my troubles were over--that in another moment I would emerge through that enchanted door and face the sea. The more so, as the sand was wet under my feet, showing that the tide had but recently left it.

But alas! instead of a broad shining doorway, and open arms of freedom wide-spread for me to leap into, I came at last to a mere long narrow slit--through which I could gaze as a man gazes through a prison window at the sky.

The entrance had once been wide and free, but a mass of rock had fallen from above and blocked it up, leaving only a long crack through which the tides passed to and fro.

I was still in my trap; it seemed more terrible than ever, now that I could see freedom so close and shining, her very robe rustling within a few feet of me, her very voice calling to me, singing the morning song of the sea. But in the caverns behind me, I heard another mocking song, and I felt a cold breath on my cheek, for Death stood by my side a-grin.

"The treasure!" he whispered, "I need you to guard that. The treasure you have risked all to win--the treasure for which you have lost--your treasure! You cannot escape. Go back and count your gold. 'It is all good money'! Ha! ha! 'it is all good money'!"

The illusion seemed so real to me that I cried aloud: "I will not die! I will not die!"--cried it so loud, that any one in a passing boat might have heard me, and shuddered, wondering what poor ghost it was wailing among the rocks.

But the fright had done me good, and I nerved myself for another effort. I examined the long crevice through which the sea was glittering so near. It was not so narrow as at first it had seemed, and I reckoned that it was some twenty feet through. On my side, it was a little over a foot across. Wouldn't it be possible to wedge myself through? I tried it at the opening, and found, that, with my arms extended sidewise, it was comparatively easy to enter it, though it was something of a tight fit. If it only kept the same width all through, I ought to be able to manage it, inch by inch, if it took all day. But, did it? On the contrary, it seemed to me that it narrowed slightly toward the middle, and--judging by the way the light fell on the other side--that it widened out again farther on.

If only I could wriggle past that contraction in the middle, I should be safe. And if I stuck fast midway! But the more I measured the width with my eye, the less the narrowing seemed to be. To be so slightly perceptible, it could hardly be enough to make much difference. Caution whispered that it might be enough to make the difference between life and death. But already my choice of those two august alternatives was so limited as hardly to be called a choice. On the one hand, I could worm my way back through the caves and tunnels through which I had passed, and try my luck again at the other end.

"With half-a-dozen matches!" sneered a voice that sounded like Tobias's-- "Precisely" ... and the horror of it was more than I dared face again any way. So there was nothing for it but this aperture, hardly wider than one of those deep stone slits that stood for windows in a Norman castle. It was my last chance, and I meant to take it like a man.

I stood for a moment nerving myself and taking deep breaths, as though I expected to take but few more. Then, my left arm extended, I entered sidewise, and began to edge myself along. It was easy enough for a yard or two, after which it was plain that it was beginning to narrow. Very slightly indeed, but still a little. However, I could still go on, and--I could still go back. I went on--more slowly it is true, yet still I progressed. But the rock was perceptibly closer to me. I had to struggle harder. It was beginning to hug me--very gently--but it was beginning.

I paused to take breath. I could not turn my head to look back, but I judged that I had come over a third of the way. I was coming up to the waist that I had feared, but I could still go on--very slowly, scarce more than an inch at every effort; yet every inch counted, and I had lots of time. My feet and head were free--which was the main thing. Another good push or two, and I should be at the waist--should know my fate.

I gave the good push or two, and suddenly the arms of the rock were around me. Tight and close, this time, they hugged me. They held me fast, like a rude lover, and would not let me go. My knees and feet were fast, and the walls on each side pressed my cheeks. My head too was fast. I could not move an inch forward--and it was too late to go back!

Panic swept over me. I felt that my hair must be turning white. Presently I ceased to struggle. But the rocks held me in their giant embrace. There was no need for me to do anything. I could go on resting there--it was very comfortable--till--

And then I felt something touching my feet, running away and then touching them again. O God! It was the incoming tide! It would--And then I prepared myself to die. I suppose I was lightheaded, with the strain and the lack of food, for, after the first panic, I found myself dreamily, almost luxuriously, making pictures of how brave men had died in the past--brave women too. I fancied myself in one and another situation. But the picture that persisted was that of the Conciergerie during the French Revolution. I was a noble, talking gaily to beautiful ladies also under the shadow of death, and, right in the middle of a jest, a gloomy fellow had just come in--to lead me to the guillotine. The door was opening, and I kissed my hand in farewell--

Then the picture vanished, as I felt the swish of the tide round my ankles. It would soon be up to my knees--

It *was* up to my knees--it was creeping past them--and it was making that hollow song in the caves behind me that had seemed so kind to me that very morning, the song it had made to Calypso ... that far-off night under the moon.

I turned my eyes over the sea--I could move *them,* at all events; how gloriously it was shining out there! And here was I, helpless, with arms extended, as one crucified. I closed my eyes in anguish, and let my body relax; perhaps I dozed, or perhaps I fainted--but, suddenly, what was that that had aroused me, summoned me back to life? It seemed a short, sharp sound--then another, and then another--surely it was the sound of firing! I opened my eyes and looked out to sea, and then I gave a great cry:

"Calypso! Calypso!" I cried. "Calypso!"--and it seemed as though a giant's strength were in me--that I could rend the rocks apart. I made a mighty effort, and, whether or not my relaxing had made a readjustment of my position, I found that for some reason I could move forward again, and, with one desperate wriggle, I had my head through the narrow space. To wrench my shoulders and legs after it was comparatively easy, and, in a moment, I was safe on the outer side, where, as I had surmised, the aperture did widen out again. Within a few moments, I was on the edge of the sea, had dived, and was swimming madly toward--

But let me tell what I had seen, as I hung there, so helpless, in that crevice in the rocks.

# CHAPTER XVII

### *Action.*

I had seen, close in shore, a two-masted schooner under full sail sweeping by, as if pursued, and three negroes kneeling on deck, with levelled rifles. As I looked, a shot rang out, from my right, where I could not see, and one of the negroes rolled over. Another shot, and the negro next him fell sprawling with his arms over the bulwark.

At that moment, two other negroes emerged from the cabin hatchway, half dragging and half carrying a woman. She was struggling bravely, but in vain. The negroes--evidently acting under orders of a white man, who stood over them with a revolver--were dragging her toward the mainmast. Her head was bare, her hair in disorder, and one shoulder from which her dress had been torn in the struggle, gleamed white in the sunlight. Yet her eyes were flashing splendid scornful fires at her captors; and her laughter of defiance came ringing to me over the sea. It was then that I had cried "Calypso!" and wrenched myself free.

The next moment there came dashing in sight a sloop also under full canvas, and at its bow, a huge white man, with a levelled rifle that still smoked. At a glance, I knew him for Charlie Webster. He had been about to fire again, but, as the man dragged Calypso for'ard, he paused, calm as a rock, waiting, with his keen sportsman's eyes on Tobias--for, of course, it was he.

"You--coward!" I heard his voice roar across the rapidly diminishing distance between the two boats, for the sloop was running with power as well as sails.

Meanwhile, the men had lashed Calypso to the mast, and even in my agony my eyes recorded the glory of her beauty as she stood proudly there--the great sails spread above her, and the sea for her background.

"Now, do your worst," cried Tobias, his evil face white as wax in the sunlight.

"Fire, fire--don't be afraid," rang out Calypso's voice, like singing gold. At the same instant, as she called, Tobias sprang toward her with raised revolver.

"Another word, and I fire," shouted the voice of the brute.

But the rifle that never missed its mark spoke again. Tobias's arm fell shattered, and he staggered away screaming. Still once more, Charlie Webster's gun spoke, and the staggering figure fell with a crash on the deck.

"Now, boys, ready," I heard Charlie's voice roar out again, as the sloop tore alongside the schooner--where the rest of the negro crew with raised arms had fallen on their knees, crying for mercy.

All this I saw from the water, as I swam wildly toward the two boats, which now had closed on each other, a mass of thundering canvas, and screaming and cursing men--and Calypso there, like a beautiful statue, still lashed to the mast, a proud smile on her lovely lips.

Another moment, and Charlie had sprung aboard, and, seizing a knife from one of the screaming negroes, he cut her free.

His deep calm voice came to me over the water.

"That's what I call courage," he said. "I could never have done it."

The "King" had been right. He knew his daughter.

By this I was nearing the boats, though as yet no one had seen me. They were all too busy with the confusion on deck, where four men lay dead, and three others still kept up their gibberish of fear.

I saw Calypso and Charlie Webster stand a moment looking down at the figure of Tobias, prostrate at their feet.

"I am sorry I had to kill him," I heard Charlie's deep growl. "I meant to keep him for the hangman."

But suddenly I saw him start forward and stamp heavily on something.

"No, you don't," I heard him roar--and I learned afterward that Tobias, though mortally wounded, was not yet dead, and that, as the two had stood looking down on him, they had seen his hand furtively moving toward the fallen revolver that lay a few inches from him on the deck. Just as he had grasped it, Charlie's heavy boot had come down on his wrist. But Tobias was still game.

"Not alive, you English brute!" he was heard to groan out, and, snatching free his wrist too swiftly to be prevented, he had gathered up all his remaining strength, and hurled himself over the side into the sea.

I was but a dozen yards away from him, as he fell; and, as he rose again, it was for his dying eyes to fix with a glare upon me. They dilated with terror, as though he had seen a ghost. Then he gave one strange scream, and fell back into the sea, and we saw him no more.

*     *     *     *     *

It will be easier for the reader to imagine, than for me to describe, the look on the faces of Calypso and Charlie Webster when they saw me appear at almost the same spot where poor Tobias had just gone bubbling down. Words I had none, for I was at the end of my strength, and I broke down and sobbed like a child.

"Thank God you are safe--my treasure, my treasure!" was all I could say, after they had lifted me aboard, and I lay face down on the deck, at her feet. Swiftly she knelt by my side, and caressed my shoulder with her dear hand.

All of which--particularly my reference to "my treasure"--must have been much to the bewilderment of the good simple-hearted Charlie, towering, innocent-eyed, above us. I believe I stayed a little longer at her feet than I really had need to, for the comfort of her being so near and kind; but, presently, we were all aroused by a voice from the cliffs above. It was the "King," with his bodyguard, Erebus and the crew of the *Flamingo*--no Samson, alas! The sound of the firing had reached them in the woods, and they had come hurrying to discover its cause.

So we deferred asking our questions, and telling our several stories, till we were pulled ashore.

As Calypso was folded in her father's arms, he turned to me:

"Didn't I tell you that I knew my daughter?" he said.

"And I told you something too, O King," I replied--my eyes daring at last to rest on Calypso with the love and pride of my heart.

"And where on earth have *you* been, young man?" he asked, laughing. "Did Tobias kidnap you too?"

It was very hard, as you will have seen, to astonish the "King."

# CHAPTER XVIII

### *Gathering Up the Threads.*

But, though it was hard to astonish and almost impossible to alarm the "King," his sense of wonder was quite another matter, and the boyish delight with which he listened to our several stories would have made it worth while to undergo tenfold the perils we had faced. And the best of it was that we each had a new audience in the others--for none of us knew what had happened to the rest, and how it chanced that we should all come to meet at that moment of crisis on the sea. Our stories, said the "King," were quite in the manner of "The Arabian Nights," dovetailing one into the other.

"And now," he added, "we will begin with the Story of the Murdered Slave and the Stolen Lady."

Calypso told her story simply and in a few words. The first part of it, of which the poor murdered Samson had been the eloquent witness, needed no further telling. He had done his brave best--poor fellow--but Tobias had had six men with him, and it was soon over. Her they had gagged and bound and carried in a sort of improvised sedan-chair; Tobias had done the thing with a certain style and--she had to admit--with absolute courtesy.

When they had gone a mile or two from the house, he had had the gag taken from her mouth, and, on her promise not to attempt to escape (which was, of course, quite impossible) he had also had her unbound, so that her hurried journey through the woods was made as comfortable as possible. Certainly it had not been without its spice of romance, for four of the men had carried lanterns, and their progress must have had a very picturesque effect lighting up the blackness of the strange trees.

Tobias had walked at her side the whole way, without speaking a word.

They were making, she had gathered--and as we had surmised--for the northern shore, and, after about a three hours' march, she heard the sound of the sea. On the schooner she had found a cabin all nicely prepared for her--even dainty toilet necessaries--and an excellent dinner was served, on some quite pretty china, to her alone. Poor Tobias had seemed bent on showing--as he had said to Tom--that he was not the "carrion" we had thought him.

After dinner, Tobias had respectfully asked leave for a few words with her. He had apologised for his action, but explained that it was necessary--the only way he had left, he said, of protecting his own interests, and safeguarding a treasure which belonged to him and no one else, if it belonged to any living man. It had seemed to her that it was a monomania with him. His eyes had gleamed so, as he spoke of it, that she had felt a little frightened for the first time--for he seemed like a madman on the subject.

While he had been talking, she had made up her mind what she would do. She would tell him the plain truth about her doubloons, and offer him what remained of them as a ransom. This she did, and was able at last half to persuade him that, so far as any one knew, that was all the treasure there was, and that the digging among the ruins of the old house was a mere fancy of her father's. There might be something there or not--and she went so far as to give her word of honour that, if anything was found, he should have his share of it.

It was rather a woman's way, she admitted, but she thought that, so long as she kept Tobias near the island, some favouring incident might happen at any moment--that the proffered ransom, in fact, might prove the bait to a trap.

Tobias had seemed impressed, and promised his answer in the morning, leaving her to sleep--with a sentry at her cabin door. She had slept soundly, and wakened only at dawn. As soon as she was up, Tobias had come to her, saying that he had accepted her offer, and asking her to direct him to her treasure.

This she had done, and, to avoid passing the settlement, they had taken the course round the eastern end of the island. As they had approached the cave (and here Calypso turned a quizzical smile on me, which no one, of course, understood but ourselves), a sloop was seen approaching them from the westward ... and here she stopped and turned to Charlie Webster.

"Now," said the "King," "we shall hear the Story of Apollo--or, let us say, rather Ajax--the Far-Darter--He of the Arrow that never missed its mark."

And Charlie Webster, more at home with deeds than words, blushed and blushed through his part of the story, telling how--having called at the settlement--he had got our message from Sweeney, and was making up the coast for the hidden creek. He had spied what he felt sure was Tobias's schooner--had called on him "In the King's Name" to surrender--("I had in my pocket the warrant for his arrest," said Charlie, with innocent pride--"the d----d scoundrel") but had been answered with bullets. He had been terribly frightened, he owned, when Calypso had been brought on deck, but she had given him courage--he paused to beam on her, a broad-faced admiration, for which he could find no words--and, as he had never yet missed a flying duck at--I forget how many yards Charlie mentioned--well ... perhaps he oughtn't to have risked it--And so his story came to an end, amid reassuring applause.

"Now," said the "King," "for the Story of the Disappearing Gentleman and the Lighted Lantern."

And then I told my story as it is already known to the reader, and I have to confess that, when I came to the chestful of doubloons and pieces of eight, I had a very attentive audience. But, at first, the "King" shook his head with an amused smile.

"Ulysses is romancing for the benefit of my romantic second childhood," he said, and then, after his favourite manner he added--

> "I might not this believe
> Without the sensible and true avouch of mine own eyes ..."

Then, he was for starting off that very night. But, reminded of the difficult seclusion in which the treasure still lay, he was persuaded to wait till the morrow.

"At dawn then," he said, "to-morrow--'what time, the rosy-footed dawn' ... so be it. And now I am going to talk to Ajax the Far-Darter of duck-shooting."

"But wait!" I cried. "Why did 'Jack Harkaway' go to Nassau?"

Calypso blushed. The "King" chuckled.

"I prefer not to be known in Nassau, yet some of my business has to be done there. Nor is it safe for beauty like Calypso's to go unprotected. So from time to time, 'Jack Harkaway' goes for us both! And now enough of explanations!"; and he launched into talk of game and sport in various parts of the world, to the huge delight of the great simple-hearted Charlie.

But, after a time, other matters claimed the attention of his other auditors. During the flow of his discourse night had fallen. Calypso and I perceived that we were forgotten--so, by an impulse that seemed to be one, we rose and left them there, and stole out into the garden where the little fountain was dancing like a spirit under the moon, and the orange trees gave out their perfume on the night breeze. I took her hand, and we walked softly out into the moonlight, and looked down at the closed lotuses in the little pool. And then we took courage to look into each other's eyes.

"Calypso," I said, "when are you going to show me where you keep your doubloons?"--and I added, in a whisper, "Jack--when am I going to see you in boy's clothes again?"

And, with that, she was in my arms, and I felt her heart beating against my side.

"O! my treasure," I said--ever so softly--"Calypso, my treasure."

# POSTSCRIPT

Now, such readers as have been "gentle" enough to follow me so far in my story, may possibly desire to be told what lay behind those other locked doors in the underground gallery where I so nearly laid my bones.

I should like nothing better than to gratify their legitimate curiosity. But, perhaps, they will not have forgotten my friend John Saunders, Secretary to the Treasury of His Britannic Majesty's Government at Nassau.

John is a good friend, but he is a man of very rigid principles and a great stickler in regard to any matters pertaining to the interests and duties of his office. Were I to divulge--as, I confess, my pen is itching to do--the dazzling--I will even say blinding--contents of these other grim compartments (particularly if I were to give any hint of their value in bullion), no feelings of friendship would for one second weigh with him as against his duty to the august Government he so faithfully serves. He may suspect what he likes, but, so long as he actually knows nothing, we may rely on his inactivity. In fact, I know that he has no wish to be told--so far he will go with us, but no further--and, as we wish neither to sully his fine probity, nor, on the other hand, to disgorge our "illgotten gains"--for which, after all, each one of us risked his life (and for which one life, most precious of all, was placed in such terrible jeopardy)--gains too which His Britannic Majesty is quite rich enough to do without--the readers must pardon me my caution, and draw upon his imagination for what I must not tell him.

This, however, I will say: he cannot well imagine too vividly or too magnificently, and that, in fact, he may accept those hyperboles fancifully indulged in by the "King" as very slightly overshooting the mark. We do not, indeed, go disguised in cloth of gold, nor are we blinding to look upon with rings and ropes of pearls. It does not happen to be our western fashion to be so garmented. But--well--I won't say that we couldn't do so if we were so minded.

Nor will I say, either, that the "King" does not occasionally, in private, masquerade in some such splendour; though, as a rule, he still prefers that shabby tatterdemalion costume which we have still to accept as a vagary of his fantastic nature. He is still the same Eternal Child, and his latest make-believe has been to fit up those caverns, through which so miserably I wormed my way, with the grandiose luxury of the Count of Monte Cristo; that, as he says, the prophecy might be fulfilled which said: "Monte Cristo shall seem like a pauper and a penny gaff in comparison with the fantasies of our fearful wealth."

Those caverns, we afterward discovered, did actually communicate with Blackbeard's ruined mansion, and the "King," who has now rebuilt that mansion and lives in it in semi-feudal state with Calypso and me, is able to pass from one to the other by underground passages which are an unfailing source of romantic satisfaction to his dear, absurd soul.

As to whether or not the mansion and the treasure were actually Blackbeard's--that is, Edward Teach's--we are yet in doubt, though we prefer to believe that they were. At all events, we never found any evidence to connect them at all with Henry P. Tobias, whose second treasure, we have every reason to think, still remains undiscovered.

As for the sinister and ill-fated Henry P. Tobias, Jr., we have since learned--through Charlie Webster, who every now and again drops in with sailors from his sloop and carries off the "King" for duck-shooting--that his real name was quite different; he must have assumed, as a *nom de guerre,* the name we knew him by, to give colour to his claim. I am afraid, therefore, that he was a plain scoundrel, after all, though it seemed to me that I saw gleams in him of something better, and I shall always feel a sort of kindness toward him for the saving grace of gallant courtesy with which he invested his rascally abduction of Calypso.

Calypso.... She and I, just for fun, sometimes drop into Sweeney's store, and, when she has made her purchases, she draws up from her bosom a little bag, and, looking softly at me, lays down on the counter--a golden doubloon; and Sweeney--who, doubtless, thinks us all a little crazy--smiles indulgently on our make-believe.

Sometimes, on our way home, we come upon Tom in the plantations, superintending a gang of the "King's" janissaries--among whom Erebus is still the blackest--for Tom is now the Lord High Steward of our estate. He beams on us in a fatherly way, and I lay my hand significantly on my leftside--to his huge delight. He flashes his white teeth and wags his head from side to side with inarticulate enjoyment of the allusion. For who knows? He may be right. In so mysterious a world the smallest cause may lead up to the most august results and there is nothing too wonderful to happen.

# EPILOGUE BY THE EDITOR

*It remains for me, as sponsor for the foregoing narrative, reluctantly to add a second postscript to that of its author, bringing the fortunes of himself and his friends a little nearer to the present year of grace. Not that anything untoward has happened to any of them. Their lives are still lived happily in the sun, and their treasure is still safe--somewhere carefully out of the sun. But neither their lives nor their treasure are where my friend's postscript left them. They are, indeed, very much nearer New York than at that writing.*

*As a matter of fact, after King Alcinoues had played but a short time at being the Count of Monte Cristo in his underground palace, it gradually was borne in upon his essentially common-sense mind, as upon the minds of Calypso and her husband, that their secret was known to too many for its absolute safety. Kindly coloured people indeed, and a very friendly "Secretary to the British Treasury" ... still, there was no knowing, and, on all accounts, they gradually came to the unromantic conclusion that the safe deposit vaults of New York were more reliable than limestone caverns filled with the sound of sea. This conclusion explains the presence of my friend and his Lady of the Doubloons in the box of the Punch and Judy Theatre that, to me, eventful evening.*

*Since then, I myself have made a pilgrimage to all the places that play a part in this romance. I have crawled my way through those caves in which my friend came so near to leaving his bones, looked into those vaults once glittering with pieces of eight and all that other undivulged treasure-trove, wedged myself as far as I dared into that slit in the rocks, looking out like a narrow window on the sea.*

*All those places are real; any one, with a mind to, can find them; but, should any one care to undertake the pilgrimage, he will note, as I did, that those baronial halls of Edward Teach--for a while the playground of King Alcinoues--are rapidly being reclaimed by the savage wilderness, fiercely swallowed minute by minute by the fanged and serpentine vegetation--which, after all, was only stayed for a moment, and which, humanly speaking, will now submerge them for all eternity.*

*Once more, to employ one of the favourite quotations of King Alcinoues, "I PASSED BY THE WALLS OF BALCLUTHA, AND THEY WERE DESOLATE." The King, I may be allowed to add, finds New York quite a good place to talk in--though he is frank in saying that he prefers a coral island.*

R. Le G.

THE END

www.bookjungle.com *email: sales@bookjungle.com fax: 630-214-0564 mail: Book Jungle  PO Box 2226  Champaign, IL 61825*

### The Codes Of Hammurabi And Moses
### W. W. Davies

QTY

The discovery of the Hammurabi Code is one of the greatest achievements of archaeology, and is of paramount interest, not only to the student of the Bible, but also to all those interested in ancient history...

**Religion**    **ISBN:** *1-59462-338-4*    **Pages:132**
*MSRP $12.95*

### The Theory of Moral Sentiments
### Adam Smith

QTY

This work from 1749. contains original theories of conscience amd moral judgment and it is the foundation for systemof morals.

**Philosophy**  **ISBN:** *1-59462-777-0*    **Pages:536**
*MSRP $19.95*

### Jessica's First Prayer
### Hesba Stretton

QTY

In a screened and secluded corner of one of the many railway-bridges which span the streets of London there could be seen a few years ago, from five o'clock every morning until half past eight, a tidily set-out coffee-stall, consisting of a trestle and board, upon which stood two large tin cans, with a small fire of charcoal burning under each so as to keep the coffee boiling during the early hours of the morning when the work-people were thronging into the city on their way to their daily toil...

**Childrens**    **ISBN:** *1-59462-373-2*    **Pages:84**
*MSRP $9.95*

### My Life and Work
### Henry Ford

QTY

Henry Ford revolutionized the world with his implementation of mass production for the Model T automobile.  Gain valuable business insight into his life and work with his own auto-biography... "We have only started on our development of our country we have not as yet, with all our talk of wonderful progress, done more than scratch the surface. The progress has been wonderful enough but..."

**Biographies/**    **ISBN:** *1-59462-198-5*    **Pages:300**
*MSRP $21.95*

## The Art of Cross-Examination
## Francis Wellman

I presume it is the experience of every author, after his first book is published upon an important subject, to be almost overwhelmed with a wealth of ideas and illustrations which could readily have been included in his book, and which to his own mind, at least, seem to make a second edition inevitable. Such certainly was the case with me; and when the first edition had reached its sixth impression in five months, I rejoiced to learn that it seemed to my publishers that the book had met with a sufficiently favorable reception to justify a second and considerably enlarged edition. ..

QTY

**Pages:412**

Reference ISBN: *1-59462-647-2* *MSRP $19.95*

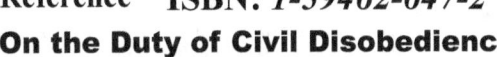

## On the Duty of Civil Disobedience
## Henry David Thoreau

QTY

Thoreau wrote his famous essay, On the Duty of Civil Disobedience, as a protest against an unjust but popular war and the immoral but popular institution of slave-owning. He did more than write—he declined to pay his taxes, and was hauled off to gaol in consequence. Who can say how much this refusal of his hastened the end of the war and of slavery ?

Law ISBN: *1-59462-747-9*

**Pages:48**
*MSRP $7.45*

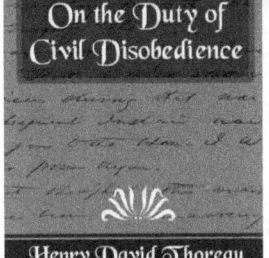

## Dream Psychology Psychoanalysis for Beginners
## Sigmund Freud

QTY

Sigmund Freud, born Sigismund Schlomo Freud (May 6, 1856 - September 23, 1939), was a Jewish-Austrian neurologist and psychiatrist who co-founded the psychoanalytic school of psychology. Freud is best known for his theories of the unconscious mind, especially involving the mechanism of repression; his redefinition of sexual desire as mobile and directed towards a wide variety of objects; and his therapeutic techniques, especially his understanding of transference in the therapeutic relationship and the presumed value of dreams as sources of insight into unconscious desires.

Psychology ISBN: *1-59462-905-6*

**Pages:196**
*MSRP $15.45*

## The Miracle of Right Thought
## Orison Swett Marden

QTY

Believe with all of your heart that you will do what you were made to do. When the mind has once formed the habit of holding cheerful, happy, prosperous pictures, it will not be easy to form the opposite habit. It does not matter how improbable or how far away this realization may see, or how dark the prospects may be, if we visualize them as best we can, as vividly as possible, hold tenaciously to them and vigorously struggle to attain them, they will gradually become actualized, realized in the life. But a desire, a longing without endeavor, a yearning abandoned or held indifferently will vanish without realization.

**Pages:360**

Self Help ISBN: *1-59462-644-8* *MSRP $25.45*

QTY

**The Rosicrucian Cosmo-Conception Mystic Christianity** *by Max Heindel*  ISBN: 1-59462-188-8  **$38.95**
*The Rosicrucian Cosmo-conception is not dogmatic, neither does it appeal to any other authority than the reason of the student. It is: not controversial, but is: sent forth in the, hope that it may help to clear...*  New Age/Religion Pages 646

**Abandonment To Divine Providence** *by Jean-Pierre de Caussade*  ISBN: 1-59462-228-0  **$25.95**
*"The Rev. Jean Pierre de Caussade was one of the most remarkable spiritual writers of the Society of Jesus in France in the 18th Century. His death took place at Toulouse in 1751. His works have gone through many editions and have been republished...*  Inspirational/Religion Pages 400

**Mental Chemistry** *by Charles Haanel*  ISBN: 1-59462-192-6  **$23.95**
*Mental Chemistry allows the change of material conditions by combining and appropriately utilizing the power of the mind. Much like applied chemistry creates something new and unique out of careful combinations of chemicals the mastery of mental chemistry...*  New Age Pages 354

**The Letters of Robert Browning and Elizabeth Barret Barrett 1845-1846 vol II**  ISBN: 1-59462-193-4  **$35.95**
*by Robert Browning and Elizabeth Barrett*
Biographies Pages 596

**Gleanings In Genesis (volume I)** *by Arthur W. Pink*  ISBN: 1-59462-130-6  **$27.45**
*Appropriately has Genesis been termed "the seed plot of the Bible" for in it we have, in germ form, almost all of the great doctrines which are afterwards fully developed in the books of Scripture which follow...*  Religion/Inspirational Pages 420

**The Master Key** *by L. W. de Laurence*  ISBN: 1-59462-001-6  **$30.95**
*In no branch of human knowledge has there been a more lively increase of the spirit of research during the past few years than in the study of Psychology, Concentration and Mental Discipline. The requests for authentic lessons in Thought Control, Mental Discipline and...*  New Age/Business Pages 422

**The Lesser Key Of Solomon Goetia** *by L. W. de Laurence*  ISBN: 1-59462-092-X  **$9.95**
*This translation of the first book of the "Lernegton" which is now for the first time made accessible to students of Talismanic Magic was done, after careful collation and edition, from numerous Ancient Manuscripts in Hebrew, Latin, and French...*  New Age/Occult Pages 92

**Rubaiyat Of Omar Khayyam** *by Edward Fitzgerald*  ISBN:1-59462-332-5  **$13.95**
*Edward Fitzgerald, whom the world has already learned, in spite of his own efforts to remain within the shadow of anonymity, to look upon as one of the rarest poets of the century, was born at Bredfield, in Suffolk, on the 31st of March, 1809. He was the third son of John Purcell...*  Music Pages 172

**Ancient Law** *by Henry Maine*  ISBN: 1-59462-128-4  **$29.95**
*The chief object of the following pages is to indicate some of the earliest ideas of mankind, as they are reflected in Ancient Law, and to point out the relation of those ideas to modern thought.*  Religion/History Pages 452

**Far-Away Stories** *by William J. Locke*  ISBN: 1-59462-129-2  **$19.45**
*"Good wine needs no bush, but a collection of mixed vintages does. And this book is just such a collection. Some of the stories I do not want to remain buried for ever in the museum files of dead magazine-numbers an author's not unpardonable vanity..."*  Fiction Pages 272

**Life of David Crockett** *by David Crockett*  ISBN: 1-59462-250-7  **$27.45**
*"Colonel David Crockett was one of the most remarkable men of the times in which he lived. Born in humble life, but gifted with a strong will, an indomitable courage, and unremitting perseverance...*  Biographies/New Age Pages 424

**Lip-Reading** *by Edward Nitchie*  ISBN: 1-59462-206-X  **$25.95**
*Edward B. Nitchie, founder of the New York School for the Hard of Hearing, now the Nitchie School of Lip-Reading, Inc, wrote "LIP-READING Principles and Practice". The development and perfecting of this meritorious work on lip-reading was an undertaking...*  How-to Pages 400

**A Handbook of Suggestive Therapeutics, Applied Hypnotism, Psychic Science**  ISBN: 1-59462-214-0  **$24.95**
*by Henry Munro*  Health/New Age/Health/Self-help Pages 376

**A Doll's House: and Two Other Plays** *by Henrik Ibsen*  ISBN: 1-59462-112-8  **$19.95**
*Henrik Ibsen created this classic when in revolutionary 1848 Rome. Introducing some striking concepts in playwriting for the realist genre, this play has been studied the world over.*  Fiction/Classics/Plays 308

**The Light of Asia** *by sir Edwin Arnold*  ISBN: 1-59462-204-3  **$13.95**
*In this poetic masterpiece, Edwin Arnold describes the life and teachings of Buddha. The man who was to become known as Buddha to the world was born as Prince Gautama of India but he rejected the worldly riches and abandoned the reigns of power when...*  Religion/History/Biographies Pages 170

**The Complete Works of Guy de Maupassant** *by Guy de Maupassant*  ISBN: 1-59462-157-8  **$16.95**
*"For days and days, nights and nights, I had dreamed of that first kiss which was to consecrate our engagement, and I knew not on what spot I should put my lips..."*  Fiction/Classics Pages 240

**The Art of Cross-Examination** *by Francis L. Wellman*  ISBN: 1-59462-309-0  **$26.95**
*Written by a renowned trial lawyer, Wellman imparts his experience and uses case studies to explain how to use psychology to extract desired information through questioning.*  How-to/Science/Reference Pages 408

**Answered or Unanswered?** *by Louisa Vaughan*  ISBN: 1-59462-248-5  **$10.95**
*Miracles of Faith in China*  Religion Pages 112

**The Edinburgh Lectures on Mental Science (1909)** *by Thomas*  ISBN: 1-59462-008-3  **$11.95**
*This book contains the substance of a course of lectures recently given by the writer in the Queen Street Hall, Edinburgh. Its purpose is to indicate the Natural Principles governing the relation between Mental Action and Material Conditions...*  New Age/Psychology Pages 148

**Ayesha** *by H. Rider Haggard*  ISBN: 1-59462-301-5  **$24.95**
*Verily and indeed it is the unexpected that happens! Probably if there was one person upon the earth from whom the Editor of this, and of a certain previous history, did not expect to hear again...*  Classics Pages 380

**Ayala's Angel** *by Anthony Trollope*  ISBN: 1-59462-352-X  **$29.95**
*The two girls were both pretty, but Lucy who was twenty-one who supposed to be simple and comparatively unattractive, whereas Ayala was credited, as her Bombwhat romantic name might show, with poetic charm and a taste for romance. Ayala when her father died was nineteen...*  Fiction Pages 484

**The American Commonwealth** *by James Bryce*  ISBN: 1-59462-286-8  **$34.45**
*An interpretation of American democratic political theory. It examines political mechanics and society from the perspective of Scotsman James Bryce*  Politics Pages 572

**Stories of the Pilgrims** *by Margaret P. Pumphrey*  ISBN: 1-59462-116-0  **$17.95**
*This book explores pilgrims religious oppression in England as well as their escape to Holland and eventual crossing to America on the Mayflower, and their early days in New England...*  History Pages 268

**QTY**

**The Fasting Cure** *by Sinclair Upton*                                    ISBN: *1-59462-222-1*  **$13.95**
*In the Cosmopolitan Magazine for May, 1910, and in the Contemporary Review (London) for April, 1910, I published an article dealing with my experi-
ences in fasting. I have written a great many magazine articles, but never one which attracted so much attention...  New Age/Self Help/Health Pages 164*

**Hebrew Astrology** *by Sepharial*                                    ISBN: *1-59462-308-2*  **$13.45**
*In these days of advanced thinking it is a matter of common observation that we have left many of the old landmarks behind and that we are now pressing
forward to greater heights and to a wider horizon than that which represented the mind-content of our progenitors...                    Astrology Pages 144*

**Thought Vibration or The Law of Attraction in the Thought World**      ISBN: *1-59462-127-6*  **$12.95**

*by William Walker Atkinson*                                       *Psychology/Religion Pages 144*

**Optimism** *by Helen Keller*                                         ISBN: *1-59462-108-X*  **$15.95**
*Helen Keller was blind, deaf, and mute since 19 months old, yet famously learned how to overcome these handicaps, communicate with the world, and
spread her lectures promoting optimism.  An inspiring read for everyone...                       Biographies/Inspirational Pages 84*

**Sara Crewe** *by Frances Burnett*                                    ISBN: *1-59462-360-0*  **$9.45**
*In the first place, Miss Minchin lived in London. Her home was a large, dull, tall one, in a large, dull square, where all the houses were alike, and all the
sparrows were alike, and where all the door-knockers made the same heavy sound...                   Childrens/Classic Pages 88*

**The Autobiography of Benjamin Franklin** *by Benjamin Franklin*      ISBN: *1-59462-135-7*  **$24.95**
*The Autobiography of Benjamin Franklin has probably been more extensively read than any other American historical work, and no other book of its kind
has had such ups and downs of fortune. Franklin lived for many years in England, where he was agent...           Biographies/History Pages 332*

| Name | |
|---|---|
| Email | |
| Telephone | |
| Address | |
| | |
| City, State ZIP | |

☐ **Credit Card**          ☐ **Check / Money Order**

| Credit Card Number | |
|---|---|
| Expiration Date | |
| Signature | |

*Please Mail to:*  Book Jungle
PO Box 2226
Champaign, IL 61825
*or Fax to:*          630-214-0564

## ORDERING INFORMATION

**web***: www.bookjungle.com*
**email***: sales@bookjungle.com*
**fax***: 630-214-0564*
**mail***: Book Jungle  PO Box 2226  Champaign, IL 61825*
**or PayPal** *to sales@bookjungle.com*

*Please contact us for bulk discounts*

## DIRECT-ORDER TERMS

**20% Discount if You Order
Two or More Books**
Free Domestic Shipping!
Accepted: Master Card, Visa,
Discover, American Express

www.ingramcontent.com/pod-product-compliance
Lightning Source LLC
Chambersburg PA
CBHW080907020726
47502CB00008B/2376